Kiss Me Kate

THE ENGLISH BROTHERS, BOOK #6
THE BLUEBERRY LANE SERIES

KATY REGNERY

SPENCER
HILL
PRESS

Please visit www.katyregnery.com

First Edition: February 2015
Katy Regnery

Kiss Me Kate: a novel / by Katy Regnery—1st ed.
ISBN: 978-1-63392-077-4
Library of Congress Cataloging-in-Publication Data available upon request

Published in the United States by Spencer Hill Press
This is a Spencer Hill Contemporary Romance, Spencer Hill
Contemporary is an imprint of Spencer Hill Press.
For more information on our titles visit www.spencerhillpress.com

Distributed by Midpoint Trade Books
www.midpointtrade.com

Cover design by: Marianne Nowicki
Interior layout by: Scribe, Inc.
The World of Blueberry Lane Map designed by: Paul Siegel

Printed in the United States of America

The Blueberry Lane Series

THE ENGLISH BROTHERS
Breaking Up with Barrett
Falling for Fitz
Anyone but Alex
Seduced by Stratton
Wild about Weston
Kiss Me Kate
Marrying Mr. English

THE WINSLOW BROTHERS
Bidding on Brooks
Proposing to Preston
Crazy about Cameron
Campaigning for Christopher

THE ROUSSEAUS
Jonquils for Jax
Coming August 2016

Marry Me Mad
Coming September 2016

J.C. and the Bijoux Jolis
Coming October 2016

THE STORY SISTERS
Four novels
Coming 2017

THE AMBLERS
Three novels
Coming 2018

Based on the best-selling series by Katy Regnery,

The World of...

The Rousseaus of Chateau Nouvelle
Jax, Mad, J.C.
Jonquils for Jax • Marry Me Mad
J.C. and the Bijoux Jolis

The Story Sisters of Forrester
Priscilla, Alice, Elizabeth, Jane
Coming Summer 2017

The Winslow Brothers of Westerly
Brooks, Preston, Cameron, Christopher
Bidding on Brooks • Proposing to Preston
Crazy About Cameron • Campaigning for Christopher

The Amblers of Greens Farms
Bree, Dash, Sloane
Coming Summer 2018

The English Brothers of Haverford Park
Barrett, Fitz, Alex, Stratton, Weston, Kate
Breaking up with Barrett • Falling for Fitz
Anyone but Alex • Seduced by Stratton
Wild about Weston • Kiss Me Kate
Marrying Mr. English

Things aren't always as they seem.
That's the truth.
Sometimes it's the only truth that matters.

And to Dr. J.M.
Thank you.

CONTENTS

"Two households, both alike in dignity
In fair Verona, where we lay our scene . . ."
—William Shakespeare, *Romeo & Juliet*

Chapter 1

From the moment Kate English found out about Étienne Rousseau's accident, she'd secretly been stalking him on Facebook.

What made this especially challenging—and monumentally pathetic—was that Étienne Rousseau didn't, in fact, have a Facebook page. So she had essentially been stalking him by proxy, via the Facebook page of his younger sister, Jax.

If Jax Rousseau had been curious about a sudden Friend Request from Kate English, she hadn't let on. It was common knowledge in their shared social circle that Kate had recently moved from New York City to Philadelphia, so Jax probably just assumed Kate was reaching out to her now that she was living locally.

She wasn't.

She was creeping on Jax's brother . . .

. . . which, for myriad reasons, was such a bad idea, it made Kate cringe as she entered her username and password, promising herself—for the hundredth time—this would also be the *last* time. A successful lawyer and confident businesswoman, Kate wasn't the type to lurk around Facebook for mentions of an ex, was she? She didn't want to think of herself like that. And yet, here she sat on her lonely bed at ten o'clock on a Saturday night, scanning

Jax's Facebook page for any mention of Étienne, who had once—a long, long time ago—broken Kate's heart into a million pieces . . . begging the question:

Why did she give a damn about Étienne Rousseau when he'd never given a damn about her?

Kate grabbed her glass of wine off the bedside table and sipped the Pinot Grigio as her index finger continued its snooping and her brain tried unsuccessfully to ignore the nagging question.

The fact of the matter was that Kate didn't have a good answer. She supposed, if she had to come up with something, she'd admit that she'd never totally gotten over him. Like any other normal, hot-blooded woman who'd ever been dumped and forgotten by an ex, she had a compulsive interest in him that was enabled by the ease of social media. Finding out these tiny tidbits about his life was this strange, irresistible weakness she couldn't seem to overcome. And yes, there was this, too: the only way someone can break your heart into a million pieces is if you gave it to them in the first place, and Kate had done just that. As a gullible and innocent girl, she had believed herself deeply in love with Étienne and had ended up giving him her heart and much, much more.

And you never really get over your first, she thought bitterly. *Especially when you move back to the city where it all happened.*

Touching the mouse on her laptop gingerly, she scrolled through a series of Jax-selfies taken an hour ago at the same party Kate had been attending: Jax looking dark-haired, dark-eyed, and fierce, hand on a jutted hip in front of a skyscraper-shaped ice sculpture . . . Jax and her twin sister, Mad, pursing their red, shiny lips for the camera . . . Jax posing with one of the Ambler sisters, her index finger caught between her teeth, somehow managing to look both sexy and bored-to-tears at once . . .

Kate kept skating through pictures and status updates, chuckling softly at a quip about stiletto heels and rainy spring nights. Though they'd been childhood acquaintances, Kate had only recently gotten to know adult-Jax through a month's worth of online lurking, and she liked the feisty young brunette. Plus, Jax updated her Facebook account about twenty times a day, which meant that mentions of Étienne, while occasional, still popped up a couple times a week to feed Kate's obsession.

Peeking at the laptop screen over the rim of her glass as she took another sip of wine, Kate almost missed what she was looking for. Her eyes widened, and she jerked her finger on the mouse, scrolling back quickly. Changing her sip to a gulp, she read Jax's status from earlier today:

> JACQUELINE "JAX" ROUSSEAU: *Big Bro getting his cast off tomorrow! Gird your loins, females of Philly. Ten'll be back in action soooooon, bitches!*

Staring at the screen, Kate read the post three more times before snapping the laptop closed and swinging her legs over the side of her bed with disgust. She huffed softly, causing Oliver, her latest rescue cat, to leap off the bed and hide beneath it, while Annie, the marmalade tabby she'd rescued two years ago, gave Kate the stink eye from the end of the bed for disrupting her sleep.

Kate's baggy pajama bottoms whooshed softly as she marched through the halls of her rented condo, heading for the kitchen to refill her wineglass.

"Gird your loins," she muttered to Cinderella, a blue-eyed Himalayan who followed her mistress to the kitchen. Kate was fostering the HIV-positive feline until the local shelter could find a family equipped to care for her.

Kate's contact at PAWS for LOVE had called again this morning to ask if she could foster one more, and while Kate hated to say no, she had no choice but to refuse. Until she had a house of her own with some grounds to build a small kennel for orphans and strays, her condo couldn't accommodate another body. Not to mention, one more cat and she'd be approaching "crazy cat lady" territory, which was a little too pitiful for Kate to bear.

Looking down at the pretty gray-and-white kitten, Kate sniffed derisively, "Back in action, huh? Back to whoring, more like. Oh, I wish I'd never met him. I wish I'd never even known how it felt . . ."

Cinderella meowed as Kate's voice trailed off. Wishes were futile. She *had* met him. She *did* know. She couldn't *unknow* the feeling of being with Étienne, but she wished she could somehow forget it. It didn't seem fair that their short liaison should still haunt her after so many years.

Pursing her lips and bracing her hands on the kitchen counter, she bowed her head in frustration, grappling for strength and direction. Although it was impossible to turn back time and make different choices, *or* erase her tenacious memories, she was a strong, smart woman, and she could certainly take control of her behavior *now*. Sternly promising herself—for the hundredth and first time—that she'd unfollow Jax and stop cyber-stalking Étienne on Facebook, she turned her back to the counter, leaning against it and crossing her arms over her ample chest.

After all, thought Kate, *it really isn't fair to Tony.*

Tony Reddington, the son of her father's business partner, had been kind enough to take Kate out for dinner when she'd first relocated to Philadelphia two months ago and had since turned into a pseudo-boyfriend of sorts. Her go-to escort for parties and galas, Tony was well-educated, cultured, and charming, filling their evenings with amusing observations and witty conversation. When he picked up Kate in his shiny, spotless Mercedes, he always had flowers waiting, and when he dropped her off at the end of their dates, he never groped or pushed, opting for a chaste kiss on the cheek or a peck on the lips, followed by a playful wink and a promise to call her. A promise he always kept.

Tony was a gentleman of the highest order, and Kate knew she should be blissfully happy on his arm, maybe even with the possibility of long-awaited wedding bells echoing in her head.

So what was the problem?

Kate's cheeks flushed as she considered the shameful answer.

After six weeks of delightful conversation, gorgeous flowers and chaste kisses, Kate wanted more . . . but not necessarily from Tony. Kate's dirty little secret was that she couldn't shake memories of Étienne since returning to Philly. She wanted hot, wet, sweet, messy, filthy kisses that would make her toes curl. She wanted fingers that burned her skin like fire, lips that sucked until she screamed, and a tongue that could make stars burst behind closed eyes. She wanted thick and hot sliding into her core over and over again, until her muscles tensed and strained and her body finally exploded into a million pieces of delight, only pulled back to earth and put back together by lips that sought hers hungrily

all.

over.

again.

As far as Kate was concerned, that kind of burning and cooling, falling apart and coming together, sweet and filthy heaven only existed in one man—the only man with whom Kate had ever experienced all of those things at once: Étienne Rousseau.

Kate's body wanted him bad.

Which was a shame, because Étienne Rousseau was also the one man on earth Kate English could never, ever have. Not ever again. Not if she had any self-respect whatsoever.

Buzz. Buzz buzz.

Jolted out of her reverie, she placed cool palms on hot cheeks and glanced at her phone.

Stratton. Hmm.

Kate's cousin, Stratton English, had looked pretty content when Kate and Tony left him at the benefit an hour ago. Cozy in a corner with his new girlfriend, Valeria, he'd appeared more socially comfortable than Kate had ever seen him, and that was saying something, since Stratton loathed parties.

She pressed *Talk.* "Why are you calling me? Why aren't you at home making out with Val?"

Waiting for his answer, she cradled the phone between her ear and shoulder, opening the refrigerator door.

He chuckled softly. "It's on the agenda." Then he got quiet, his voice taking on a slight edge. "Are *you* busy? Is, uh, Tony there?"

Yeah, right.

Kate picked up the bottle on the door and kicked the fridge closed. She thought about asking Stratton if he thought it was normal for a guy to stay in the "chaste kiss" zone after six weeks of dating, but she just wasn't in the mood to talk about it. Her cousins, Stratton especially, were very protective of Kate, approved of Tony, and would have no issue whatsoever with Tony moving as slow as molasses until Kate's blonde hair turned gray. This was a far better conversation for her close girlfriends, who included her cousins' wives, fiancées, and girlfriends.

She pursed her lips as she set the bottle on the counter.

No, not them either. They'd all go home and share Kate's question with their significant others and her cousins would end up weighing in anyway. No. She didn't need advice. She liked Tony. Quite a lot. And she felt sure that he liked her too. Things would eventually heat up, right? She just needed to give Tony a little more time to make his move, and in the meantime she needed to stop letting thoughts of Étienne get her all hot and bothered.

Unfollow Jax. Unfollow Jax. For the love of Pete, unfollow Jax.

Kate rolled her eyes. "Tony was a perfect gentleman."

"Glad to hear it," said Stratton, edge gone.

"So, what's up?" she asked, uncorking the half-drunk bottle of wine. "Are you still at the party?"

"Just leaving," he said, and his voice instantly got more serious. "Hey . . . are you sitting down?"

"Nope. But I'm drinking. Will that do?"

"I guess it'll have to," said Stratton.

"Why are you using your doomsday voice, cuz?"

"Because . . . well, for starters, I'm pissed at Barrett."

"Huh?" Barrett was Stratton's oldest brother and the CEO of English & Company, where Kate worked as a lawyer and Stratton was the acting CFO. Since Stratton was incredibly loyal to his brothers and a generally easygoing person, if he was upset with Barrett, there was a good chance it was work-related. "I thought we all agreed no work at parties."

"A rule Barrett disregards at every turn, at every party, every weekend."

This was true. When it came to business, the only "off" button Barrett knew was his fiancée, Emily Edwards. Otherwise, business was *always* on the table.

"And usually you don't care."

"This time I do."

Kate grinned. "Okay. Tell me . . . what company did Barrett just agree to buy?"

Stratton sighed heavily. "Here's the deal—no, wait. Before I say anything else, I want you to know . . . we're going to fix this, Kate. I promise."

This was suddenly sounding a little more serious. Kate grimaced lightly, then took a swig directly from the bottle before recorking it and putting it back in the fridge.

If Kate was a classic optimist (yes, with closet stalker tendencies), her favorite cousin, Stratton, was a classic fixer, with extreme tunnel vision when it came to those he loved. Kate understood Stratton's compulsion to "fix" things for the people he loved, because she would—literally—do anything for the people she cared about.

In fact, she thought, thinking of her hot laptop and cold, ungirded loins, that was probably why she couldn't stay away from Jax's Facebook page.

Despite the years between Kate's fleeting week with Étienne and now—despite the way he'd hurt her so long ago—the second she'd heard about Étienne's car accident, she'd irrationally longed to race to his bedside and hold his hand. She wasn't under any illusion about his feelings for her. He'd never *really* cared for her—his actions had made that abundantly clear long ago. Hell, at this point, she didn't even know if he still *remembered* her—she hadn't seen him or heard from him in over twelve years, and in that twelve years, by all accounts, Étienne hadn't been lonely. (Ah-hem.)

But even at fifteen years old, Étienne Rousseau was more insouciant, irreverent, and untouchable than anyone Kate had ever met, which pretty much made him the brooding nip to Kate's curious cat. Back then, in addition to his lips on hers and his hands all over her body, she'd desperately wanted to connect with him, understand him, matter to him, belong to him. And for a brief, heartbreaking, and mind-bendingly beautiful moment, she had. Or thought she had. Instead—she remembered, stiffening her spine—he took her virginity and she never saw his face again.

Suddenly she had a sharp sense of foreboding as she turned back to the conversation. "You're making me nervous, Strat."

"I don't know how this happened, but . . . Barrett just got into bed with the Rousseau Trust," he blurted out. "The *fucking* Rousseaus."

The Rousseau Trust. Étienne's family trust.

"Oh," she murmured, a fluttering hand pressing against her heart.

Whatever news she'd expected to hear, the possibility of a business deal between English & Company and the Rousseau Trust hadn't cracked the list. Just hearing his name threatened to knock the wind out of her, not because it was so outlandish that the English brothers would work with the Rousseaus, but because a deal meant she might have to actually see him. Étienne. In the flesh. It was one thing to sneak onto Facebook and indulge an unhealthy, but harmless, fantasy. It was quite another to sit across a boardroom table from the object of that fantasy and be expected to deliver coherent sentences.

To cover up the fierce and sudden hammering of her heart, Kate scrambled to remember the last thing Stratton said . . . *into bed with the Rousseau Trust* . . . and quipped, "Is Emily okay with that?"

"Kate," said Stratton gently, no stranger to Kate's method of using humor to lighten uncomfortable situations, "I'm serious."

She groaned, picking up her wineglass and walking through the kitchen and dining room to the bright-white painted French doors that led to Kate's favorite room in the condo: a sunroom furnished with a white wicker sofa and rocker, complete with comfy cushions as plump as Kate's backside. "Okay. I'm sitting down. Catch me up."

"Are you still drinking?"

"I think it's best," she said weakly, taking a big gulp.

"So Barrett, Emily, Val, and I were hanging out at the bar. Suddenly J.C. Rousseau sidles up, all oily with his stupid toothy smile, and starts talking to Barrett about some piece of property that he and his siblings own in New Orleans, and how they want to unload it."

Only Stratton would call J.C. Rousseau—a man so darkly handsome women literally swooned when he smiled—oily and toothy. She grinned, then refocused.

"Property?" she asked.

"Shipbuilding."

"Oh." Kate's lips dropped open. This was interesting. For months Barrett had been seeking a third shipbuilding company to add to the two he'd already merged in England and New York. A presence in Louisiana would be the perfect complement. "Wow, that's actually . . . amazing. If the specs pan out, it could be perfect."

Stratton huffed with annoyance. "You aren't seeing the big picture, Kate."

"Which is?"

"We'd be working with the Rousseaus. *You'd* be working with the Rousseaus."

Kate took a deep breath, leaning back in the rocker and resting her bare feet on a glass coffee table. *Working with Étienne. Shaking hands with Étienne. Staring at Étienne's beautiful green eyes across a mahogany conference room table. Wondering if Étienne still made that noise in the back of his throat when he—*

Her toes curled against the cold surface even as her cheeks—and other parts of Kate's anatomy—flooded with heat.

"Kate? You still there? There's more."

She swallowed another big sip of wine. "Yeah, um . . ."

"I didn't know this, but the legal structure of Louisiana is still based on—"

"The Napoleonic code," murmured Kate.

"Yeah. Which means that you'd be working directly with the Rousseaus' legal counsel to hammer out the deal. You'd be *on point* with their in-house lawyer . . . do you know who that is?"

Of course she did. She'd been cyber-stalking him by proxy for weeks.

"Étienne." She sighed, hating the way her stomach buzzed and her breathing hitched, as though her brain hadn't yet shared the message with her body that Étienne Rousseau was absolutely, positively, *eternally* off-limits.

"So *now* do you get it?" asked Stratton.

"Étienne and I would be working together on the deal," she said softly, examining the words in her mind as she said them and trying to ignore the fierce fluttering of her heart.

"Side-by-side," said Stratton. "It's terrible. I already ripped Barrett a new one and said that he'd have to figure out a way to get out of it, so I don't want you to wor—"

"Wait," said Kate, eyebrows crinkling together as she snapped out of her swoony state and focused on the business angle of Stratton's news. "It's a good opportunity, right? For English & Company?"

"Theoretically, yes, it *could* be . . . but we wouldn't dream of—"

She uncurled her toes and placed them squarely on the floor. "Stratton. Take Étienne out of the equation and give it to me straight."

He paused before answering. "Fine. Yes. Adding the Rousseaus' company to the Harrison-Lowry merger would make our tri-headquartered company the ninth largest shipbuilder in the world."

History with Étienne was one thing . . . but Kate's last name was just as English as Barrett's: business was business.

Kate took a deep breath and gulped the last of her wine. Maybe she was crazy, because she knew if she said the word, her cousins, Fitz, Alex, and Stratton, would pressure Barrett to drop the deal, and out of loyalty to Kate, Barrett would walk away. But with a swift and sudden certainty, Kate knew that wasn't what she wanted for two reasons.

One, she truly wanted what was best for English & Company, even at the price of her own comfort, and,

Two, some strange, masochistic part of her didn't want to pass up this opportunity to be in the same room as Étienne. He lived—gorgeous, smoldering, and larger-than-life—in her mind, glamorized over their years apart and her recent flirtation with social media. Yes, Kate had been drawn to him long ago, but the boy she'd fallen for had broken her heart too, a fact she frequently ignored while ogling months-old pictures of him on Jax's timeline.

How better to banish him from her head and her heart than to remind herself—in an up close and personal way—of what a self-centered, brooding bore he could be? One look into his eyes should also reconfirm that he had zero interest in her and kill any ridiculous fantasies she still harbored about him. Yes, of course. She wanted to get rid of thoughts of Étienne and clear the runway for Tony, right? Well then, she needed to spend some time with Étienne and remember what a jerk he could be. Thanks to Barrett, such an opportunity had just been served up to Kate on a silver platter.

"Stratton," Kate said, her voice calm, but firm, "business is business. You can't turn down deals every time an ex-boyfriend of mine shows up."

"Étienne's a bastard," spat her cousin. "Damn the Rousseaus anyway."

Kate drew her bottom lip into her mouth and dropped her eyes guiltily, even though Stratton wasn't standing right in front of her. Étienne had slept with her, then disappeared, and Kate had never heard from him again. That had hurt her, but he'd never promised her anything either. A part of Kate—a very small part of Kate—couldn't completely get on board with hating Étienne. Despite the fact that he'd hurt her so terribly, a corner of her heart had always hoped that someday she'd understand the reason for his actions and be in a position to forgive him.

"That may be true, and I appreciate your concern, but I insist that you all take me and Étienne out of the equation. If English & Company can profit by acquiring a property held by the Rousseau Trust, I won't be responsible for standing in the way of such a transaction. In fact . . . I *insist* we pursue it."

There was a long silence on the other end of the phone before Stratton spoke again. "Kate, we can find another company to buy. There will be other opportunities."

Knowing her cousin as she did, it was important to convince him that her feelings were neutral, or she knew he'd intercede on her behalf and cancel the deal. "I mean it Stratton. This is business. Nothing more, nothing less."

"Think carefully. Are you sure about this?"

No. Her heart fluttered with a strange mixture of hope, anticipation, and dread.

"We need to do what's best for English & Company," she said firmly. She paused before adding softly, "Anyway, Étienne and I are ancient history."

Meeting Étienne

Fifteen-year-old Kate English didn't mind spending spring break with her aunt, uncle, and three of her five cousins in Haverford, Pennsylvania, while her parents completed a two-week tour of Europe. In addition to the fact that she adored her cousins, the freedom from her parents' strict and old-fashioned rules felt like heaven. Although sometimes—like right now—she wished one of those cousins had been born a girl, because it sure would be nice to have someone to talk to. She briefly considered calling her best friend, Libitz, back in New York, then remembered Libitz had gone to Cancun for the week. Kate sighed. She was on her own.

Walking down the grand staircase, she passed seventeen-year-old Alex in running clothes on his way upstairs for a shower, glistening with sweat and smelling like a cross between BO and a stale distillery. She wrinkled her nose at him, which earned her a broad smile.

"Wanna smell my pits?" he asked, raising an arm, blue eyes twinkling.

"Gross!" she cried, dodging past him.

She heard his throaty chuckle ascend behind her as she continued down the stairs. Turning into the front foyer, she headed back to the kitchen to see if she could find some breakfast. Before last night, Kate had never had more than a few sips of champagne at Christmas and New Year's under her father's watchful eye. Drinking three beers on the back-yard trampoline with Betsy Story and the Rousseau sisters had been well over her limit, and her stomach was woozy this morning. Still, it had been worth it, if only because Jax and Mad's older brother, Étienne, came looking for them.

Shivers ran down Kate's arms, and she bit her upper lip, recalling the way Étienne had sauntered out of the bushes, making his leisurely way to the trampoline. He was barefooted and wore his jeans slung low on his hips. His pale, chiseled face was so beautiful in the moonlight. Kate's lips had dropped open, her heart skipping and stuttering. Jet-black hair, thick and unruly, slightly curled at the ends, fell just past his shirt collar and framed his face. Her fingers had twitched, longing to reach out and bury themselves in its softness.

He hadn't smiled when Jax introduced them, his eyes staying flat and disinterested as though on purpose. He'd held out his hand, however, and when Kate took it, his flesh—unexpectedly warm and dry—had pressed flush against hers, making her breath catch as her entire body turned on, like it had been plugged in for the first time in her life. His lips—the memory of which had kept her up well past midnight—were torturing her. Remembering the way he'd slowly licked them while their hands were clasped together made Kate breathe funny, made her tummy flip over and flutter. She'd had small crushes on a few of the boys at Trinity, the private prep school she attended in New York City, but nothing like this. Nothing like the way her skin puckered at the memory of their hands touching—the way secret, hidden muscles deep inside her body clenched every time his beautiful face floated through her mind. What was happening to her?

"Hey Kate!" exclaimed twelve-year-old Weston, darting out of the kitchen's double doors at the end of the hallway. "Mom said if I want to go riding I gotta get you or Alex to go with me."

"Why's that, slick?"

"Aw, she doesn't trust me after I jumped the Amblers' fence last week."

Kate pursed her lips. "You *did* almost kill yourself."

"One lousy fall isn't going to kill me."

"Sprained your finger, though."

Weston rolled his eyes. "Big deal! Will you go with me? Please? Alex is such a jerk. Whenever we run into someone we know, he calls me 'Romper Room' on purpose. I hate him."

"No, you don't," said Kate, chuckling as she ruffled his hair. She'd never seen a kid who worshipped his older brothers as much as Weston English.

"Okay, I don't. Will you go? Come on! Please, Kate?"

She had already been riding with Weston yesterday and knew the riding trails around Blueberry Lane rambled through the backyards of most of the estates, including the Rousseaus'.

"Sure," she said, cheeks flushing like she'd just told a lie. "I'll go. Just let me get some breakfast first."

Pushing open the swinging doors, Kate wasn't surprised to find her fourteen-year-old cousin, Stratton, sitting at the long chrome counter in the center of the kitchen, reading a book, with a plate of cold, half-finished waffles in front of him.

"Morning, Strat," she said.

"Hey, Kate," he answered without looking up.

Kate gave him a hard look before pulling up a stool across from him. Alex was a tease and Weston was too young . . . with Barrett and Fitz away at college, Stratton was her best immediate option for a chat. She propped her elbows on the counter and stared at him.

"*What?*" he finally asked, looking at her, blue eyes exasperated to be interrupted while reading.

"Étienne Rousseau."

"Hmm," said Stratton, folding down the corner of his page and giving her a cautious look. "What about him?"

"What's his story?"

Stratton sighed, pursing his lips and shaking his head. "He's one of four. His older brother, J.C., goes to Princeton. His sisters, Mad and Jax, are in junior high. He's a sophomore at St. Michael's with me and Alex. They moved here from France about ten years ago. He thinks he's better than everyone else . . . and he used to cheat at hide-and-seek."

"Hmm. Not a big fan, huh? What else?"

Stratton rolled his eyes. "It's not like we're friends, Kate."

"You go to the same school. You've lived on the same road together for years. You've got to know more about him. Come on, Strat."

Stratton sighed, looking deeply annoyed. "He's on the swim team, and I think he paints. He won some award last year for a painting. The Rousseaus are sort of . . . *fast*. I mean, I've seen Étienne drunk more than once. He's been caught smoking behind school, and that's illegal at his age. I've also seen him driving his dad's car and he's only fifteen, which means he's pretty comfortable breaking the law. And . . ." Stratton lowered his voice, but it didn't conceal the wide ribbon of jealousy threaded through his words. "Girls are always staring at him."

I bet they are.

Kate wetted her lips, dropping Stratton's eyes. "Is he dating anyone?"

"Like I'd know. He's a year older than me and way more popular." He tapped twice on the metal counter. "Why all the questions?"

Kate slid off the stool and turned for the coffeemaker, pouring herself a cup and stirring in a little milk. "I met him last night."

"And . . . ?"

Fireworks. Dazzling, blinding, gorgeous fireworks.

Her cheeks felt hot. "I was hanging out with his sisters and he stopped by. That's all. I'm just curious about him."

Stratton cleared his throat. "Nothing against Jax and Mad, but why not hang out with the Story sisters instead? Or Emily Edwards? She's probably close to your age."

Um, because neither the Story sisters, nor the gardener's daughter, are able to scorch a path to my heart with a single touch.

"Yeah, okay." She gave her cousin a small smile as he stood, taking his book off the counter.

As Stratton neared the mudroom door, he turned. "You *really* want to know what I think?"

"Uh-huh."

"I don't like Étienne. Never have. That's my opinion." He swallowed, blinking twice before leveling her with his eyes. "Your parents wouldn't like him either."

Kate cast her eyes down quickly, her cheeks flaring with embarrassment. He was right. Her parents had a strict rule that Kate wasn't allowed to date until she was sixteen, and even then the boy needed to be "well-heeled" and from one of the "right" families. No way the racy, French-born Rousseaus would crack that list.

Stratton must have sensed he'd shamed her because his voice was gentle when he followed up. "I care about you, Kate, and the Englishes and Rousseaus don't mix. Steer clear, okay?"

Looking up, Kate smiled at him in the well-practiced way she smiled at her parents when they'd just rejected her request to attend a school dance or sleepover at a friend's house whose parents they didn't know.

"Of course. Will do. Thanks, Strat."

Kate watched him leave, settling back on her stool and taking a long sip of coffee as the image of a beautiful, green-eyed, dark-haired boy flooded her mind. Goosebumps rose up all over her innocent, goody-two-shoes body just thinking about his bad-boy ways.

Though their entire meeting had only consisted of brief eye contact and a single, electrifying handshake before he'd herded his sisters home, Kate had sensed something in his energy: something edgy and mysterious she desperately wanted to learn more about. She pulled her bottom lip into her mouth, chewing on it distractedly until Weston came to find her to go riding.

She only knew two things for sure:

One? Her parents were far, far away in Brussels.

And two, despite Stratton's warning, Kate had no intention of staying away from Étienne Rousseau.

Chapter 2

Hailing a cab in front of his apartment building on Monday morning, Étienne Rousseau took a deep, cleansing breath of fresh spring air and smiled.

After nine weeks in a fiberglass cast from knee to ankle, Étienne was so grateful to be back on his own two feet, he didn't care that he needed the help of a cane to walk. Finally able to leave his apartment without crutches, he felt reinvigorated, rested, and ready to resume—or restart—his life.

Adding to the figurative spring in his step was the profound relief he felt in being wholly, completely, one hundred percent single for the first time in years. Right before his accident, Étienne's psycho, master manipulator of an exgirlfriend, Amy Colson, had broken up with him by informing him of her plan to marry a man she'd met in Japan on a recent business trip—a man she claimed to have fallen in love with over the course of two weeks.

And while his five years with Amy hadn't exactly been a picnic, being dumped so she could suddenly marry someone else—who was, in fact, a total and complete stranger—had hurt.

While dating Amy casually during their senior year at Swarthmore, Étienne wasn't sold on her as girlfriend material. She texted him too much, was always calling to "check in," and seemed to want to know where he was at all times. Adorable, with an ass to die for, she was simply too clingy for Étienne's taste, and he decided, after dating her for about a month, that it was time to cut bait.

However, on the evening he planned to break up with her, Amy had received the terrible news that both of her parents had died in a sudden accident. Such a tragic and unexpected loss had immediately vaulted their relationship from casual to far-more-serious overnight as Amy turned to Étienne for comfort in her grief. Étienne, who was moved by her sadness and somewhat trapped into staying with her, had supported her emotionally through months of deep melancholy. By graduation, their feelings had blossomed into love.

Or so Étienne had thought.

The reality was that Amy and Étienne were dysfunctional from the beginning. The fractured nature of their courtship meant they hadn't dated long enough for Étienne to get to know Amy very well during the few weeks they dated before her parents' death, and the Amy he knew after their loss wasn't the "real" everyday Amy either—she was "grieving" Amy.

Two years into his relationship with her, Étienne could barely remember the cute, clingy, slightly cloying Amy he'd dated in the way beginning. Grieving Amy was giving way to someone else entirely. He didn't know it, but he was finally getting a chance to meet the "real" Amy.

Suspicious and jealous to an extreme, she'd constantly accuse him of cheating on her, which would lead to emotional fights, tearful break-ups, passionate make-ups, and exhausting, persistent, nonstop drama. They'd break up for a week or two, and Étienne would go out with someone else, which Amy would call cheating to anyone who would listen. Meanwhile, her favorite revenge ploy was to sleep over at Stratton English's apartment during these brief break-ups and then allude to the fabulous, unforgettable night she'd had with him. Étienne's own jealousy would rise up, hot and possessive, he'd race over to her apartment, they'd fight again, somehow end up fucking again, and wind up together—totally fucked up—yet again.

And still—even though it wasn't healthy and even though it might never have been real . . . Amy had belonged to Étienne for so long, he barely knew what life looked like without her. Even though he didn't *like* her all that much, when he wasn't with her, he missed her. And when he thought of someone else touching her—like Stratton-fucking-English—he wanted to put his fist through a wall.

So, when Amy announced during one of their famous break-ups that she'd become engaged to a man she'd met on a business trip, whom she'd agreed to marry after an acquaintance of a week, Étienne had been furious and hurt. Invited out for drinks with his brother, Jean Christian, and other friends, Étienne had partied way too hard and tried to drive home drunk, which had led to his car wrapped around a tree and landed him in a fiberglass cast for nine weeks. But during those nine weeks trapped in a cast, trapped at home, *no longer* trapped with Amy? He'd had a unique chance to review his relationship with her. Unsurprisingly, he'd quickly arrived at a place of deep relief.

And now?

Cast-free and Amy-free, Étienne was finally ready to embrace his freedom. He had no one to answer to, no one to account to. He was ready to swing his dick around and see where it landed. But under no circumstances—*none, absolutely none*—would he permit himself to engage in a new *relationship*. After five rollercoaster years of insanity with Amy, Étienne Rousseau was finally free, and that's exactly how he was going to stay.

Étienne opened the door of the cab and slid across the backseat, giving himself space to spread out his left leg. He gave the driver his office address then cracked his window, enjoying the cool morning air on his cheeks.

Thanks to some poor choices as a jackass teenage lothario and Amy's delusional rants to her loudmouthed girlfriends, Étienne had been painted in their social circles as a black-hearted, ruthless, philandering cad, so frankly, he didn't think that remaining single would be much of a challenge. He saw the way women looked at him—they definitely wanted to take him for a spin, but they weren't anxious to take him home. Fine by him. He'd had enough fucked-up-serious to last a lifetime.

The truth? he mused, tapping his lips with one tapered index finger as he looked out the window at a park dotted with cheerful pink dogwood trees. The truth was that he'd never, not once, cheated on Amy Colson when they were together. When they were broken up, which was multiple times every year due to her crazy accusations, yes, he'd sampled some other goodies, just as she had with Stratton. And he certainly couldn't help the way women looked at him and came on to him. That wasn't his fault, and it's not like he encouraged it, even though it made Amy insanely jealous. Étienne knew he was good-looking, and he could certainly be charming, and his sister, Jax, told him that women swooned for the slight French accent in his and his brother's speech.

But the truth?

The truth was that Amy was not self-confident enough to be Étienne's girlfriend, something he would have learned long ago if they'd had the opportunity to date a little longer before her parents' accident.

The truth was that when Étienne and Amy were together, despite her incessant suspicions and near-constant jealousy, Étienne had been faithful to her.

That was the truth, and frankly, it didn't matter to Étienne who knew it. Flashing back twelve years in the blink of an eye, his face hardened as he remembered a certain incident with Alex English. He'd learned a long time ago that it was impossible to control what people believed, and there was no sense in spitting into the wind. *He* knew the truth, and as far as he was concerned, that's all that mattered.

Arriving in front of his office building, he paid the driver and took his time exiting the cab, careful to balance his weight on the cane before setting forth into the building. Putting thoughts of Amy from his mind for once and for all, he looked forward to seeing what deals Jean Christian and Jax had been cooking up during his recovery. They'd sent home a little work here and there, but anxious not to tire him out, law student Jax had taken over much of the simple legal work in Étienne's absence.

Pushing the button on the elevator, he was surprised to find his thoughts lingering not on Amy, but on Alex—or more specifically, on the circumstances that had led to the incident with Alex. Though Étienne made an effort not to think about her very often, he couldn't deny that all these years later, it still hurt to remember Kate English. He'd fucked many since, and spent five years with crazy Amy, but if he was honest, Kate was the one girl who'd ever *really* gotten under his skin. Sometimes he wondered about her— did she ever think of him? Did she ever wish their short affair could have turned into something more? Of course not. After the incident with Alex, he'd never heard from her again.

The elevator door opened suddenly, and Étienne looked up and smiled to see J.C. waiting for him behind glass doors.

"Étienne!" greeted his brother, holding open the door to the offices of the Rousseau Trust as Étienne hobbled from the elevator into the reception area. His leg still ached, but the doctor said he should be using it regularly now that the cast had been removed, so he pushed forward.

"*Merci, Jean Christian*," he said in their native French before stepping haltingly through the glass door.

Étienne's brother Jean Christian, or J.C. as he was more well-known among their friends and acquaintances, was five years older than Étienne, and one of his best friends. When their father had passed away a few years ago, they'd started the Rousseau Trust together as a way of investing his vast fortune. Last year, Jax had come on board after making the decision to attend law school. Their other sister, Mad, had gone a completely different direction with her life, and was the assistant children's librarian at one of the larger branches of the Philadelphia Public Library. Mad didn't have the stomach for business—of all the Rousseau children, Madeleine Rousseau was the sweetest, kindest, most tenderhearted. Which is why it was no surprise she was standing just behind J.C., grinning at Étienne in welcome.

"How does it feel to be back?" she asked, stepping forward to kiss both of his cheeks and embrace him.

Though he'd just seen Mad at his place for dinner last Friday, her hugs and kisses were always welcome.

"*Tres bien, belle seour*," he answered, patting her back gently with his free hand. "What are you doing here?"

"Just came to welcome you back," she said, dark eyes sparkling.

Étienne narrowed his eyes. "Hey, why do you look so beautiful?"

"Oh." Mad's lips parted but she quickly lowered her eyes as her cheeks flushed pink. "I, um, I just—"

"I was right! I thought I smelled a huge ego all the way from my office!" Jax strode into the reception area in a black pencil skirt, hands on her hips, attitude in full swing, and offered Étienne a big smile.

"*Your* office? Don't you mean mine, little sister?"

J.C. cleared his throat. "We couldn't have her working in the broom closet."

"So you gave her my office?"

"Nah," said Jax, winking at J.C. "He had the kitchenette redesigned as an office for me."

Étienne whipped his eyes to his brother. "My espresso machine?"

"Safely relocated to your office," said J.C., chuckling as his phone buzzed in his hand. "I have to take this. I'll let these two harass you for a while. When you're settled in, give me a shout so we can talk . . . new deal starting today and I . . . uh, I need to get you up to speed." He clapped Étienne gently on the shoulder as he turned to leave. "Good to have you back, Ten."

Étienne watched his brother go before turning his attention back to the twins. "So, Mad was just about to tell me—"

Jax reached out and took Étienne's arm. "Let me help you to your office!"

Étienne gave her a look then turned back to Mad, who picked up her coat from an armchair and quickly shrugged into it.

"I have to get back to the library," she said, giving her brother a quick kiss, her cheeks still flaming.

"Already?"

"She's very important," said Jax, waving good-bye to Mad and tugging Étienne forward. "Young minds to mold and all that."

"Dinner on Friday night?" Étienne called after Mad.

"Yes. At J.C.'s place," she said, stepping into the waiting elevator as the glass door whooshed closed.

He turned back to Jax. "What's up with her?"

"Boy, you're dense."

"Am I?"

"Hells yes." Jax cocked her head to the side. "Can't you tell? She's in love. Obvi."

"What? What the hell? With who?"

"Whom," corrected Jax.

"With *whom* is our baby sister in love?" he asked, realizing that Jax had somehow maneuvered him down the hall to his office.

"I could tell you," said Jax, "but then I'd have to kill you. And I like you way too much for murder."

"Why is death on the table?"

"Because you're not going to like it."

His next thought was totally irrational—and likely prompted by his early musings—but he couldn't help it. "One of the goddamned English brothers?"

Jax widened her eyes with glee, a slow grin spreading across her face. "Close, but no cigar. Last I checked, they're all taken."

"How did *that* happen?"

"Didn't you hear? They're irresistible."

Étienne scrunched up his face in distaste. "What unlucky girl landed Alex-fucking-English?"

Jax's face remained impassive, even though Alex English was an accepted villain in their immediate family. She picked a piece of lint off her black cashmere sweater. "He fell hook, line, and sinker for Jessica Winslow. Wedding this summer."

"Little Jessie Winslow, huh? My condolences. I bet Christopher's a wreck."

"I don't know. Winslows and Englishes seem pretty cozy, actually."

"Yeah. They always *were* tight. So, Jessie and Alex, huh? Break your leg and you miss a year's worth of gossip." He narrowed his eyes at Jax. "And you're telling me that awkward-as-hell, Stratton-fucking-English is off the market too?"

"Seems that way. He's screwing some dancer chick named Valeria who has a sizeable ass," she said, making a lewd hand gesture as she sat down in a guest chair in front of her brother's desk.

Étienne chuckled. An ass-man himself, he respected Stratton's choice even though he despised Stratton English with the heat of a thousand fires for getting involved in his on-again, off-again situation with Amy.

"I totally understand why you hate Alex . . . but, I don't think you have cause to hate Stratton," said Jax with a knowing look. "Come on. Do you seriously think he ever banged Amy? I mean, I think it's more likely—because she was certi-fucking-fiable—that they were just friends and Crazy Amy just made it *sound* like there was more going on."

"I know she slept over at his place, Jax. A lot. Every time we broke up, she ended up there, because she loved calling me from the landline. What the hell do you think they were doing? Watching chick flicks? Eating ice cream? Playing tiddly winks?"

Jax scoffed. "I grant you, tiddly winks would've been a great waste of Stratton English's godlike body, but I'm telling you . . . he's hardcore into this Italian chick. I don't think he and Amy were ever a thing, no matter how she made it look. I don't think he's the type that could downshift that fast."

"Fucking Amy," muttered Étienne, sitting down heavily in his desk chair and leaning his cane against the desk. "Psycho."

"You can say that again," agreed Jax.

"I still don't like him."

"That's your prerogative."

"As long as we're talking about my favorite family from the old neighborhood," he said acidly, "are you saying that Weston English and Connie Atwell are a done deal? Because last I heard, she went to Italy without him."

"Nope. He and Connie went their separate ways, and he met a cutie pie named Molly at Fitz's wedding. Tiny tits, too many freckles, sorta had this Midwestern 'aw, shucks' thing going for her."

Étienne rolled his eyes. "Perfect."

"Pretty much."

"So, all of the Englishes are finally off the market," said Étienne, taking a deep breath and refusing to explore the slight squeeze of his heart as he said these words, and wishing he'd specified "brothers."

"Not *all* of the Englishes," said Jax, giving him a sly grin.

Étienne stared at her with hard eyes, daring her to go there, his lips narrowed to an unamused line. "Leave it alone, Jax."

"I know you still think about her," said his sister softly, lowering her lashes. While Étienne and Jax spoke freely about every other aspect of their lives, Jax knew that Kate English was not a comfortable or welcome conversation topic for her brother.

Refusing to rise to her bait, Étienne opted for silence, pulling his bottom lip into his mouth and biting it hard as he tried to banish the image of Kate's soft, blonde hair and trusting, blue eyes from his mind.

"Okay, fine," said Jax, realizing they were at a stalemate. Her usual dry, witty demeanor took on a more serious edge. "But, I think you need to have a conversation with Jean Christian *tout de suite* about this new deal."

Étienne looked up at his sister, wrinkling his forehead, thoughts of Kate English scattering. "Why?"

Jax got up from her seat and pushed the chair back under the lip of her brother's desk. "Just trust me. You're going to want to have a conversation ASAP."

"Why can't *you* tell me what's going on?"

"Because I'm not a partner," she said evenly. "I'm staying out of it. Plus," she said, glancing at her diamond-encrusted

Cartier watch, "I'm going to be late for class. Catch you later?"

"Friday?" asked Étienne distractedly, staring at the back of his hand, which lay flat on his desk.

"See you at J.C.'s," she said, sailing out of his office door.

As soon as she was gone, Étienne turned his gaze away from the small white scars on the backs of his knuckles, fisting his hand as he turned in his chair. His view from the fourth floor wasn't spectacular—all he could really see was the office building across the street—but he sat back in his chair for a moment, annoyed that the English family was stealing so much of his peace of mind this morning. What the hell? Was there no escape from that fucking family?

He didn't want to think about Kate. He'd learned from experience that rehashing those memories did nothing but put him in a nasty, bitter funk for hours. And yet, even as he fought himself, he could feel thoughts of their week together—as warm, lush, and golden as Kate's hair—pooling in his head, on the brink of flooding his mind with overwhelming and unwelcome feelings.

In an attempt to escape them, he stood up, grabbed his cane, and hobbled from his office to J.C.'s, opening the door without knocking.

"Tell me about the new deal."

J.C. looked up from his desk in surprise. "Settled in already?"

Étienne dropped his body to the red leather sofa across from J.C.'s desk. "Cut the shit. Jax was being all weird about it. What do I need to know?"

J.C. leaned back in his chair, cocking his head to the side. "We agreed when we started this business that we'd leave our personal crap at the door, right?"

Étienne nodded stiffly.

"Okay. So, that established, I made a good deal that you might not like."

"In ink?"

J.C. shook his head back and forth slowly. "Not yet."

Étienne relaxed into the couch. "Good. Now tell me the deal isn't with the English brothers . . ." As J.C. started to respond, Étienne held up his hand to stop him. ". . . because you are *my* brother and you know my history with that family and 'personal crap at the door' or not, I know you wouldn't force me into a position in which I was required to work with them."

"Ten . . ." started J.C.

"Just tell me it's not the English brothers."

"It is."

"*Fuck!*" exclaimed Étienne, lurching forward, then wincing when his recently-injured knee banged into the coffee table in front of him. He rubbed it, huffing with anger as he looked back at his brother. "Are you kidding me? *Merde!* What were you thinking?"

"God, you got into a little scrape with Alex over ten years ago—"

"*A little scrape?* Are you crazy? He got me *expelled* from St. Michael's, Jean Christi—"

"You were kids."

"He broke my fucking nose!"

"The surgeon did a great job fixing it," said J.C. amicably.

"And Stratton-fucking-Eng—"

"Give me a break. I'd be surprised if he actually knew what to *do* with his dick, and you think he boned Amy? No way. I'm with Jax. You gotta let that one go."

"Nice to know you and Jax have been gossiping about my private life. And just for your information, Amy spent a lot of time at his place."

"On the couch, I'm betting. No, wait. I bet *he* slept on the couch and gave *her* the bed. You were just too close to all of it to see she was playing you both like fiddles." J.C. grimaced. "Bitch. You are so well rid of her."

It was gratifying that Étienne didn't feel like punching his brother for insulting Amy. All he felt was silent agreement, which confirmed that he was well and truly finished with her and gave him the perspective to say, "This isn't about Amy. It isn't even about Alex and Stratton. It's about you entering into a deal with people I fucking hate. Thank God you didn't ink it."

"I lied," said J.C.

"What about?"

"I inked it."

"What the *fuck*, J.C.?" His knee clobbered the table again and he let out another loud "*fuck*" as he leaned forward and rubbed it again.

"We can get out of it, but there'll be a penalty. A big one."

Étienne raked his hands through his hair, bending his neck and staring at the floor. "I can't believe you did this."

"Sorry. But I can promise you this, little brother. You won't have to work with Alex. He's in London. And I'll handle Stratton. You'll just be on point with their legal counsel."

Étienne looked up at J.C., giving him a sour look. "Well, that's just great. Weston English is about as hotheaded as they come. He's going to be as difficult as possible."

"Then be glad you won't be working with Weston. He took a job at the D.A.'s office at the end of February."

"Huh." Étienne wrinkled his nose in thought. "Fitz?"

At least Fitz, who was also a lawyer, was even-tempered and level-headed. Plus, he had the added benefit of being one of the few English brothers with whom Étienne didn't have a mired personal history.

"Nope. Not Fitz."

Étienne shook his head, trying to figure out where J.C. was going with this. "Well, I find it really hard to believe that English & Sons has hired non-family counsel for this—"

"Kate."

Étienne's head snapped back like he'd been smacked. "What?"

"Kate. Kate English. She lives in Philly now. She's been lead counsel for English & Company since March."

Kate English. Fuck.

Étienne stared at J.C. long and hard before looking back down at his hand, which he flexed and fisted reflexively.

Staring daggers at J.C., he finally said quietly, "I can't work with her. Jax'll have to do it."

"Impossible. The deal's in New Orleans, and you're schooled in Napoleonic code. She isn't."

His eyes must have been like pinwheels, zeroing in on his brother's slightly sheepish, slightly amused face.

"*Shit!*" yelled Étienne, picking up his cane and throwing it across the room.

Kate. KateKateKateKateKate.

Her name reverberated in his head, making it ache, making it long for something he hadn't seen or touched or reached for in twelve years, making it yearn for something he could never have again, something he should never have had in the first place, something that had changed the whole trajectory of his life, catastrophically, at the time.

Étienne looked up at J.C. "You're *not* my brother."

"Yeah, I am," he answered, his eyes compassionate.

"What's the penalty if we back out?" Étienne asked softly.

"Four million."

Étienne's eyes flashed with despair. Was avoiding his personal history with the English family worth four million dollars? The answer arrived, grim and quick: it was not.

"No other way out?"

"If it helps, we stand to make a lot in the sale, Ten. We're unloading that shipbuilding company that's always been the oddball in our portfolio."

"Fuck," muttered Étienne, before looking up at J.C. in anger and surrender. "It better be a *fantastic* goddamned deal."

Meeting Kate

Fifteen-year-old Étienne Rousseau leaned down so his mother could kiss his cheek then looked up and gave his father a confident grin.

His father winked at him before turning to Jean Christian, who stood beside Étienne. "You're in charge while we're away, son. Look after Étienne and the girls."

"Of course, father," answered newly twenty-one-year-old Jean Christian, who hadn't been very happy about "babysitting" his siblings during spring break. When his parents had sweetened the deal by offering J.C. a thousand dollars for his time, he'd—unsurprisingly—capitulated and agreed to live at Chateau Nouvelle while their parents spent the week in Hong Kong for business.

Lilliane Rousseau beamed at Jacqueline and Madeline, who had recently insisted they be called Jax and Mad in an episode of ridiculous teenage folly that would almost certainly blow over by next week.

"Be good for your brother," their mother said gently, kissing each of her daughters on the cheek. "Make good choices."

The four siblings followed their parents to the front walkway, waving good-bye as the hired car crunched over the gravel of their driveway, bearing their parents swiftly to the airport.

"See ya, suckers!" exclaimed Jean Christian as soon as the car was out of sight. He turned to his younger brother and sisters. "Well, it's only six o'clock. If I hustle, I can be back on campus for the first spring break fiesta!"

Étienne looked up at J.C. with wide eyes. "But Papa said—"

"Princeton's only an hour away, butt plug. Besides, I'll stop by tomorrow," said J.C. He chucked Mad under the chin. "And I'll take you two out for ice cream, too."

"Are you going to be staying overnight on campus all week?"

"That's the plan." J.C. flashed a grin at his siblings as he strode over to his car with keys jangling. "Julien and Marie will be here if you need anything," he said, referring to their gardener and housekeeper. "Don't miss me too much . . . and don't burn the place down!"

Étienne stood beside his sisters as J.C. zoomed down the driveway in his shiny red Saab, heading north toward New Jersey, leaving them alone without proper adult supervision.

Julien and Marie lived in an apartment over the garage and would be around a lot, of course, but that wasn't the same as having their parents or J.C. in residence, as evidenced when Jax turned to Mad with a giggle. "Let's go out!"

"Hey, I don't know . . ." said Étienne, but his words were wasted as Jax grabbed Mad's hand and they slipped back inside.

Étienne stood stunned and alone on the front walkway for a moment before following his sisters inside. With his brother gone and his sisters entertaining each other, it was going to be a long week for him. He wondered who else was around . . . the Winslows were still living in London and Étienne was steering clear of the Story sisters for now. For solid reasons of his own, he couldn't stand the English brothers, but maybe he'd head over to Dash Ambler's in a bit and see if he was around, or maybe he'd just relish having the remote all to himself for once and spend some quiet time at home alone.

Although Étienne was popular, he was also somewhat of a loner by nature. Or by nurture. When his parents had moved their family to the United States eight years ago, seven-year-old Étienne didn't speak a word of English. His sisters were enrolled in a nursery school program and J.C., who was several years older, had had the benefit of four years of English back in France.

Étienne, enrolled in the second grade program at a private Catholic school, had been an odd-man-out for months as he struggled to learn English and fit in with the American kids who didn't have much use for his bumbling speech and clumsy grammar. It hadn't been an especially easy transition, but his parents, who often employed tough-love strategies with their four children, had thought it best for Étienne to assimilate immediately without coddling. The experience had made him quiet and careful with his words. He spoke sparingly when he wasn't with his family, and while this might be adorable to teenage girls, who fancied him brooding, the truth was that his confidence had taken a hit at a young age. Silence was simply safer unless he trusted the person with whom he was speaking.

While he was trying to decide between company and quiet, the twins bounded down the stairs, changed from their school uniforms into jeans and tank tops.

"We're going over to Betsy Story's house," said Mad, pulling on tennis shoes.

"And we're taking beer," said Jax, racing ahead to the kitchen.

Étienne turned to Mad. "That's not a good idea and you know it."

"*Ferme la bouche, Étienne*," said Mad with a giggle. "Don't spoil our fun. *You* drink beer."

"I'm fifteen."

"Two years older. Big deal."

"Be back by ten," he called as she disappeared into the kitchen to find Jax.

A few hours later, Étienne checked his watch, surprised he'd been watching TV and dozing on and off for almost three hours. He briefly considered swinging over to Dash's house, but checking his watch again, he decided against it. It was almost ten and he hadn't heard the girls come in yet. Remembering his father's parting words *to J.C.* about looking after the twins, he decided to go find them.

Heading out the side door of the recreation room where he'd been watching TV, he didn't realize he'd forgotten to put shoes on until his toes sank into the freezing, wet grass beyond the heated flagstone patio. Looking up at the night sky dotted with stars, he realized he didn't mind. Though the spring night was chilly and the grass was an odd mixture of soft and prickly between his toes, he kind of liked the strangeness of it.

The distant sound of giggling coming from the English estate, Haverford Park, made him head in that direction.

Trekking quietly across the grounds of the dark, empty Winslow estate, Westerly, the laughter grew louder until he parted the bushes and stepped into the well-lit backyard of Haverford Park. And there, about ten yards in front of him, was a trampoline, with four girls sitting in a circle.

Mad noticed him first. "Ten!"

"It's late," he whispered back loudly, striding across the lawn.

He scanned the trampoline quickly, catching sight of Betsy Story sitting beside another girl, who glanced at him briefly before turning back around. For a second he was distracted by her thick blonde hair tumbling in waves over the collar of her denim jacket, and he wondered who she was.

Betsy cleared her throat loudly.

"Hey, Bets," he offered.

"Hi," said Betsy coolly, looking away from him.

He'd kissed her a few months ago and she'd let him touch her tits, for which he was grateful. But later he'd heard through the grapevine that her feelings were hurt when he didn't follow up afterwards and ask her out. She'd called him a "user jerk" and her older sister, Alice, who went to Princeton with J.C., told him that "your little brother's a prick for dissing my sister."

Girls were so stupid like that. Did Betsy expect a marriage proposal just because they'd fooled around? Whatever. Kissing and touching? He lived for it, he *loved* it, but it was all for fun. She offered, he took. The contract was as simple as that and didn't include dinner. It didn't *mean* anything. In fact, Étienne had yet to meet a girl who'd made him feel something other than his dick hardening with anticipation.

"Étienne," said Jax, drawing his attention to the girl with the blonde hair with a wave of her hand, "this is Kate. Kate English."

Étienne looked at her as she turned around slowly. As she moved, a cloud slid away from the moon, illuminating the trampoline, creating a moonlight halo out of her hair.

"Hi," she said, offering him a shy smile as she pushed a lock of gold behind her ear.

Étienne felt like he'd been sucker-punched, because suddenly his lungs were depleted, frozen, and still as he stared at her. His fingers twitched by his sides, wanting to touch that lock of soft blonde hair, wanting to gently brush his fingertips against the perfect shell of her ear. His lungs burned as he stared back at her, unsmiling, shocked by his reaction to this unknown girl.

He opened his mouth to say hello, but he couldn't seem to form the word, so he closed his lips, watching her eyes trail down his face and rest on his mouth for several moments before skating back to his eyes.

"I'm Kate," she said, her smile widening just a touch, even though he hadn't offered her any encouragement.

His hand moved of its own volition, reaching out to her, and she answered his invitation, raising her own hand and enveloping his with her cool, soft skin.

Maybe it was the moonlight . . . or the soft, wet grass . . . or the clean, crisp air.

Maybe it was the way the world had tilted and the moon had backlit Kate like an angel.

Maybe it was her smile—so open and warm, so pure and unspoiled—or her blue eyes, the color of which he could just make out by moonlight.

He couldn't account for it, but in clasping Kate's hand he found everything that had been missing with every other girl he'd kissed and groped. He *felt* something. It slammed into him like a freight train—like destiny, like grace—and even at fifteen-stupid-years old, Étienne knew it mattered.

Kate's hand grew warmer against his the longer they touched, and his body reacted violently, his blood sluicing through his veins, hot and dirty, sweet and good. He settled and resettled his fingers against her skin, fighting hard against the impulse to entwine his fingers with hers.

Feeling off-balance and undone, he searched her face frantically, lingering on her lips, which made him lick his own with involuntary yearning.

"He's such a weirdo," said Jax, shaking her head.

"I guess it's time to go," agreed Mad with an embarrassed sigh.

The twins shimmied to the edge of the trampoline, making it ripple and breaking his connection to Kate as she unclasped his hand.

His fingers idled, limp and abandoned, before he snatched them away, shoving his hand into the back of his jeans. He ran his free hand through his hair, trying to figure out what had just happened.

Who the hell was she? A long-lost English sister? A cousin? He grimaced. Of all the families on Blueberry Lane, she had to be a part of that one, right? Well, that was fucking inconvenient, he thought as he tried to steady his ragged breathing. Why did touching her hand make him feel so much, want so much? And God, why did it suck so much to think of walking away from her now?

He flicked his glance back to Kate, but she wasn't looking at him anymore—why should she? He hadn't even managed to utter a word to her. She was hugging his sisters good-bye. Étienne clenched his jaw and turned around, stalking back in the direction from whence he'd come, the soft footfalls of his little sisters following behind a moment later.

At the wide border of daffodils in front of the hedge that separated Westerly from Haverford Park, he turned back around to see Kate English thoughtfully watching his retreat. She raised her hand in farewell, but he turned and stepped forward quickly, disappearing into the hedge before she could claim anymore territory in his throbbing, yearning, ridiculous heart.

Chapter 3

The English were skirmishing.

Kate's Uncle Tom had convened a meeting that included her, Barrett, Fitz, and Stratton, to vote on whether or not English & Company would pursue the acquisition of Rousseau Shipbuilding. Despite Kate's assurances that she didn't mind working with the Rousseaus, the conversation had still dissolved into a family quarrel.

"Have we forgotten our history with that family?" demanded Stratton, looking sideways at Kate.

Barrett sighed heavily, shaking his head in consternation.

Fitz and Stratton were passionately against any business venture that included the Rousseaus, while Barrett and Tom both insisted that the best business decision would be to pursue the purchase. Before it turned into a deadlock, Kate decided to cast her vote.

"I'm with Barrett and Uncle Tom. It's in our best interest to buy. And that's not all . . . I *want* to run lead on this."

Fitz whipped his head to look at Kate. "I'm a lawyer, too, Kate. Let me do it."

Her uncle shot down that suggestion. "You're having a baby in six weeks, son. You won't be reliable."

"I can do it. I took a few legal courses," said Stratton.

Kate cocked her head to the side, leaning close to Stratton's ear and whispering, "You're really making me angry."

"I'm trying to protect you," he shot back.

Meanwhile, Fitz was trying to convince his father and Barrett that he could handle the legal side of the deal and Daisy's pregnancy at the same time.

That was it. Kate slapped her hand down on the conference table hard enough to make her uncle's coffee jump and said, "Listen!"

Five pairs of blue eyes turned to Kate in surprise.

"English & Company will benefit from this acquisition, so forget any thoughts of sidelining the Rousseaus *right now*." Barrett's lips quirked up slightly, and he nodded at her with pride and respect. "And *I* am the legal counsel for English & Company. Not Fitz, and certainly not Stratton. *Me*. Kate. So *I* will be on point with Rousseau's counsel on this deal." Stratton started to say something, but she raised her voice and rode right over him. "We are family and I love all of you very much. But this is business, and if any of you *ever* use my personal life to isolate me from a project again, I will consider bringing a discriminatory suit against this company. Is that clear?" Kate checked off the eyes of her cousins and uncle one by one before turning to Stratton. "How about you, Mr. CFO? You ready to see me as a full business partner?"

"It's your grave, Kate," murmured Stratton, adjusting his glasses as he stared down at the table. "I hope you don't regret it."

"I won't," she answered evenly, then softened her voice and added, "I won't because I will be legal counsel for the ninth-largest shipbuilding company in the world."

She looked across the table to see Barrett smiling. "Way to go, Kate. I couldn't have said it better myself."

"Barrett," she continued, gathering her files and standing up, "I'll need your notes so I can get up to speed. Have them on my desk within an hour."

"Oh," he said. "One thing . . . I already scheduled a meeting. Today. With J.C. and Étienne Rousseau at their offices."

Kate's breath caught, but she nodded without a hitch. "Great. What time?"

"You don't have to go."

"Barrett . . ." she warned him.

"Four o'clock."

"Four's fine," answered Kate crisply, heading back to her office to slog through the legal documents associated with the acquisition and force herself not to anticipate seeing Étienne in a few short hours.

Six hours later, Kate looked at the clock, shocked to see that it was after three. Her desk was covered with half-filled coffee cups, an open bag of chips, an empty muffin wrapper, open highlighters, two law books, and several piles of sorted paper. Amazingly, the time had flown by once Kate had hit stride, throwing herself into the legal issues that she'd need to manage for this deal to take place.

It was a pretty simple deal, actually. English & Company would acquire Rousseau Shipbuilding for a sum of $180 million and would then merge the new acquisition to the other two they owned. There would be some staffing redundancies, but that would be up to Barrett to handle after the merger. The only tricky bit Kate could see was that the company had been inherited, and since it was based in Louisiana, she needed to figure out if the state laws would bring any unexpected paperwork to the sale. That, she assumed, would be Étienne's bailiwick.

Étienne.

Her hand trembled as she picked up one of the coffee cups for a bracing sip. She'd see him in just a few short minutes, which seemed impossible after so long, and her heart thundered in anticipation.

"You almost ready to go?" Barrett said suddenly from the doorway. Kate jerked in surprise, spilling a healthy splash of black coffee on the front of her dress. She winced, patting at the cool wetness.

"At least you're wearing brown," said Barrett, giving her a lopsided smile. "You can't really see it. Meet me downstairs. I'll get us a cab."

Kate shoveled a pile of papers into her briefcase, still swiping at the top of her dress as she made her way to the elevator bank.

Good Lord, thought Kate, looking at herself in the shiny brass door of the elevator. Her hair stuck out of its once-tidy bun in haphazard chunks and wisps, and she pulled two pencils from said bun with wonder. The splotch of coffee on her dress looked like a nursing leak over her right boob, and her skirt was wrinkled with tiny crumbs of muffin sticking to the sweater-like material. She'd thought the simple brown sweater dress chic at one point, but she had to admit, it had seen better days. It had stretched out over the years, losing its shape, and the cowl neck in the front revealed a little more than was proper if she let it fall victim to gravity. She messed with it, covering the deep line of exposed cleavage and brushed off the sack-like, shapeless skirt.

Huffing at her reflection, which didn't look much better than it had two minutes before, she reminded herself that she wasn't going out on a date—the reason for the meeting was business.

Business, business, business, she repeated in a mantra as she stepped onto the elevator.

Any notions of Étienne Rousseau—as anything other than her legal co-counsel—needed to be banished from her mind. And with any luck, he'd be a complete and total jerk and make it easier on her.

The elevator arrived in the lobby and Kate lifted her chin, stepping forward and clutching her briefcase with sweaty palms as she exited the building and found Barrett waiting in a cab at the curb.

"Sorry," she said, sliding in next to him.

"No problem. We're not late."

Kate gave her cousin a brief smile, noticing his strange expression. "What?"

"You have . . . um . . ." He reached over and pulled pencil number three from her hair.

"It's a bad habit," she explained, "from law school. I was always losing pencils, so a friend of mine told me that every morning she made a bun in her hair and stuck pencils in it. I copied her idea and always had my own supply after that."

"Smart," said Barrett, chuckling softly.

Kate opened her purse and took out a brush, loosening her hair and brushing out the long waves. "I guess I should try to look a little more presentable."

"Not on my account," said Barrett.

As she went to bind her hair back into a ponytail, the rubber band in her fingers snapped. "Damn." Looking through her purse, she realized she didn't have a replacement. She'd just have to wear her hair down. Twisting it as tightly as she could, she laid it over her shoulder, then jammed her brush back into her purse.

"Don't be nervous," said Barrett gently, watching her fuss. "It'll be okay."

"Oh, I'm fine," answered Kate a little too quickly.

Barrett gave her a look.

"Okay," she admitted. "I'm a little nervous."

"What happened between you two? You and Étienne? I've heard the stories, of course, but I was at college at the time so all of my information was secondhand."

Kate shook her head then shrugged. "He was a spring break fling."

Lie. He was much, much more than that.

"Were you in love with him?" asked Barrett, crossing his arms over his chest and looking at her thoughtfully.

"Yes."

"Are you still?" he asked.

"No," she answered, though the blunt sound of her denial felt oversimplified or maybe even cowardly, and it sat like rotten egg smell on her lips, making her wrinkle her nose. It felt like a half-truth or a third-lie or just not the right word at all. She pushed back on this feeling as hard as she could, and added, "I think he's a jackass."

"No arguments here."

"Anyway, there's Tony, and he's—"

"Yeah, Tony. He seems nice."

"He *is* nice." *And eventually, one day when he's ready, he will draw me into his elegant arms, and—*

"So, you two are . . . serious?"

Kate paused before answering. *Were they?* She and Tony had been more or less exclusive for weeks, but it didn't feel serious. Sometimes it didn't even feel substantial enough to be relevant. Tony certainly hadn't made her feel—yet, she still had hopes—the way that Étienne made her feel all those years ago. Then again, *no one* had ever made Kate feel as Étienne had. Despite several college boyfriends and a serious relationship a few years ago in New York, memories of Étienne still felt more vibrant than real life.

Which is why you need to be reminded of how things ended, not how they began.

"I don't know," she said cautiously, offering Barrett a small smile as she answered his question about Tony. "We'll see."

They lapsed into silence, but despite her best efforts, her mind wouldn't settle, as one heart-thumping thought circled round and round in her brain: in a matter of minutes she'd be face-to-face with the man to whom she'd willingly and lovingly surrendered her virginity.

Looking through the rain-covered window, Kate thought of the last time she ever saw his face in person: She'd turned and looked back at him once more before slipping through the hedge and returning to her aunt and uncle's house. Her body had still been warm from his, the space between her legs tender, her skin sensitive, and her heart thundering. The way he'd gazed at her, with such profound tenderness and wonder as she waved good-bye, had made her eyes brim with tears of gratitude and love. It had been pure hell to leave him, but she had forced one foot in front of the other, secure in the knowledge that even though she'd leave for New York in the morning, and despite the guaranteed disapproval of her parents if they ever found out, her love story with Étienne was just beginning.

She winced at her blurry reflection. Later she'd discovered—over the silent days and weeks that followed—that it wasn't beginning at all. In fact, their short romance was already over.

And yet, she couldn't help wondering as she watched the drops of rain slip soundlessly down the glass like so many tears . . . Would he still speak in that low, silky, accented voice that had so captivated her as a teenager? Would his hair still be black and thick, tousled and unruly like he just rolled out of bed? Would he tease her with backhanded compliments and sexy smirks? Would his eyes seize hers as they used to, searching and direct?

Would he recognize her?

Would he be kind?

"We're here, Kate."

She looked up as they stopped in front of a nondescript office building. Barrett paid the fare, and Kate stepped out of the cab, taking a deep breath. Barrett opened an umbrella, placing his hand under her elbow as they walked briskly across the wet sidewalk and up the steps to the office building lobby.

Stepping off the elevator on the fourth floor, they were greeted by glass doors directly in front of them that read *Rousseau Trust*. As Barrett pushed the door open for his cousin, he leaned down and whispered in her ear, "Breathe. It's just business."

Kate smiled at him gratefully, steeling her resolve to put forth only the most professional demeanor with Étienne, regardless of their history.

"Good afternoon," said an administrative assistant, who looked up as Kate and Barrett entered the small reception area. "May I help you?"

"Hello," said Kate, tucking a strand of blonde hair behind her ear and offering a warm smile, despite the fierce hammering of her heart. "Kate and Barrett English here to see—"

"Me."

Étienne would have known her anywhere.

His eyes drank in her loveliness after such a long absence from it—the golden blonde of her thick, wavy hair that beckoned him with its softness, wordlessly urging him to touch the glossy lock recently tucked behind one ear. His fingers curled around the crooked curve of his cane, bracing himself as she turned from the receptionist, raised her chin, and trained her summer-sky blue eyes on his. They widened just slightly as her lips parted, tilting up in a small smile as her breath caught with a barely-there gasp of wonder. Her face softened in recognition or remembrance as Étienne gazed back at her—her features at once so familiar and so missed, he wouldn't have thought it possible after so many years. But the way his heart lurched and galloped confirmed what Étienne already knew: Kate English was still a weakness for him. Even all these years later, she was Kate and he was Étienne—and once upon a time, he had loved her madly.

"Étienne," she finally said in a quiet, slightly husky voice. She held out her hand, which trembled just a little. "It's been a long time."

He was a fool to expect he could take her hand without experiencing the same jolt of electricity he'd felt the first time he ever touched her, but it still surprised him. The way their hands fit together, the way his blood rushed fast and hot, gushing through his thundering heart like it hadn't been twelve years since he'd held her soft, naked, willing body against his, but only twelve days, twelve hours, twelve minutes ago instead. Staring at their joined hands, he swallowed thickly, then—distracted by Barrett clearing his throat behind her—dropped her hand and took a clumsy step back.

"Hello, Kate. Thank you for coming." Then he turned quickly to Barrett—knowing his cheeks were uncharacteristically flushed—determined to stay professional. "Barrett."

"Ten," said Barrett, extending his hand with a cool nod.

"J.C. is waiting for us in the conference room."

"Lead the way," said Barrett, placing his hand on the small of Kate's back.

Étienne turned, leaning on his cane, hating the way he probably looked—weak and hobbled—while she looked as vibrant and strong and beautiful as the day he'd met her. He could smell her perfume just behind him, something clean and fresh like soap, or fresh laundry, or fresh cut grass, cool between his toes on a starry spring night. Hobbling carefully down the hallway, he asked himself why the hell he didn't let J.C. greet them, but realized he hadn't given the matter any thought. The moment he'd heard the light squeak of the glass reception doors, he'd bolted up from his seat near the conference room door and made his way down the hallway, as if pulled to her. It had been more than a decade since he'd seen her face, but suddenly it was like he wasn't able to bear the separation another second. It made no sense at all, especially because he was so determined to protect his newfound freedom.

"Here we are," he said, stopping at the conference room door to allow Barrett and Kate to precede him into the room.

"Barrett. Kate. Thanks for coming today," said J.C., standing and reaching across the table to shake hands. "Shall we sit?"

"I think Kate should come with me," said Étienne without thinking.

J.C., who'd already sat back down, looked up in surprise. "Oh?"

"Mmm. We, uh, well, *we* have to discuss the legal issues, and *your* time would be better spent discussing the merger plans."

J.C. looked at Barrett, who shrugged as he took a seat at the table. "Does that work for you, Kate?"

Kate had been staring at Étienne since he uttered her name, but now she jerked her eyes to her cousin. "Yes. Fine. Work. We're all here for work. I'm here for . . . work."

Étienne's lips twitched as he looked down, still holding open the conference room door. She was just as nervous as he was, and damn it, it made him want to smile because he was reminded of how flustered she could get and how much he used to like it.

Kate pivoted quickly, passing by him as she stepped back into the corridor. He closed the conference room door and led the way down the hall wordlessly, listening for her footfalls behind him. Stopping at his office, he opened the door and held it for her, clenching his jaw as she swept past him, trying to remind himself that the woman who was addling his mind right now was the same girl who'd looked into his eyes with devotion and then had promptly forgotten he ever existed.

Tightening his lips and narrowing his eyes, he trailed behind her, cursing his cane as he made his way slowly to his desk, finally lowering his body to the chair with relief.

Kate glanced at him, and then looked quickly around the room before taking a step toward one of two guest chairs in front of his desk, placing her briefcase in one and pulling out the other to sit. She unsnapped her briefcase, opening it and repositioning it to face her, then took a deep breath and looked up at him with clear, defiant eyes.

"Shall we get started?"

My God, she's magnificent.

He had no idea where the thought came from, but it sat full and heavy in his head, edging out all other notions as he stared back at her. His lips twitched again, and he allowed them to form a small, teasing smile. He couldn't help it.

"Shouldn't we say hello first, *chaton*?"

Kitten. Her eyes flared at his use of the old nickname and color flooded her cheeks.

"No," she said. "I don't think so."

"Kate—"

"Fine." She tilted her head to the side and offered him a polite smile that didn't reach her eyes. "I was sorry to hear about your accident. How are you?"

"Much better now," he answered.

She licked her lips nervously and looked around the room, finally gesturing to the painting over the small love seat in a cozy alcove. "One of yours?"

It surprised him that she should remember his love of painting. He looked over at the artwork, a piece he'd completed at Chateau Nouvelle last summer. "Yes."

She stared at it for an extra beat before turning back to him. "It's good. You were always talented, Étienne."

"You look good, Kate." It wasn't an appropriate thing to say, but he was starting to realize that he didn't have much control over his words around her . . . which was the only way he could account for what came out of his mouth next. "Except for that dress."

She took a deep, sharp breath, blinking at him in shock.

"Still hiding your curves."

Her eyes widened and her cheeks flushed further as she looked down at her briefcase, picking up a sheet of paper and laying it flat on his desk.

"Shall we focus on business?" she asked, her voice tight.

"If you'll recall, I was a fan of them."

She stared at him, holding her breath, stunned and completely flustered.

"Sorry I said that about your dress," he said, biting on his lower lip. "Seeing you again is . . . throwing me off. I-I haven't been in the office for a while. This is my first day back and—"

"You know what, Étienne?" she interrupted, her eyes flashing with fury as they cut to his. "I'm not here for your amusement . . . or for a walk down memory lane . . . or for your obnoxious comments and backhanded compliments. I am here to review the legal issues arising from our acquisition of your—"

"Are you seeing anyone?" he blurted, ignoring her minitirade.

She sighed, shaking her head like she couldn't believe his insolence. He watched her carefully as she decided whether or not to answer the question, tensing and releasing her jaw before finally saying, "Not that it's any of your business, but yes, I am."

"Who?"

"Tony Reddington."

"Don't know him."

She blinked at him again before smoothing her hand over the document on his desk. "Yes, well, perhaps we should—"

"Want to know if I'm seeing anyone?"

"Not especially," she huffed, sitting back in her chair with her arms crossed over her chest. She searched his eyes for a moment and he read wariness, distrust and uncertainty in hers . . . but there, simmering below her indignation: curiosity. *There you are. Kate English, my curious cat, my kitten, my chaton.* He wasn't at all surprised when she finally asked softly, trying to sound disinterested, "Are you?"

He shook his head. "No. I just broke up with someone."

Suddenly her lips tilted up in a mocking smirk that he didn't find attractive at all. "Oh, is *that* how you're spinning it?"

So she knew about Amy. Of course she did. She was Stratton's cousin. Sitting back in his own chair, he stared at her, suddenly feeling more guarded and less flirtatious.

"Fine," he said evenly, with a little shrug of ennui. "She broke up with me."

"Smart girl."

Étienne felt his face harden, hurt feelings from long ago flooding back and crashing over him with fury. He'd been so sure Kate loved him all those years ago, but she hadn't, of course. She'd left Haverford after their night together and he'd never heard from her again. Not a phone call. Not a letter. Nothing. She'd obviously believed Alex's version of events as God's truth and turned her back on him without giving him any chance to explain. And it still hurt. Even now.

"Oh, I see. *You* know Amy so well?" He shook his head, a mean smile spreading his thin, angry lips. "No. The person you know so well is Stratton, so I'm curious to know if he confessed that he banged my girlfriend every time she and I broke up for half an hour, or did he edit out that part of the story?"

Kate gasped, lurching forward and slamming her palm on his desk. "Don't you *dare* talk about my cousin that way! He would *never—*"

"*He would never!* You're still a naïve little princess with stars in your eyes, aren't you, *chaton*? And *so* offended. Why don't you go run and get Barrett to beat me up?"

She stared at him, her face the picture of righteous indignation, her chest heaving up and down with the force of her breathing. Finally she said in a low voice laced with contempt, "You are *ridiculous.*"

He flinched. Did she have any idea of the price he'd paid when Alex beat his face to a pulp in the courtyard of St. Michael's? How he'd been expelled? Forced by his parents to leave Haverford and attend military school far away in Mississippi? Of course she knew. Her cousins would have told her everything.

"*I'm* ridiculous? Fine. I'm ridiculous. You know, Kate, you're right. We *should* focus on work. Let's get this over with." He reached forward, sliding the paper she'd placed on the desk closer to him and perusing it quickly. "Good idea. One of us needs to write a letter of intent. I'd ask you to do it, but if memory serves, letter writing was never your strong suit, so why don't I prepare it? I'll messenger it to English & Company tomorrow for your review."

As he spoke, she flinched, sitting back in her chair slowly and staring at him in shock, like she was trying not to cry. And as much as he hated her in that moment, his heart clutched with the knowledge that he'd somehow managed to hurt her.

"Fine," she murmured, looking away.

The fact that Kate had sent over thirty letters to Étienne after their week together—one a day for a month, none of which had ever been answered—made his comment so painful, it was as though he'd reached across the desk and slapped her. She dropped her eyes to her lap, biting the inside her cheek and forcing her eyes not to water.

So, she had one of her answers: he'd received her letters, but didn't feel that letter writing was her "strong suit." She sucked in a ragged breath, thinking about the flowery words of love she'd used so long ago to tell him how she felt, how much she missed him, how much she loved him, how she couldn't wait to see him again. He'd read them and ignored them—or worse, laughed at them.

As if that wasn't bad enough, he'd had the audacity to accuse Stratton of sleeping with Amy? Her blood boiled and her tears receded. Stratton had been nothing but kind to Étienne's ex-girlfriend. It was one thing to hurl insults at *her*. It was quite another to attack her cousin.

Well, she had gotten her wish. Étienne was being an utter and complete jerk, which should make it easy to thrust him from her head and heart, and focus all of her attention on sweet, polite Tony.

And yet.

And yet.

Kate sensed she had hurt him when she called Amy a "smart girl" for dumping him and to her surprise—and shame—that didn't feel very satisfying at all. It felt low and petty to take a cheap shot like that, and if he hadn't made that stupid comment about Barrett beating him up, she would have apologized. How had their conversation run off the rails so quickly?

She peeked at him quickly before glancing down again. He was still so beautiful, it almost hurt to look at him because she suddenly remembered every expression, every look, every word he ever said to her. She wanted to stare at him for hours, to reclaim the contours of his face, to run her fingertips over his lips then bury them in his hair.

When her eyes had slammed into his at the reception desk, she'd felt it all the way through to her marrow—he still owned some part of her all these years later. He would *always* matter to her, despite the way he'd hurt her.

However he'd also reminded her, in short order, of what a jackass he could be. If she hadn't been so shocked by his rude comment about her dress, she would have laughed because she agreed with him—it wasn't one of her prettier outfits. But then he'd chased it with that compliment about her curves, his eyes smoldering as he reminded her that he'd been a fan of them, and all reasonable thoughts had flown from her head.

Damn it. This meeting was a disaster, and she had no idea how to work with him moving forward. She was feeling just as off-kilter as she'd felt when she'd fallen for him so long ago, and she couldn't afford to walk down that road again. Unrequited longing might be a rite of passage for teenage girls, but it looked pathetic when worn by an adult woman. She wanted to focus on his rudeness and meanness, but being alone with him was making it impossible for her to control her weakness for him. There was only one solution: She needed to leave. Now.

"This was . . . unproductive." Kate reached for her brief-case, snapping it closed. She looked up at him, keeping her face impassive. "I think it would be best if we communicate via e-mail from here on out, don't you agree?"

"Fine," he said, trying to keep his brilliant green eyes flat and bored, but unable to hide the churning of emotion just below the surface.

Why did she have this strong, inexplicable feeling that he was somehow harboring hurt feelings too? It didn't make any sense. If he had snapped his fingers back then, she would have defied her parents and run to him, but he couldn't even be bothered to write back to her. Thirty unanswered letters had broken *her* heart. He wasn't the victim here, she was. She shoved her misguided intuition to the side and stood, extending her hand.

"I can't say it's been a pleasure, but—"

Just then, Étienne's office door opened with a whoosh. Kate turned to see J.C. and Barrett enter the room, both looking frazzled.

"You've probably figured out the same thing we have: the oil rig portion of the company is in violation of antitrust laws when added to the production of Harrison-Lowry," announced J.C., raking a hand through his hair. "It constitutes a monopoly. You two need to head down to Louisiana next week and find a buyer for the rigging business, or we'll be held up in arbitration by the U.S. government indefinitely."

Damn it, thought Kate, *I missed it*. She'd been so distracted by Étienne, she had missed a potential pothole in the deal.

Chastising herself, Kate slowly turned her head back to Étienne, who leaned back in his chair and smirked.

"*Ça va*. New Orleans in the spring? How delightful," he said, his soft French accent like silk. She read the challenge in his mocking eyes—he was daring her to refuse the trip and trash the deal.

Kate raised her chin at him in defiance and turned back to Barrett, making a silent promise to herself that her unfinished business with Étienne wouldn't jeopardize this deal again.

"Business is business. When do we leave?"

Flirting

Although she wasn't supposed to, Kate had let Weston ride ahead on his own, then slipped down from her own horse and grabbed the reins so she could make her way more leisurely on the section of the bridle path that abutted the Rousseau property. Flicking her glance at the house every few feet, but trying not to be obvious, she walked slowly with Stewart nickering his disapproval from just behind.

"I. Am. Ridiculous," she said softly to the brown pony after five minutes of walking without a glimpse of human life.

"I. Am. Étienne," said a laughing voice from behind her.

Kate gasped, spinning around so fast she dropped Stewart's reins and almost landed on her butt.

"Where di . . . how long have you been . . . ?" She reached down to pick up the leather strap, treating him to a widescreen view of her derriere in her haste.

"Following you?" He looked meaningfully at her backside then grinned at her, his lips turning up slowly. "Long enough to sing the entire song 'Baby Got Back' in my head."

Kate gasped, her eyes widening as she processed his unflattering words. She turned away from him as her cheeks flushed. "You're a jerk."

"That's what they tell me."

"Well, they're right."

"Here's the thing, though . . . I suspect your ass really isn't as huge as it looks in those jodhpurs. They add six inches on each side."

Kate started walking again, ignoring the burn behind her eyes. Her body shape was, and had always been, a source of insecurity for her, though she'd never met anyone who'd pointed it out in such a bald, offensive way. It's not that she was fat; she just wasn't super skinny like most of the girls she knew. Her breasts and hips had developed earlier, giving Kate a more womanly look that made her stick out a little from her peers.

"Umm . . . did my words somehow convey to you that the size of your ass bothers me?"

She turned on the heel of her riding boot to face him, face hot, eyes furious. "You know what? I couldn't care less if it bothers you." Swinging back around, she started walking away briskly. "And stop following me!"

"Because it doesn't," he called from behind her.

Kate spun around to face him, placing her hands on her hips as her larger-than-average breasts heaved uncomfortably against a thin white T-shirt. But as she processed what he'd just said, indignance was slowly replaced by confusion and she felt her brows knit together as she stared at him.

"It doesn't *what?*"

His eyes flicked to her lips as he took a step forward. Then another. Then another, until he was so close to her, she could smell him, and he smelled like men's shampoo, which pretty much smelled like heaven.

"Let me put this another way . . . As far as I'm concerned, the size of your ass," he said slowly, eyes still locked on her lips, only lifting at the final second, "is perfect."

The flush that had started in her cheeks suddenly spread into her scalp, down her neck and shoulders, resting over her breasts, then sliding like warm honey to her belly.

"Oh," she murmured.

He shrugged, offering her an adorable smile as he raked a hand through his floppy hair. "What can I say? I'm an ass-man."

He started walking again, and Kate took a deep, ragged breath, trying to fill her lungs before hurrying to fall into step beside him. Had he just insulted her or complimented her? He'd somehow managed to call her fat-assed and perfect at the same time, which was sort of mean, but sort of amazing. With Stratton's words from this morning—*steer clear*—still resonating in her head, she had to admit she was fascinated by him: he was edgy and teasing, brooding and provocative, crazy handsome and way too sexy for a teenager. Just being near him was making her body hot and shivery at the same time. There was no way she was cutting bait yet.

"Where do you go to school?" he asked conversationally once she'd caught up with him.

"Trinity Prep."

"In Manhattan?" He turned to her with slightly narrowed eyes. "You're not from Philadelphia?"

"Just visiting," she managed. *Me and my fat, perfect ass.* "Where, um, where do you go to school?"

"St. Michael's," he said. "With your cousins."

"Yeah, that's what Stratton said."

"Asking around about me, huh?"

"No! No, I-I just . . . I mentioned that I met you. Last night. On the trampoline." *On the trampoline? Really, Kate?*

"I wasn't actually *on* the trampoline," he pointed out.

No, you were barefoot and beautiful beside it.

"Are you friends with Betsy?" he asked.

"Yeah, I know her from summer camp."

"So, I bet you've heard a lot about me."

No, actually. Kate had never heard of him until last night.

She twisted her neck to look at him, her breath catching at the sight of his profile staring straight ahead as he walked beside her. His skin was pale, which made his long black lashes look extra dark and thick. His cheekbones were chiseled and manly, making him look much older than fifteen, and when Kate's eyes dropped to his lips, she felt another rush of heat in her belly.

"Um . . . heard like, um, what?"

"Like I don't have girlfriends," he informed her, his voice confident and cool, like he was a college guy or a character in a movie. "I have flings."

Whoa.

No, Betsy had definitely not shared this shocking, riveting bit of information with Kate. It seemed like an awfully bold thing for him to tell her, but Kate couldn't help the way it made her feel—all nervous and excited and suddenly out of breath. She had to work hard to control the whimper that lodged in her throat, threatening to squeak free.

"F-flings?"

"Mm-hmm," he purred, and was it her imagination, or was his toe-curling French accent getting that much thicker? "In fact . . . I'm looking for one this week."

"A fling."

"Mm-hmm."

His shoulder brushed into hers and it made her heart pump so fast, so loud, she wondered if he could hear it too. "Oh."

"What are *you* looking for this week, Kate?"

She stopped walking, handling the leather strap as she looked up at him earnestly. Kate knew she wasn't as cool as he was, nor, she suspected, anywhere near as experienced. She wasn't even totally sure he was kind, but from the moment she saw him last night, he'd zoomed up her list of the most intriguing, captivating people she'd ever met. And all she wanted was to spend her week scratching through that pseudo-cool, smooth, flippant, smirky exterior and to discover what was underneath. At a loss about how to say all of this without appearing psycho and desperate, she deferred with,

"I don't know."

He cocked his head to the side. "Because it kind of seemed like you were looking for me, too."

Her breath hitched again, but then something occurred to her. She lifted her eyes to his, a more confident smile spreading her lips. "Wait. *Too?*"

His cool façade slipped, and the smile he answered her with wasn't smirky at all. It was simple and sweet, and maybe even a little sheepish—just a teenage boy grinning at a teenage girl who'd inadvertently managed to make him slip up in his game of "too cool for you."

When she was little, Kate had a pair of blue-and-red-lensed glasses, and when she wore them to read a specially encoded book, she could see messages that were invisible without the glasses. As she smiled back at Étienne Rousseau, Kate felt like she'd just slipped on those glasses. Suddenly she could *see* him: the hope in his expression, the hint of vulnerability, the whisper of longing. He was just as young as she, likely as nervous, possibly even as interested. She knew what she was looking at, because her heart was certain it was a perfect mirror of the way she was looking at him, and it gave her the courage to respond.

"You're right. I was looking for you."

He chuckled softly—happily—as he reached for her free hand, lacing his fingers through hers and sending a swift shot of something awesome straight to her heart.

"Now that you've found me, Kate English, whatever will you do with me?"

Chapter 4

After such a disastrous ~~reunion~~, er, meeting, Kate knew she needed to clear her head. The best option now that it had stopped raining was to walk the thirty minutes back to her office. Barrett tried to convince Kate to share a cab, but she handed him her briefcase and insisted on walking.

What the hell had just happened between her and Étienne? And how was she going to be professional when they traveled to New Orleans together? They could barely remain civil in the same room for fifteen minutes. And she'd missed a crucial pitfall of the merger, which made her hunch her shoulders in shame. Still, the worst of it was that they'd had to schedule another face-to-face meeting to discuss how to unload the oil rig portion of the company, and while she was grateful for the home-court advantage of having the next meeting at her office, it meant that they wouldn't be able to confine their communication to e-mail only.

Kate needed to figure out a way to handle herself before Wednesday, but she was at a total loss. There was only one solution. Fishing her phone from her purse, she speed dialed her best friend, Libitz.

"KK! 'Sup?"

Kate smiled instantly, picturing Libitz like she was standing right there on the wet sidewalk beside her: dyed black hair in a supershort Twiggy cut to match her super-skinny Twiggy body. Superbig, dark brown eyes dominating her elfin face, and some superchic, barely-there lip gloss shipped from Paris, because New York had nothing that would "do." In short—no pun intended, although Libitz was also supershort—Libitz was, well, *super*.

"Lib, it is *so good* to hear your voice."

"I'd say the same, but I know that voice. Tired, upset, and . . . yep. Tears. I hear 'em. Who needs a good pounding?"

Kate's eyes watered as she burst into a giggle. Libitz weighed in at a cool one hundred and five pounds, which meant that she couldn't "pound" anything more than a house fly. Lib looked so cosmopolitan and cool on the outside that her deep, protective streak always surprised people who didn't know her, but Kate knew from experience: Lib was fierce when it came to the people she loved, and Kate ranked high on that list.

"Étienne Rousseau," she said, shaking her head at her own stupidity.

"Wait!" exclaimed Lib. "*Who?*"

"Étienne . . . um, I don't know if you remember, but—"

"*If I remember?* Spring break '03. Believe me, KK, I remember. I was there for the months upon months of tears." Lib paused for a second. "What I don't understand is why I'm hearing his name now."

"My company's doing a deal with his, and I just . . . saw him."

"Oh my God. That's huge!"

"I know. Hugely awful."

"How does he look? Horns sprouted yet?"

Kate chuckled again, swiping away the one tear that had gotten away. "Nope. As hot as ever, I'm afraid."

"I gotta say . . . this is *interesting*, KK."

"It's *not* interesting. It was a disaster. He was rude and jerky, and smiley and he said he always loved my curves and I could barely speak and he asked me about Tony, and I told him Amy was smart for dumping him and he told me my letters sucked." Kate shook her head, sighing deeply. "Dis. Ass. Ter."

"Totally lost. Start at the beginning."

Kate told Lib all about Barrett's deal with J.C. on Saturday night, and how Kate was actually the one who insisted on following through with the merger.

"Stop there," said Lib. "How come?"

"Because it's good for business. It's a solid opportunity and I'm not going to let—"

"*Errrrh*," interrupted Lib, making the sound of a game show buzzer. "I'm calling bullshit."

"Lib, you know I'm serious about business."

"Yeah, I know. But, this guy trampled your heart. I can understand you *grudgingly* agreeing to do the deal to be professional, but you just told me that you *insisted* on doing the deal, which means"—she hummed thoughtfully—"you wanted to see him."

Kate drew her bottom lip into her mouth.

"Stop chewing your lip," said Lib. "Why do you want to see him?"

No sense in lying to Lib. She'd know.

"I thought it would help me get over him."

"I sort of thought you *were* over him."

"I *was*," said Kate glumly. "But moving back here stirred up all these old memories and I don't know . . . I can't stop thinking about him and then I became friends with his sister on Facebook and—"

"Kathryn Grey English! You're cyber-stalking him, aren't you?"

Oh God. Libitz just knew her too well!

"Um . . . a little?"

"It's all coming into focus now," said Lib dryly. "Where does 'Prince Tony, the Charming but Asexual' fit into all of this?"

"That's not fair. He's not—"

"Yeah, yeah, yeah. Fine. Just answer the question."

Kate grimaced. She'd been talking to Lib about Tony for weeks now and Lib, who was apt to have sex against the wall of her apartment if a first date went well, couldn't get her head around Kate and Tony's chaste courtship.

"I mean, I sort of wanted to see Étienne. Yes. But just to verify that he's a total asshole and convince myself I was over him so my runway would be free for Tony."

"But does Tony *want* to land his plane on your runway?"

"Libitz!"

"Well? It's a valid question. But here's a better one . . . Do you want *Étienne* to land his plane on your runway instead?"

"Lib . . ." She wasn't sure her face could get any redder.

"Press your always-abnormally-cold palms against your cheeks, Ice Cube. You'll feel better in a sec."

"It's crazy freaky when you do that," said Kate, laughing as she wedged the phone between her ear and shoulder and pressed her cool palms against her hot cheeks.

"I think I know you better than you know yourself sometimes," said Libitz thoughtfully.

"Wouldn't surprise me," answered Kate, a surge of homesickness making her eyes prickle. "*Please* tell me what to do."

"Wish I could," she answered gently. "But you've got to figure this out."

"Okay, don't tell me what to do . . . tell me what you *see*."

"Hmm. Let's see." She could see Libitz nodding sagely as she took a deep breath. "You never got over Étienne. Possibly because he was your first, maybe because he disappeared, maybe because you loved him and just never stopped. Tony? He's nice, Kate. But he's a bookmark. He's just a place saver until the real story continues."

"I've dated other—"

"You've dated other guys? Yeah. You have. Where are they now?"

"Well, they didn't work out. You don't necessarily meet 'the one' while you're in college, Lib."

"Nor does it stand to reason that it's impossible to meet him when you're fifteen."

"Étienne Rousseau was *not* 'the one,'" Kate huffed.

"Oh no? Because in one way or another, from the moment you turned your back and walked through that hedge, you've been looking for him. Truth, KK? I don't know if he's 'the one' or not. But I know you won't find 'the one' until you settle up your history with Étienne. That story needs a firm and final 'The End.' Without it? All the Tony's you ever meet will *only* be bookmarks."

"I think you might be right."

"It's widely accepted that I'm a genius."

Kate chuckled, feeling a little better. Even though she didn't love Lib's answer, she had to admit that she agreed with it. She needed to settle the past, find out why Étienne never wrote back to her, why he let her go, and if it all meant nothing to him. After she understood, she'd be able to box up her memories and kiss them good-bye. How exactly she'd manage it? She had no idea. But at least she had a better handle on the situation.

"True, true. You are brilliant, Lib. Enough about me. How are things with you?"

"Smashing. Glorious. Nonstop delight."

"Still single, huh?"

"The demand for tiny, prickly, gallery-owning Jewish girls is so high I barely know how to keep up with the offers. But

I'm not bored," she added to let Kate know that she might not have someone important in her life, but she wasn't lacking for company, either.

Kate grinned. "He's out there, superstar."

"KK, the eternal optimist."

"There's got to be an amazing guy for someone as awesome as you."

Libitz laughed her throaty, smoky, rarely-heard chuckle. "If I held my breath, I'd asphyxiate."

"Then don't hold your breath. Just trust me."

She could picture Libitz shrugging with discomfort. "I'm fine. I just hooked up with a cutie from Gaslight last night, and besides, I have my art to keep me warm."

Kate looked up, surprised to find herself in John F. Kennedy Park, famous for its iconic sculpture by Robert Indiana. "Hey, Lib . . . what would you do if you were me?"

"With Étienne? I don't know. I guess I'd either start writing the story again or figure out a solid ending. It's up to you."

Her eyes burned as she whispered, "Love you, Lib."

"Love you, K." And she hung up.

As Kate slipped the phone back into her purse, she wondered if it was a coincidence that she was four blocks off-course, standing in front of an eighteen-foot high, bright red, shiny sculpture of the word "LOVE."

Étienne had tried very hard not to think about Kate English since their fiasco of a meeting on Monday afternoon.

He'd tried very hard not to think of her as he and J.C. spent Monday afternoon brainstorming possible buyers for the oil rig portion of Rousseau Shipbuilding, and he refused to let her pass through his mind as he made himself dinner in his quiet apartment later that night. As he lay in bed staring at the ceiling, he forced himself not to linger on the shape of her mouth and forbade himself to remember what those lips felt like beneath his.

On Tuesday morning as he showered his aching, frustrated body, he tried—unsuccessfully—to choose which of the women in his social circle he should pursue for a night of pleasure, only to have Kate's face cock-block him at every turn, so he finally gave into the memories of her legs wrapped around his back and allowed himself some temporary manual relief.

Sitting at his desk as he reviewed the laws pertaining to corporate mergers in Louisiana, he tried not to imagine what Kate had been like in law school, quickly deciding she would have been serious and sassy at turns. Ten minutes later, he was thoroughly disgusted with himself when he realized he'd been staring off into space as he fantasized about the twenty-one-year-old version of her.

When Jax offered to book his travel plans, he desperately tried not to think about the fact that he and Kate would be staying at the same hotel for a night, but somehow his fingers reached for the phone, putting in a quick call to the hotel after Jax e-mailed the confirmation and requesting that he and Kate were booked on the same floor.

Over and over again, he reminded himself she was seeing someone . . . and he was recently out of a bad relationship and had no interest in starting something new—or jump-starting something old—with Kate English, of all people, but these reminders grew quieter as he barreled toward one distinct moment in time: the minute he would be in the same room with her again.

By Wednesday, it was clear that it had only taken one meeting with Kate for her to crawl under his skin again, so he gave up on trying not to think about her and forced himself to consider instead what it was he wanted.

Besides the fact that he wanted her fickle, dismissive heart pounding against his as he drove into her over and over again, he wanted answers. Why hadn't she given him the benefit of the doubt when her cousins informed her of the incident with Alex? Did she truly believe he would ever, even in the wildest, stupidest version of himself, say such ugly things about *her*? He and Kate hadn't only shared their bodies with each other; they'd shared their ideas, their hopes, their thoughts and dreams. He'd given her his heart, for fuck's sake. How could she possibly believe he'd betray her like that?

The answer came swiftly. Because she'd loved her cousins more than Étienne. Because she trusted them more. Because ultimately, she would always choose them over him, and the truth be damned.

Well, whether she wanted to know the truth or not—whether or not she'd even believe him—he was going to tell her exactly what had happened with Alex that Monday morning at St. Michael's, and he was going to make damn sure she listened. After all these years, he still had a right to clear his name, whether or not she wanted to hear it.

So, aside from wanting to fuck her, he wanted answers and he wanted a reckoning.

Then what?

Étienne didn't know.

In the absence of a productive answer, his mind—and his dick—instantly circled back to his fierce desire to fuck her. The fact was, and had always been, Kate English was like a drug to him. He was still brutally attracted to her, no less than he'd been the night he first saw her on the trampoline, bathed in moonlight. But adult Kate wasn't an endearingly nervous girl. She was all woman: confident, smart, sharp, and sexy as hell, even wearing that brown potato sack of a dress. He shifted in his desk chair as his long-ignored cock, which hadn't seen any action since before he broke his leg, sprang to eager attention.

Did he want her? Like air or water.

Could he have her? Absolutely not.

His past with Kate was mired in hurt, and while sleeping with her had been the single best moment of his adolescence, the price he'd paid for that honor was unbelievably high. Any future with Kate, beyond business, was simply too messy to contemplate. He didn't trust himself with her. He didn't trust the explosive level of their chemistry—it had already made him blindingly stupid once in his life. Not to mention, she'd indicated that she was dating someone. Besides, he'd already promised himself that he would abstain from serious relationships for a good long time, and his history with Kate was too complicated for them to date casually.

Being with Kate was simply not an option.

That fact firmly accepted, he needed to do *something* to get his mind off of Kate and move in a different direction. Étienne's eyes flicked to the invitation that J.C. had put on his desk this morning. This Saturday was the annual charity ball to benefit A Better Way, a local nonprofit group that supported extracurricular programs for inner-city youth. At first, he'd rolled his eyes at J.C., looking meaningfully at his hobbled leg, but J.C. had laughed and told him he was a crappy dancer anyway.

No doubt she'll be there with her boyfriend, thought Étienne, frowning.

Reaching for his phone without a moment's hesitation, he clicked on the address book and found the name he was looking for. Since Connie and Weston English didn't work out, he assumed she was free, especially since she'd called him upon her return from Rome. He and Connie were old friends—someone with whom he'd hooked up during his breaks with Amy, with no expectations and no hurt feelings after. As an added bonus, the Atwells and the Englishes were nothing short of mortal enemies, which meant that Kate and her insidious cousins would likely give him a wide berth with Connie on his arm.

Perfect, he thought somewhat bleakly, purposely ignoring the anxious leap of his heart as he dialed Connie's number and half-hoping that she wouldn't be free.

Kate rearranged the pictures on her desk for the twenty-sixth time and smoothed her hair again, checking for rogue pencils that might be lodged there. Her blouse felt too tight, but the sales lady yesterday afternoon had assured her it wasn't tight—it was just fitted. Still, Kate fussed with it a bit, trying to convince herself she'd bought it because she needed a new blouse, not because of anything Étienne may have said. Frankly, she was getting sick of Étienne. Waking up early this morning to take a run, Kate resented the fact that the entire hour—when she usually focused on the day ahead—had been wasted with thoughts and memories of Étienne, just like every hour from the moment she left his office on Monday.

After her conversation with Lib on Monday, Kate had turned away from LOVE and firmly decided there was no story to continue writing, but that yes, it needed an end. And that end required her to gather her courage and ask Étienne why he never responded to her, why he refused her calls, why she never heard from him again. That choice made, she was giving herself until the return trip from New Orleans to actually have the conversation. It's not like they could be deep in a discussion of antitrust laws and Kate could suddenly turn to him and demand, "Why didn't you ever write back to me?" She needed to choose a moment divorced from business, and she had to be strong enough to accept his answer, whatever it was. She wasn't there yet, but she would be. And once he told her that she'd been too awkward or too fat or too pathetic or too inexperienced to maintain his interest at the time, she would hold back her tears and thank him for his honesty.

And then what?

Then she'd have a frank conversation with Tony. She'd tell him that while he may have sensed Kate had some loose ends in her head and heart, they were firmly tied up now, and she wanted to move their relationship to the next level. Glancing at the photo of herself and Tony on her desk, her grimace softened. In a perfectly-fitted tux, with reddish-blond hair, freckles, and bright green eyes, Tony managed to look both boyish and sophisticated at once. Kate's gaze lingered on his arm around his shoulders, then skated to his broad, confident grin and laughing eyes. She jumped when her phone buzzed.

"Yes, Jodie?"

"Mr. Rousseau has arrived. Shall I direct him to your office, Miss English?"

Despite her efforts to stay calm, her heart instantly raced into a gallop. "That would be fine."

Kate flattened her palms on her desk and stood, lifting her chin and trying to look placid as her eyes fastened on the door to her office. *Be professional. Be professional. Be professional.* She heard his halting footsteps in the hallway, the plant of his cane and uneven pace of his gait, each small sound resonating in Kate's head like a drum. She sucked in a deep breath as he turned the corner and appeared in her doorway: Étienne, in all of his heartbreaking beauty.

She swallowed, propelling herself around her desk with her hand extended. "Étienne. Good to see you."

He shifted his cane to his other hand so that he could shake hers. "You too, Kate."

Trying desperately to ignore the sensation of his flesh pressed against hers, she withdrew her hand quickly and gestured to a small conference table by the windows. "Shall we sit?"

He nodded, pulling out a chair and settling himself. Kate reached for his cane, but he pulled it back from her in an awkward tug of war. "I'll keep it with me."

"Of course," she answered, heading back to her desk and picking up two manila folders. When she turned back to him, he'd shifted to look at her.

"Look, Kate. I know we have history." He clasped his hands together in his lap, his green eyes direct and serious as he continued. "I know it's making things awkward, but there's no reason we can't still work together. We're both professionals, right?"

Kate took a deep breath and nodded at him, feeling relieved. "Yes, of course."

"We can't miss another issue like this antitrust fiasco. It could blow the deal."

"Agreed."

"I'm sorry if I was inappropriate."

"Me too," she admitted, taking the chair across from him, and sitting down. "I shouldn't have said that about—"

"No recriminations. We both behaved poorly." He gave her a gentle smile, though his eyes seemed far more searching and fierce than his casual posture and quiet, level-headed words.

Kate nodded, giving him a small smile of her own. He stared back at her intently, his eyes finally softening a little.

"It *is* good to see you," he whispered intently.

"You too," she murmured, amazed to find that it was true.

After a moment, he breathed deeply and shifted his glance to the files on the table before him. "Oil rigs and antitrust. Are you up to speed?"

Kate sat up straighter in her chair. "I think so . . . unless Louisiana arbitrates differently? Why don't we talk through the situation step-by-step so we have an action plan?"

"Of course," he said, launching into a detailed discourse on the details pertaining to selling off a portion of Rousseau Shipbuilding prior to the merger.

Kate had ordered them lunch after three hours of sleeves-rolled-up review of the deal and Étienne considered her now as they sat across from one another unwrapping sandwiches.

Although his original intent in mentioning their past was to cut to the chase and explain to her exactly what had happened that morning at St. Michael's, he realized that with things so tense and awkward between them, she wouldn't be able to hear him. And it suddenly mattered to him that she heard him—that she understood. He didn't want to just blurt out what had happened at St. Michael's for the sake of thrusting his truth on her; he truly and deeply wanted her to believe him, and to reframe everything that had happened between them after by applying a new truth to the circumstances. He knew it was theoretically impossible, but what Étienne really wanted to do was rewrite history. And he couldn't do that while they were on pins and needles around each other. Before he could tell her anything, he needed to relieve the tension between them and soothe some of her uneasiness.

So far, so good. Over the past few hours not only had they made good progress on the antitrust issues and possible buyers, but Kate had loosened up considerably. The only thing that hadn't loosened up was her blouse.

A huge improvement on the brown sack she wore last time, it fitted over her breasts like a glove, highlighting their luscious curves with just enough of an opening to be sexy, not slutty. Every time Kate looked away, his eyes gravitated to her chest like a magnet, and he decided he'd been idiotic to give her fashion advice: to say her clingy blouse was distracting would be a gross understatement.

She flicked her eyes up, and he met them just in time so that she didn't catch him leering, then he grinned at her as she finished recounting a story about law school.

". . . so I decided to go with an automatism defense," she finished, laughing at herself.

"Amnesia?"

Nodding, she opened a packet of mayonnaise and squeezed it on her sandwich. "Amnesia."

"And . . . ?"

Her eyes flashed, pleased and blue, as she placed the top back on her sandwich. "I won."

He chuckled lightly. "Of course you did. That was inspired."

Kate's face was totally unguarded as she grinned back at him for a moment before remembering herself. She shrugged, dropping his eyes, her exuberance dimming a little. "Well . . . it was unexpected, I guess. I surprised the jury."

Sensing that it would make her uncomfortable to compliment her any further, he picked up his sandwich and took a bite, chewing thoughtfully before saying, "You know, I thought I saw you once. While we were in law school."

"Did you? Where?"

"At a collegiate legal convention. In Boston."

She'd been dabbing at the corner of her mouth, but her hand stilled. "In the fall of 2010."

"Yeah."

"I was there."

Surprised, he lowered the Coke bottle he'd been sipping from. "It *was* you. I called to you . . . from across a quad at Harvard."

Kate opened her mouth to say something, then closed it.

"Kate . . . Do you remember? Did you see me?" he asked, searching her face.

She looked down, placing her sandwich on its wrapper and playing with the paper corner. "I wasn't sure it was you. I didn't want to . . . I . . ." She shook her head, still staring at the table.

"Didn't want to what? I just wanted to say hello to you, Kate."

Her eyes slammed into his and he was surprised to find them glistening. "Why?"

"Because it was you. Because you were . . . important to me."

"How can you say that with a straight face?" she demanded.

He furrowed his brows as he stared back at her. "Because it's true."

She shook her head, crossing her arms over her chest and looking away from him. "Please stop."

"Kate, whatever you think—"

His words were cut off by a curt rap at her office door. Kate jumped from her seat, swiping at her eyes with her fingers and taking an audible deep breath. Étienne cut his eyes to the door, deeply annoyed by the timing of the interruption, but even more infuriated by its subject.

"Tony!" exclaimed Kate.

"Hello, sweets," he said smoothly, leaning down to kiss her cheek. "Ready for lunch?"

Étienne strained his neck to get a look at her boyfriend, his eyes hardening as he took in the tall, elegant physique of a good-looking man.

"Oh," said Kate. "Oh, no. I forgot. I'm so sorry."

"No worries," said Tony, looking over her head at Éti-enne, who still sat the small conference table. Étienne braced his hands on the tabletop and stood, nodding at fucking-Tony who had just ruined a good opportunity to untangle some of the history between him and Kate. "Tony Reddington."

"Étienne Rousseau."

Tony smiled congenially at Étienne, his eyes lingering on Étienne's for an extra beat before turning back to Kate. "Well, sweets. Looks like you're busy. Rain check?"

She nodded. "Sorry about it."

Tony leaned down and kissed the tip of her nose before straightening. "Not another word. See you Saturday?"

"Mm-hmm," she said, flicking a glance at Étienne before turning back to her boyfriend. "Saturday."

Tony looked at Étienne again, offering him a charming smile and holding his eyes, again, a single beat longer than necessary. "*Enchanté, Étienne.*"

Étienne nodded curtly.

Tony turned back into the hallway, but Kate didn't face Étienne as she closed the door quietly. Étienne couldn't totally explain the surge of jealousy he felt from meeting Tony, but it was mixed with something else—an odd feel-ing . . . something that felt like a puzzle to figure out, and the entire effect was extremely unsettling. He was feeling emotional and after promising Kate that he'd be profes-sional, he didn't trust himself to honor that promise any-more. It was time to leave.

As he gathered his files together, he said, "I assume you two are headed to the A Better Way ball on Saturday?"

"Uh, yes," said Kate, finally turning to face him, but mak-ing no move to return to the table or keep him from leaving. "Will you be there?"

"Of course." And then, because he was jealous and frustrated and stupid for her, he added, "with Constance Atwell."

Her eyes flew open and her lips parted in surprise. "Connie *Atwell*! I didn't realize—"

"You didn't realize what?" he asked innocently, perversely pleased by her shocked and disapproving reaction to Connie's name. Amy's jealousy had always felt lethal to Étienne, but Kate's felt more like salvation.

"You said you weren't dating anyone," she said indignantly, eyes flashing at him.

Étienne smirked, then looked away from her, snapping his briefcase closed and taking his cane in his other hand. He took several steps toward the door but Kate stood motionless, her eyes locked with his until Étienne was directly in front of her, his chest no more than a breath from hers. For just a second he indulged himself and stared down at her breasts, which heaved with her quickened breathing, pushing against the teasing, thin silk of her fitted blouse.

Finally tearing his gaze away from her chest with regret, he met her stormy eyes.

"Oh Kate," he purred, purposely thickening his accent, "Con and I aren't . . . dating."

His meaning unmistakable, he enjoyed the play of emotions on Kate's face before stepping to the side and sailing out the door. He was positive she hadn't meant to give away so much in her expression, but Étienne smiled all the way back to the office because her reaction had told him one very important thing:

Étienne wasn't the only one in that room who vividly remembered the last time they'd fucked the other person in it.

Painting

Étienne flicked his glance up from the canvas to look at Kate again. He had her face memorized by now, of course, but he couldn't keep himself from watching the way the sun bathed her skin in warmth, the way a passing cloud would darken her eyes just a touch, the way her little pink tongue kept slipping between her lips to wet them.

After they'd found Weston at the Amblers' place and walked him back to Haverford Park, they'd tacitly decided to spend the rest of the day together, mostly hiding out in the gardens of Westerly, the Winslows' unoccupied mansion. When he shared with her that one of his favorite hobbies was painting, Kate insisted he run home to get his paints and a canvas so that he could paint her, and surprisingly (because art was something sacred to him that he usually enjoyed in solitude) he'd immediately complied.

Grinning back at her before turning his attention to the canvas, he wondered what it was about Kate English that had him so captivated. She was pretty—her skin even and pink and her hair long and thick. The way it caught the light made it look golden, shiny, and clean and he had to keep himself from touching it. He'd already reached out once, to tuck a strand behind her ear, and a bolt of heat had shot straight to his groin, making his dick twitch.

He didn't know for sure, but he got the feeling that Kate didn't have a lot of experience—the way her cheeks colored when he cursed, the way she averted her eyes when he stared at her for too long. She seemed a lot more innocent than the Story sisters or the other girls he'd been with, but he'd quickly learned that she was very sharp as they spent the morning talking. Beautiful, smart, and inexperienced. Who knew that combination was his Kryptonite?

"Kate," he asked, spending some time on her lips, dabbing the brush into some lighter pink then blending the color with peach. He glanced up quickly, then looked back down, trying to capture their bowed shape on the canvas. "Have you ever been in a play?"

Before the break, St. Michael's had put on a production of *Romeo and Juliet* with St. Bernadette's, the local girls' school. Étienne, who was perceived as brooding, had won the part of tortured, troubled Mercutio, which he had enjoyed playing. But the reality was that he lingered in the backstage shadows during every love scene between Romeo and Juliet, memorizing their lines, uncomfortably drawn to the passionate words of love they shared with one another.

Étienne mixed his brush with peach and white paints. Catching sight of his hands, which were flecked with paint, he remembered his favorite lines:

> *If I profane with my unworthiest hand*
> *This holy shrine, the gentle fine is this:*
> *My lips, two blushing pilgrims, ready stand*
> *To smooth that rough touch with a tender kiss.*

Ever since meeting her last night, he'd longed to kiss Kate, only holding back for fear of scaring her. He'd only known her for a handful of hours, and she didn't seem like the type that made out for sport. He glanced at her lips again as she answered his question.

"Trinity just did a production of *West Side Story*," she answered.

"Huh. That's a coincidence. We just did *Romeo and Juliet*."

"Same story," she said, offering him a small grin which made his heart leap.

"Were you in it?"

Her grin faded as she shook her head. "No. My parents thought it would distract me from my studies."

"Oh—"

"No!" she said suddenly, her voice raised and indignant. "That's just what I told everyone, but I want to tell you the truth." She frowned, her forehead creasing as she looked down at her lap. "My mother thought it was too racy. There's kissing in it . . . and implied sex."

He shouldn't have been distracted by the word "sex" in such an innocent context, but he was. He totally was. He could barely think about anything else and the word—*sexsexsexsexsex*—ricocheted around in his head as his blood rushed south, hot and fast, making him hard.

He shifted on his stool, loosening his shorts. "Did you at least get to see it?"

"No. I wasn't allowed to go."

"You *are* fifteen, right?"

"Right." She sighed, still frowning.

"Do they think you don't know about sex?"

She shrugged. "They know I know. We discussed it when I was twelve—very clinically. They just . . . want to keep me as their little girl. Protect me from ugliness, from growing up too fast. My mother never wanted to raise a child in New York City—she thought it was too risqué, too vulgar—but my Dad insisted he needed to live where he worked. They compromised by putting me in private school and having nannies and chaperones watch me all the time to ensure I remained . . . unspoiled."

"So it's safe to assume you've never had a boyfriend?"

"Ha!" she scoffed. "Holding hands with you would have gotten me grounded."

"Wow. That's . . . that's kind of crazy, Kate."

Kate took a deep breath, her breasts bobbing up as her lungs expanded. Damn, this girl had no idea how sexy she was just by breathing.

Her voice took on a defensive edge. "They're just trying to protect me . . ." Then her voice brightened. "But when I'm at Libitz's house—she's my best friend—we watch R rated movies sometimes when her parents go to bed. I've seen things. I'm not a complete moron."

"I'd never call you a moron." *But you're definitely inexperienced and your parents sound whack.*

"Lib's mother is way more liberal than mine."

"I'm surprised your parents let you hang out with her," he said, wishing he could keep the edge from his voice, but it didn't sit well with him—how sheltered her parents tried to keep her.

"I've known Lib since kindergarten, which means my parents have known the Schulers at least that long. And Mr. Schuler owns the biggest, most well-regarded modern art gallery in Manhattan. It would be"—she paused, then looked at Étienne and grinned—"socially inappropriate for them to interfere with my friendship with Lib."

"And I gather that social appropriateness is second only to protecting you?"

Kate giggled. "Uh-huh."

Growing up in an expat family had exempted the Rousseaus from some of the common social norms of the American families with whom they socialized in Haverford. His parents weren't concerned with local social niceties as long as their children didn't embarrass them and defaulted—almost without exception—to the social norms of their native France. Ergo, Étienne had been drinking wine at the table since he was a child, choosing his bedtime since he was twelve, and although he was aware that these—and other behaviors—seemed racy or indulgent to the parents of his American counterparts, Étienne didn't greatly abuse or question the freedom. It was simply the way life was lived.

Kate's life, on the other hand, sounded stifling.

"I guess Libitz is pretty important to you then."

Kate nodded somberly. "I don't know what I'd do without her. I tell her everything. She keeps me sane."

"Well, I think you're lucky. I don't really have a friend like that," he said, leaning down to rinse his brush in a cup of cloudy water before blending some blue and white to paint her eyes.

"Stratton implied you were cool," said Kate, looking up at him through lowered lashes, as if sheepish to admit she was asking about him.

"I don't know about that," said Étienne, liking it that she was curious. "When we moved here, my English wasn't good. No, that's not true. It was . . . nonexistent. So, I didn't talk a lot. Even now, I'm mostly quiet, and I think people ascribe a personality to you if you don't assert one. Anyway . . . I hang out with Dash. You know the Amblers?" Kate shook her head, and Étienne jabbed a thumb toward Blueberry Lane. "They live over there. The farmhouse. I'm friends with Dash . . . and with this other guy, Kurt. Kurt Martinson." He flicked his eyes up to gauge her reaction when he said Kurt's name, but there was none. "I guess they're my best friends, but we don't really, you know, talk about real things."

"Why not?"

Étienne took a deep breath, deciding whether or not to enlighten her as to the history between the Englishes and Martinsons. "Actually we talk a little, I guess. We talked when Kurt's sister, Johanna, hurt herself earlier this year."

"Hurt herself?" asked Kate, tilting her head to the side, her brows furrowed.

"Yeah. Um . . . she used to date your cousin, Alex, and, uh—"

"Ohhhh!" said Kate, nodding in understanding. "I overheard my parents talking about that poor girl. Johanna Martinson. When Alex broke up with her, she cut her wrists."

Étienne flinched, his hand stilling as he looked up at Kate. "*Broke up?*"

"Yes," she said, her voice soft but certain. "Alex broke things off and she went a little . . . crazy, I guess. But I heard she was troubled. Parents divorcing. Other things going on."

"Johanna may have had her issues, but Alex *didn't* break up with her," Étienne blurted out defensively, remembering the conversations he'd had with Kurt, one during which Kurt had actually cried. "Alex *cheated* on her."

"I'm sure he didn't," Kate said softly, but firmly.

"I'm sure he *did*. And I live here. I'm friends with her brother. Everyone knows Alex went to a party and macked on this other chick all night and when Johanna Martinson found out at school the next day, she went home and slit her wrists open. Kurt's older brother found her, thank God."

"That's not possible," insisted Kate. "Alex wouldn't hurt someone like that."

Was she really so naïve? She blindly accepted what her parents or cousins told her without questioning it? "You should review the facts before you act like you know what you're talking about."

Her eyes widened and her mouth dropped open. "I don't like what you're insinuating about my cousin."

"Then I won't insinuate. Alex is an asshole."

She gasped, jumping up from the bench where she'd been sitting. "You have some nerve—"

"And you don't know what you're talking about!" he snapped back, plopping the brush into the cup of water, which sloshed onto his palette.

Kate's face was red and with her hands planted angrily on her hips, Étienne suddenly realized that she looked so pissed, she might leave. She might turn her back on him and run back across the lawn to Haverford Park and he'd never see her again. And he realized how terrible that would be, because he liked her—aside from being wildly attracted to her, he really, *really* liked her—and there was no way he wanted her to run away.

He shook his head, reaching a hand out to her. "Sorry."

She stared at the ground, saying nothing, and he dropped his hand, feeling helpless.

"Kate," he said softly. "I'm sorry. I shouldn't have said that about Alex. I shouldn't have yelled at you."

She looked up and her face softened a little. "It's possible my parents don't have all of the information about what happened. You're right. It's not my business to be talking about it."

"Hey . . . how about we don't talk about your cousins anymore?" he asked, taking a step toward her and offering her a hopeful smile.

"Not even when one of them calls you 'cool?'" she asked, sitting back down on the bench.

Étienne pivoted, picking up his brush as a rush of relief made his hands weak for a moment. When he looked back at her, her lips were turned up in a sweet grin.

"I don't know if I'm cool," he said, as he had a few minutes before. "I think 'cool' might just be a convenient euphemism for no one really knowing the real me."

He painted a ring of sky blue around the black pupil of her eye then looked up to stare at the real thing. She stared back at him, her gaze strong and steady, and he could feel the sparks snap and crackle between them, like just being around each other somehow *created* electricity, somehow produced a charge.

"*I'm* getting to know the real you," she finally said softly.

His throbbing heart should have signaled danger, because falling can hurt and he wasn't just falling, he was slipping, sliding, plunging, and tumbling. He was hurtling headlong toward Kate English with every breath he drew, with every sweet word she spoke.

"Yeah," he said, wishing this week never, ever had to end. "You are."

Chapter 5

Kate whipped the matronly black cocktail dress off her body and hurled it across the room, knocking over her bedside lamp and eliciting an angry growl from Oliver, who jumped off the bed and scurried out of her bedroom.

"Sorry, Ol," she called, plopping down on her bed and staring at her open closet with frustration. Tony was due to pick her up in forty-five minutes, and Kate hadn't even chosen a dress yet, let alone done her makeup or hair, which still needed to be twisted into an elegant, conservative chignon.

She groaned, staring at the veritable wall of drab black, brown, and gray fabric before her and conceded that Étienne was one hundred percent correct. Except for the simple white blouse she'd purchased for her meeting with him on Wednesday, almost everything Kate owned was too big, too baggy, and as plain as the Amish on Sunday. Glancing over at the pile of expensive, boring dresses flung haphazardly across her bed, it was a mountain of neutral colors, every dress just a little larger than necessary, all making Kate's body look utterly shapeless. Not one was youthful. Not one was sexy.

When exactly had Kate sidelined herself from being found attractive by the opposite sex? Or worse, being found attractive at all? Had she always been like this? Afraid of her body? Embarrassed by her curves?

Standing up in her black strapless bra, black underwear, and black Spanx pantyhose, she checked herself out in the floor length mirror on the back of her closet door.

Kate was a solid size sixteen, which, she decided objectively, wasn't really that enormous. No, she wasn't about to win a runway modeling contract, but she wasn't exactly an elephant either. She was tall and big-boned, not delicate, and a good deal of her weight gathered in her breasts, hips, and backside, leaving her a nice waist and a soft, but relatively flat, stomach. She stuck out her breasts a little and stifled a giggle. They were full but pert, like a '40s pinup girl, and a tingling swept up the back of her neck, flushing her face, as she remembered Étienne's stark perusal of them before he left her office on Wednesday.

Right after he told her about him and Connie.

She grimaced, twitching her lips. She had no right to feel jealous—she had no right to feel *anything*—when Étienne mentioned he was attending tonight's event with Connie Atwell, but she couldn't help the sudden rush of fury she'd felt imagining them together. Connie, who had dated Kate's cousin, Weston, for a while, was a whiny, manipulative brat, and Kate should be glad that Étienne was saddled with her. But she wasn't.

"I wish he was saddled with me," she whispered softly, then gasped as she realized what she had said.

"No, no, no, I take it back," she insisted to her reflection in a strong, defiant voice. "I don't wish that! I don't!"

But the words were already out, mixing it up with the dreariest cocktail dresses ever made. The reality Kate was forced to finally, grudgingly accept? She *did* wish it. Part of her wished for a second chance with beautiful, complicated Étienne. The more time she spent with him, the more uncertain she became about their shared history. She couldn't shake the feeling that before Tony had interrupted them on Wednesday, he'd been about to tell her something important. His eyes had been searing and honest as he admitted, "*Because it was you. Because you were . . . import-ant to me.*" While it had moved her to tears to hear him say those words, and everything about the way he said them sounded credible, Kate wasn't totally sure how they could be true. If she'd really been important to him, he would've con-nected with her after they parted ways that night, right? She frowned at her reflection. Something wasn't adding up, and even as she felt nervous about digging back into their pain-ful past, she still felt an urgency to figure out what exactly had happened.

Her phone buzzed on her bed, and Kate grabbed it, find-ing a message from Tony reconfirming that he was picking her up at eight o'clock. Kate felt a shot of guilt as she realized that despite the fact that Tony was picking her up in a few minutes, the only man she was thinking about tonight was Étienne. She shrugged. What Tony didn't know wouldn't hurt him. And besides, Étienne had always been a force for her heart to reckon with—suddenly working with him again was mucking up everything in the past that should probably be left behind. If she could . . .

But she couldn't, and when the thought of model-slim Connie Atwell flitted through Kate's mind again she made a quick decision. No, Kate couldn't compete with adorably tiny size-two Connie, but she wouldn't be wearing a size-eighteen black, long-sleeved sweater dress tonight either. She wasn't a sexpot, but she could make more of an effort to dress her age.

Reaching forward, she shoved her drab dresses to the right side of the closet and licked her lips as she looked at four colorful dresses hidden to the far left: bridesmaid dresses. Hmm. In the mantra of every bride since the beginning of time, Kate had been assured that she'd be able to wear the dresses again, and damn if she wasn't about to put that promise to the test.

Hands on her hips, she narrowed her eyes and evaluated her choices:

1. An Alfred Angelo floor-length satin dress in emerald green with an asymmetric draped neckline, gathered natural waistband, and fitted skirt.
2. A Monique Lhuillier plum, strapless, floor-length gown with a bandeau neckline and Watteau back.
3. A Badgley Mischka knee-length, champagne-colored strapless dress with a sweetheart neckline and unflattering peplum pop at the waist.
4. And finally . . . a Watters & Watters strapless lace sheath in cobalt blue that fell just above the knees with an A-line skirt and shirred, fitted sweetheart bodice.

Kate reached for the blue dress, turning it toward her with one hand and fingering the heart peaks of the bodice with the other. She remembered how boldly it had accentuated her breasts and recalled that her dance partners had tripled at that particular wedding, despite the fact that Kate had felt immodest and exposed in the wisp of dress.

Considering it, she pulled it from its mates and held it against her body, turning to the mirror and feeling a smile spread across her face as she realized that the color was just a little deeper than her eyes. She tossed her messy curls around her shoulders and her smile grew broader. Placing the dress gently on her bed, she sucked her bottom lip between her teeth and grinned.

Tonight she wasn't going to be elegant, conservative Kate. Tonight she was going to be twenty-seven years old and sexy, damn it!

Whether Étienne notices or not doesn't matter, Kate told herself as she dusted slightly-darker-than-usual eye shadow on her lids and chose a glossy pink lipstick from the bottom of her makeup bag. She brushed out her hair and instead of twisting it up in a tight updo, she found a crystal pin in her jewelry box and pinned one curl behind her ear. Fishing out the sapphire teardrop earrings she almost never wore, she fastened them into her ears and added the sapphire-and-diamond tennis bracelet her parents had given her for her twenty-first birthday.

Her excitement chasing away any misgivings or nerves, she marched back into her room and took the dress off the bed, shimmying it over her hips and reaching behind to zip it. She must have lost a couple of pounds since wearing it last summer because she didn't need to suck in her breath to fasten the top clasp, and though the little dress looked fitted, it didn't look ready to burst.

Placing one hand on her hip, she looked back at her reflection and chuckled lightly, looking at herself with wonder.

Before this moment, Kate hadn't even known she could look like this. She'd wondered from time to time if she could turn on the sexy at will, but she hadn't felt the confidence or need to venture out from the comfortable, acceptable elegance she'd become accustomed to. Smiling at herself in the mirror for an extra minute, she jumped when she heard her doorbell ring. She still needed to choose shoes, a wrap, and a purse, but Tony could fix them a drink while she finished getting ready.

Heading for the front door in bare feet, she felt a pang of guilt as she reminded herself that her date tonight was Tony, despite the fact that it was Étienne who had been her motivation for changing things up. Then again, she thought, trying to make herself feel better, perhaps dressing a little sexier tonight would be just the thing to move her relationship with Tony to the next level. A girl could hope.

Kate opened the door with a flourish, offering Tony a playful smile.

"Kate!" he exclaimed, his brows screwing up in confusion as his eyes traveled from her face to her dress to her bare feet and back up again. "What have you done to yourself?"

Her heart plummeted.

"What do you mean?" she squeaked.

He gestured to her hair first, then her dress, with an elegant hand. "What is this?"

The flush in her cheeks was so hot, it was almost painful. How embarrassing. How outrageously embarrassing. He didn't think she looked hot. He looked surprised, and maybe even a little disapproving.

She stepped back, allowing him into her apartment, keeping her eyes down and trying not to cry. If she cried, she'd completely wreck her eye makeup, since she'd gone extra heavy with the mascara.

"Oh, sweets," he said, chucking her playfully under the chin gently. "What a cad I am."

Kate looked up at him as he closed the door.

"You just look different. I'm used to my solid Kate in reliable black."

"Well," she said, searching his face, and feeling a bit of pique rise up inside at being called solid and reliable, "I decided to make a change tonight."

"You sure did," he replied, giving her an encouraging smile.

She chuckled softly. "Is it really awful, Tony?"

"No, no. It's just . . . different," he reassured her unconvincingly, heading to the kitchen to make them each a martini. "Maybe add a sweater or something? You're bound to get chilly in that tiny little dress."

A part of Kate wanted to take his disappointing appraisal and apply it immediately: run to her room, put on a basic, black cocktail dress, wipe off her extra makeup and twist up her hair.

Except, Kate thought as she walked silently back to her room to the music of Tony pouring and shaking, *I like how I look tonight*.

Prior to Tony's disapproval, Kate had felt playful and optimistic, sexy and strong. For the first time in a long time, she was anticipating a social event with excitement, and she wasn't counting down the minutes until she could return to her apartment, change into pajamas, drink wine, and lurk on Facebook. For the first time in a long time, Kate wanted to go out. Kate felt . . . like a woman.

And suddenly she realized that no amount of time would fix what was wrong between her and Tony. He was elegant, charming (*most of the time*, she conceded with a slight eye roll), and eligible, but he wasn't for her. Not now. Not ever. He was safe because she felt so little for him, and she knew that Lib was right—Tony was just a place saver, not a true contender for her heart.

Slipping into black peep-toe heels Kate had only worn once, she filched a black velvet wrap from the top shelf of her closet and found the matching blue bag she'd carried at the wedding where she'd worn this bridesmaid dress.

Yes, she'd attend tonight's ball with Tony. But after tonight, it was time to say good-bye.

Connie had run into her sisters, Felicity and Hope, when they'd arrived in the hotel ballroom, and after exchanging pleasantries with her sisters, Étienne had told her to meet him at the bar. He wasn't in the mood to listen to Atwell gossip. Truth told, he wasn't in the mood for anything from an Atwell at all. The only thing he *was* in the mood for was a certain English . . . which rather sucked, because the only one he wanted to see didn't appear to be in attendance yet.

"Come on, brother," said J.C., appearing behind him and throwing his arm around Étienne's shoulders. "Let's get a drink while the Atwells are busy."

Led by J.C., Étienne walked haltingly across the room to the bar, leaning on his cane, turning back occasionally to check and see if Kate had arrived yet.

"Seems like you're looking for someone," commented J.C.

"Nope," denied Étienne, ordering a vodka on the rocks.

"How are things going with Kate English?"

"Superb," he answered tersely, taking his glass from the bartender and throwing back the drink, only to hold out the glass, asking for another. He wasn't in the mood to talk to his brother—or anyone else—about Kate.

"Well, speak of the devil," murmured J.C., nudging his brother gently in the side.

Étienne had been raising the glass to his lips, but his hand stilled as he caught sight of Kate English walking into the ballroom.

He stared at her, gaping, unable to move, unable to look away, because *oh my God*, she looked so fucking hot, just staring at her made heat shoot like a bullet to his groin. She wore a short blue dress with a plunging neckline that barely held her creamy breasts in place but created the most delectable valley between them. Shiny black heels encased her feet and her hair fell around her shoulders in waves, with only one small portion pinned back behind her ear.

"Jesus," he hissed.

"That's not *really* Kate English, is it? We just saw her on Monday and she definitely did not look like that."

"Shut up," said Étienne, cutting his eyes to his brother and making sure J.C. understood that any further comments about Kate would be unwelcome. Étienne threw back his second drink in one gulp, then slapped the glass on the counter, turning back to stare at Kate.

Was it absurd to wonder if this transformation because of him? Was it madness to hope that it was?

He didn't consciously make a decision to move toward her, but just as his feet had propelled him to meet her in the reception area on the afternoon of their first meeting, he couldn't seem to stop himself from moving closer to her. She smiled at her date as he took two glasses of champagne off a passing tray and handed one to her, but her smile dimmed as she caught sight of Étienne approaching. She lifted her chin and swallowed nervously, as if daring him to comment on this dress as he had on the other.

"Kate," he said, staring into her eyes with a boldness that her date should have taken issue with.

"Étienne," she answered, taking a sip of champagne.

"You look"—he saw her brace herself, stiffen her spine, clench her jaw, and lower her glass, as if waiting to be insulted—"unbelievable."

Her shoulders relaxed just a touch, but her eyes were still uncertain as she raised her glass and let the rest of her champagne slide down her throat.

"Stunning," he clarified in an intense murmur, leaning closer to her ear and pressing his lips to her skin in a kiss hello. "Dazzling."

When he drew back, a small, pleased chuckle slipped from her lips.

"Thank you," she said, her voice soft and genuine.

The relief in her eyes was unmistakable, and it pissed him off. Hadn't her date—*fucking-Tony*—told her how phenomenal, how breathtaking and sexy and captivating, she looked tonight? And if not, why the fuck not? Étienne shifted his eyes to Tony, who grinned at Étienne like a fool.

"Étienne," said Tony, wetting his lips with a slow flick of his tongue. "How delightful to see you again so soon."

Oh.

Oh, no.

Étienne's eyes grew wide as he put together the disconnect he'd sensed in Kate's office when he'd met Tony on Wednesday, *and* he knew the reason why Kate had appeared unsure of her appearance tonight. Any man interested in women would have been dumbstruck by Kate's transformation, would be bracing himself to fight off all the other guys in that ballroom. But Tony wasn't looking at Kate. He was looking at Étienne.

Fuck. Kate wasn't Tony's girlfriend, she was his beard. But from the way she'd spoken about Tony, he didn't believe Kate was aware of this arrangement. And frankly, from the way Tony had treated her, with pet names and kisses, Étienne hadn't put it together immediately either. His lip curled, his anger toward the other man so white-hot and searing, he could barely keep himself from throwing a punch.

He had an immediate flashback to lying on Kate's stomach, watching cloud bunnies fuck merrily in a spring sky . . . At that time, he'd just been getting to know her, but she'd been like an open book, her heart so vulnerable, so full of trusting goodness, it had terrified him to know that it would eventually get her hurt. Suddenly, he wanted to *murder* Tony.

Instead he wiped the sneer off his face and offered his most charming smile, raising his eyebrows in a gesture of interest. "Delightful. Indeed."

"Kate tells me you're a lawyer. I'd love to get your opinion on a . . . personal matter."

What the fuck was this jackassery? Kate was standing directly beside this douchebag and he was making a not-so-subtle pass at Étienne? His fist curled in anger, but he forced himself to nod.

"Shall we get better acquainted while Kate gets a refill?" asked Étienne. He turned to Kate, his eyes beseeching her to trust him as he spoke to her gently, "I saw your cousins over there by the bar."

"Oh, yes. Perfect. Yes," said Tony quickly, licking his lips again before glancing down at Kate. "You should go say hello to your family. We'll find you in a little bit, sweets."

Kate looked at Tony, then Étienne uncertainly, left with little choice. "I guess I'll go say hello."

Étienne watched her go, taking in the sway of her hips, her long legs in sexy heels, the way her gorgeous ass bobbed up and down, matching her stride. It was almost enough to make him forget Tony and run after her, pull her into his arms, and show her how much he missed her after all these years.

When Tony cleared his throat, Étienne was unsurprised to find Tony staring at *him*, not at Kate.

"Join me?" said Étienne congenially, gesturing to a dimly-lit corner.

Tony's lips tilted up in an expectant smirk as he led the way.

When Tony reached the corner, he turned to Étienne with a satisfied smile. "You're very subtle. I admit, I wasn't sure, except the cut of your suit is utterly perfect and—"

"Does she know?" asked Étienne, in a voice that would slice through steel.

"Know?"

"Does Kate know you're gay?"

Tony's smile dimmed, and he crossed his arms over his chest defensively. "I'm sure she does. We spend a lot of time together."

"She doesn't know," said Étienne in a low growl. "I can tell."

Tony waved his hand dismissively before tucking it back under his arm. "It's an arrangement. She's my date to events. I'm hers. I assure you, she doesn't generally look like *that*." Tony gestured toward her with his chin. "She usually looks like my grandmo—"

"Shut your mouth," growled Étienne, taking a deep breath as his nose twitched with distaste. He had nothing against gay men—he'd had several good friendships with homosexual men in his life, and his favorite cousin was bisexual. What he took issue with was willful deception at Kate English's expense. "I'm going to make myself very clear."

"About what?" asked Tony, his voice still hanging onto some hopeful flirtation.

"You will tell her the truth tonight. You will offer her the chance to continue dating you until she can break up with you in some public way so that no one suspects she was your beard."

Tony's eyes narrowed. "You have balls of steel, *mon ami.* Tell me, why would I—"

"Why would you do that? Well, if you don't," continued Étienne in a lethally-smooth, low voice, "I will *ruin* you. I'll do whatever it takes. Nothing off-limits. I will dig up everything I can. Every embarrassing episode. Anything you ever did that would mortify your family, question your ethics, and ruin your reputation. I. Will. *Ruin.* You," he promised again.

Tony flinched, his face furious. "Why do you care? Why do you even—"

"It's none of your business," he said sharply, keeping his eyes locked with Tony's. "Have I made myself understood?"

Tony's lips were thin and his jaw was set like stone as he nodded curtly. "Yes."

"Terrific. Now go join your date," he said, looking at Tony like he was garbage. "And before you tell her that you're gay, tell her she looks like a fucking knockout."

As he watched Tony scurry away to tell Kate how great she looked, it occurred to Étienne that some part of him should feel relief that Kate wasn't taken after all. But he didn't. He couldn't. Not until he was sure her heart was safe.

Tony was acting very strange.

After spending five minutes talking to Étienne, he had bee-lined for Kate, exclaiming about how nice she looked, then nervously excusing himself to talk to a business associate across the room. Kate hadn't seen him again since, and she wondered what Étienne had said to him. Not that she'd reversed her decision to break things off with Tony tonight, but what right did Étienne have to sabotage her relationship with Tony?

Visiting with her family, her anger rising, she noticed Étienne still standing by the wall where he and Tony had chatted, watching her. She locked eyes with him, looked meaningfully at the French doors to her left that led to a private, secluded terrace outside, then glanced back at him. He nodded to confirm he'd join her, and Kate grabbed her champagne glass off the bar and wove through the crowd toward the French doors. If she was going to demand answers from him, she didn't want an audience.

The cool air was welcome after the warmth of the ballroom, and Kate placed her glass on the cement balustrade before her, waiting to hear Étienne's footsteps behind her. It didn't take long. When she heard the doors latch closed, she turned to face him.

The terrace was very intimate suddenly—about the length of the doors that led back inside—and through sheer curtains, light from the ballroom warmed the small space. Ivy vines grew along the brick of the building and drooped prettily over the doors like a garland, which framed the beauty of Étienne Rousseau standing before her in the scarce moonlight and ambient city light. It fleetingly occurred to Kate that aside from his office and hers, it was the first time they'd been alone for a reason other than business since the night they'd lost their virginity to each other, and her breath caught from the sudden rush of memory. His skin, his smell, the noises he made in the back of his throat, the low rumble of his laugh, the reverent touch of his fingertips against her—

"No," she said softly, swaying toward him, then away. Trying to ignore the fierce beating of her heart, she leaned back against the balustrade and raised an eyebrow.

"No?" he asked, holding back a slight smile, reading her face like a book.

She wetted her lips nervously and lifted her chin. Étienne leaned back against the closed doors, staring at her, waiting.

"What did you and Tony talk about?" she asked, hating the breathlessness of her voice.

"His sexual orientation."

Kate blinked. "*His what?*"

"We talked about the fact that he's gay."

"He's not," hissed Kate, her heart ramping into an uncomfortably fast rhythm that made her press a palm to her chest. She turned away from Étienne, her denial still heavy in the air between them even as puzzle pieces fit together beautifully in Kate's mind—the lack of passionate kisses, the comfortable rapport between them, his tepid reaction to her sexier outfit tonight. He'd confused her with his solicitous interest, his pet names and flowers, and chaste—but persistent—kisses. But it all made sense now. She'd been dating a gay man.

She lifted her eyes to Étienne, struggling to maintain some shred of dignity. "He's not. He's . . ."

"He is," said Étienne firmly. "He's using you, Kate."

Kate winced, her breath hitching with surprise and humiliation. Of all the people in the world to out her boyfriend and make a fool of Kate, it *had* to be Étienne, the other man who'd used her and forgotten her. Cursing fate, she shook her head, blinking furiously, finally turning to Étienne.

"What an amusing anecdote for you," she said through quick, angry breaths.

"I take no pleasure in this," he said softly.

"Of course you do! You hate my cousins. You hate me," she gasped. "The only way someone like Tony could ever be interested in someone like me is if he was gay. Is that about right? The only reason he'd date me is to use me, right?"

Étienne flinched, narrowing his eyes and taking a step toward her.

"I am *barely* holding it together," he warned her. "Don't you *dare* tell me what I think or how I feel, Kathryn Grey."

As her full name rolled off his tongue so easily, she blinked back tears, taking a step toward him, bowing her head in shame.

"He's gay," she whispered in defeat, "and I'm an idiot."

He crooked his finger and placed it under her chin, raising her head to look at him. The tenderness in his eyes was so familiar, a balm and a blessing, tolerance and kindness from the unlikeliest possible source.

Palming her cheek, his breath brushed her skin when he answered, "You're magnificent. Any heterosexual man would agree with me. From the moment you walked into this ballroom, I couldn't look away from you, not even for a second. Don't you see that, Kate? Can't you see?"

"See *what*?" she managed to ask, though her knees threatened to buckle beneath her.

He threw his cane to the ground and slipped his arms around her waist, pulling her into his arms roughly, possessively. Her nipples beaded, pushing against the bodice of her dress as she stared up into his smoldering eyes, which seized hers, holding them ruthlessly.

"How much I fucking want you. How much I have *always* wanted you."

He lowered his head, and his lips, which she'd dreamed about since the moment she'd last tasted them, landed flush and full on hers, hot and demanding. Closing her eyes in surrender, Kate's lips parted to allow his tongue entrance, her palms flattening on his chest as his arms tightened around her.

Deep inside, Kate knew she shouldn't want him so desperately, shouldn't be standing in the moonlight letting him kiss her when their second ending would likely be as heartbreaking as their first. And yet, she couldn't keep herself away. She whimpered as his fingers curled on her lower back, pushing her urgently against the hardness of his erection and proving to her that every word he said about wanting her was true. She leaned against him as his tongue swept into her mouth over and over again, swirling around hers, making her dizzy and electric.

"Étienne," she said on a sigh, her fingers flexing against the wall of his chest as she dropped her forehead, panting against his throat. "No more."

"*Chaton, chaton, ma belle chaton*," he whispered, his breath warming her temple, the touch of his lips pressed against her skin making her tremble. "Kate, I've missed you so."

"Missed me?" she murmured, her head in the clouds, still drunk with desire and breathless from his kiss.

"We both made mistakes, *non*?"

And just like that, Kate fell back to earth.

Mistakes? Like not writing back to me? Like acting like what we'd shared was nothing? Righteous indignation gave her the strength to straighten up and push him away. Kate *hadn't* made any mistakes with Étienne as far as she was concerned. She'd written faithfully. She'd called. She'd dismissed her pride and even stopped by his house that summer. Despite all of her efforts, she'd never heard from him again.

"No," she said, pushing against his chest. She shook her head at him, pulling away from his arms as a tear rolled down her cheek, glistening in the moonlight like a diamond. "No, Étienne. *I* didn't make any mistakes."

He winced, dropping his arms from around her, his face hardening. His expression was a mix of deep hurt and great anger, and Kate swallowed, tilting her chin up. She wouldn't admit to wrongdoing when she hadn't done anything wrong. She wouldn't share blame when it all belonged to him. If there was any chance for a future between her and Étienne, he would need to admit his mistreatment of her and offer her an explanation of his behavior. Only then could she forgive him and consider moving forward.

Leaning down, he picked up his cane, catching her eyes one more time as he straightened. She forced herself not to wince as he said, "I understand. Good night, Kate."

She watched him go back inside, then braced her hands on the balustrade and let her tears fall.

Tony found her outside half an hour later, and Kate asked him to take her home right away. After a quiet and awkward car ride home, Tony pulled up in front of her apartment building, cut the engine and turned to her.

"May I walk you up?"

Kate faced him. "It's true, isn't it? You're gay."

Tony nodded. "I thought you knew."

"I don't believe that," she said gently. "I think you were using me."

"Funny," said Tony, with just a hint of bitterness. "Because I think you were using me too."

Kate nodded. "I guess I was. You were safe. You were nice. You always brought me pretty flowers."

Tony gave her an apologetic smile. "I'm sorry, Kate."

"Me too," she answered, holding out her hand. "Friends?"

"Of course," he answered, shaking hers. "You won't tell anyone, will you?"

"It's not my secret to tell," she answered, dropping his hand. "But why are you hiding it?"

"It would break my father's heart, and his health is fragile. There's just . . . no reason to tell my parents. They're very old and very old-fashioned. I don't want to hurt them."

Kate nodded in compassion and understanding. "It's going to come out eventually. No pun intended."

"When they're gone. Then I won't care who knows."

"Good night, Tony."

Kate gave him a sad smile then turned to reach for the door.

His voice stopped her. "Hey Kate?"

"Hmm?"

"That guy . . . Étienne. He threatened me, you know. He said if I hurt you, he'd ruin me . . . and come to think of it, if he wasn't walking with a cane, I'm fairly certain he would have kicked my ass."

"I'll call him off," said Kate, looking down and trying to hide the smile that wanted to turn up the corners of her lips. He had tried to protect her and she had gotten angry with him. She owed him an apology.

"He's beautiful," said Tony softly.

Kate nodded, remembering the way his eyes had burned just before he'd kissed her.

"He's in love with you."

"No," said Kate, shaking her head.

"Yeah," said Tony, looking over at her, "he is. There's something very real there. I felt it. I'm sure of it."

"We have history," said Kate. "You're just picking up on that."

"What happened?" asked Tony, leaning back against his headrest to settle in for a story.

"Hmm . . ." Kate sighed, looking out the windshield at the empty street. "It didn't work out."

"You broke up with him?"

"No," said Kate wistfully, thoughts of their kiss tonight mixing seamlessly with memories of the first one they'd ever shared. "No, I didn't break up with him. I wanted him. He was the one that let me go."

Falling

"That one," she said, giggling so the vibrations made his head bounce slightly in a way that was making him so happy and so hard, he was grateful she was staring at the sky and missed the tent getting higher and higher in his pants.

Étienne looked at the cloud cluster she was pointing to. "Bunnies fucking."

She gasped in surprise then giggled again and his head, which rested on her belly, jostled merrily.

"That one!" she said, pointing up again.

"Umm," he hummed, drawing out his answer, even though she knew what was coming. "Raccoons fucking."

"Ten!" she cried, using his nickname, but the laughing had already started again.

Étienne closed his eyes and listened to the sound of happiness, forcing himself not to dwell on the fact that it was already Tuesday and Kate was heading back to New York on Saturday.

After painting and talking all afternoon and into the evening, they'd only said "good-bye" last night when it was too dark to see their hands in front of their faces. Étienne had considered pulling her against him for a kiss as he'd walked her back to the hedges that separated Haverford Park from the Winslow place. They'd held hands for most of the day, after all; he couldn't imagine she'd refuse him, but he'd chickened out at the last minute.

"What're you doing tomorrow?" he'd asked her instead, grabbing her other hand too and tightening his grip around her fingers.

"I don't know," she had answered, but he'd heard the smile in her words. "You tell me."

Kate English was fresh-faced and sunny, thoughtful and interesting. They'd wandered for hours yesterday, walking the bridle trail together holding hands and talking. He'd told her all about St. Michael's, she'd told him all about Trinity Prep, and they'd even discovered some acquaintances they had in common. He'd been surprised to learn that Mock Courtroom was her favorite club (his too!) and swimming was her favorite sport (he was the only sophomore on the varsity team!) But they didn't have everything in common . . . where he preferred studio art, Kate liked music and drama better. And when he complained about having three siblings, Kate had shared how much she wished she had any. By the end of the day, he knew more about Kate than he knew about any student at St. Michael's, many of whom he'd known since second grade.

She was easy to talk to, of course, but it was more than that. When she wasn't listening carefully to him and asking insightful questions, she was engaging him with her stories and observations. She laughed and giggled at herself in this self-deprecating way that was at once confident and shy, and Étienne found himself chuckling with her more than once. She didn't take herself too seriously, but she wasn't flighty and unsubstantial either. As he'd painted her, he'd watched her, feeling himself fall harder with every passing moment. He liked her. He liked her so much it made his chest hurt, it made his heart ache, it made him want to be witty and sharp to keep her laughing, it made him want to slow down and listen to her words, or speed up to progress faster, from hand-holding to more.

More.

When her blue eyes, earnest but uncertain, found his, he felt it in his toes—how much he wanted her, how much he didn't want to do anything wrong that could possibly cut short the precious time he had with her. With any other girl, he'd have definitely kissed her by now, copped a feel up top, and be pressing his advantage to get into her pants. With Kate? He'd met her on Sunday night and here it was, Tuesday afternoon, and he had yet to steal a kiss.

"Now you do one," he said.

"Okay. Which?"

Étienne stared at the bright blue spring sky, looking for a cluster of clouds, and finally found one, pointing right over her head. "Those. What do you see?"

"Hmmm," she murmured. She'd had her hands pillowed under her head, but she moved them lower now, resting them on her rib cage, just above his head. He reached up with his closest hand, weaving his fingers through hers and drawing her knuckles to his face. He kissed them gently, running the ridges back and forth over the sensitive skin of his moistened lips. It was the most forward he'd been with her yet, and he felt her sharp intake of breath under the back of his head.

"Tell me what you see, *chaton*," he said gently with his cheek against the back of her hand.

"*Ch-Chaton?*" she asked him in a breathless murmur.

"It means kitten," he said, pressing one last kiss to her skin, before lowering their joined hands to rest together over his heart.

"Étienne," she whispered, "what's happening between us?"

His heart skipped a beat, but he kept his voice level. "What do you see in the clouds?"

"Well . . . I see, um, a girl and a boy . . ."

He rubbed his thumb over the base of hers in acceptance and encouragement.

". . . and, um, they're sort of . . ."

"Sort of what, *chaton*?"

"Falling for each other."

"Mm-hmm. I see it too," he said softly, raising her hand to his lips again.

"But the girl doesn't know what she's doing and she's nervous and she just . . ."

"She just?"

"She's just never felt like this before."

He clenched his jaw together, surprised by the impact her words had on his entire body, making him want to draw her into his arms and hold her close to him forever. She was going to get herself hurt being this honest, leaving her heart so open to plunder. He wanted to protect her. He wanted to make sure no one ever, ever hurt her, ever mangled her whole, trusting heart. And for the first time in his life, with the first girl, she made him want to be just as honest as she was. No game playing, just the truth. So he whispered,

"Neither has he."

He released her hand and flipped around, leaning his elbows on the grass, his chin still resting on her belly. Her shirt had ridden up a little, and he bent his neck to press his lips to the pale strip of exposed skin there that smelled of clean cotton and sunshine, and just a little bit—he realized with a thrill—like him. When he leaned back up, she had her eyes closed, and her bottom lip was caught her teeth. Her breathing was quick and shallow.

And he suddenly knew if they moved any faster right this minute, it could scare her off, it could be a mistake. And if he made a mistake—like yelling at her yesterday—and she ran away, it would mean losing time with her when there was so little left to begin with. He couldn't afford that. He wouldn't surrender a moment—no, not even a second—of the time he had with Kate. He wouldn't risk it.

Taking a deep breath, he stood up.

"Kate," he said.

Her brows wrinkled together and she opened her eyes, surprised to find him standing over her. "What?"

"Let's go get ice cream, and then I'm going to finish your painting."

"Ice cream," she repeated, shielding her eyes from the sun and looking both disappointed and the tiniest bit relieved.

Étienne reached down for her hands to help her up. She giggled as he pulled her to her feet, and he couldn't stand it anymore. He needed to touch her. He needed to feel her. He pulled her into his arms, locking them around her back. His chest pushed into hers as his breathing grew ragged with her body soft and flush against his for the first time.

Burying his face in her clean-smelling hair, he muttered, "Why'd you have to be from New York?"

"At least I'm not from California," she said, soft in his arms, her breath warm against the skin of his neck. "Or Sydney. Or London."

He closed his eyes and grinned, savoring this moment, trying to memorize it for the rest of his life. Finally, he opened his eyes and pulled away from her, running his fingertips down her arm until he found her hand and tucked it securely in his.

"Can you keep a secret?" he asked.

Kate grinned and nodded.

"We're going to borrow my Dad's car."

"You're not sixteen!" she exclaimed with wide eyes. "You don't have your license yet."

"That's true," he said wickedly, grinning at her. "Do you trust me, good little *chaton*?"

She licked her lips and pursed them together before nodding mischievously.

He almost kissed her right then and there, but held back, anxious not to misstep with his Kate. Not once. Not even a little bit. He would wait. For her, he felt like he would *wait* forever if that's what it would take to *have* her forever.

"Then what are we waiting for?" he asked, pulling her behind him across the grass, her giggles light on the breeze, every moment with her filling his heart to bursting.

Chapter 6

Étienne woke up after a fitful night sleep, his leg aching from overdoing it at the ball last night and a rock-hard erection demanding relief.

He shouldn't have kissed her.

He never, ever should have kissed her.

Clenching his eyes shut and shaking his head at his own stupidity, he couldn't help the rush of hurt he felt when he recalled her words, "*No, Étienne. I didn't make any mistakes.*"

Surprised by the sudden burning behind his eyes, he whipped the covers off his body and swung his legs over the side of the bed, looking down at the scar tissue that covered the lower portion of his left leg. When he'd woken up in the hospital the morning after his accident, Mad had informed him that the lower and larger bone of his leg, the tibia, had actually cracked in half and broken through the skin from the impact of his car hitting the tree. He had no memory of the accident or his injury, but the scar was enough of a reminder of what had happened and a warning that a hurting heart could lead him to reckless behavior.

Seamlessly, he flashbacked to another time he'd made a rash decision that had ended badly.

When Étienne had been expelled from St. Michael's and subsequently been informed of his parents' decision to send him to the Chambers-Ford Military Academy in Mississippi, he'd had only one thought: Kate. If New York felt like a thousand miles away, Mississippi may as well be a million, and he wouldn't be home until summer break at the end of June. And even then, he'd only be home for a few days before heading to France for the rest of the summer. Not to mention the rules of the school—which were lengthy, strict, and well-documented in his father's tirade—only allowed for one phone call a week: to his parents and no one else. Faced with months before he'd see her face or hear her voice again, Étienne had stolen his father's car in the middle of the night and driven to New York.

Arriving at Kate's posh Fifth Avenue building, he'd given his name and demanded that the concierge call her apartment. Pacing back and forth in the lobby of her building, he'd waited for almost half an hour before her father, dressed in pajamas and a bathrobe, had finally arrived downstairs, stepping out of the elevator with a grim expression.

"You're Étienne Rousseau?" he confirmed.

"I am. I'm here to see Kate."

"I've called your father. His driver's bringing him up from Philly. He'll be here in two hours."

"My father?" Étienne shook his head. "No! No, I-I'm here to see Kate. I have to see her!"

"Absolutely not. It's three o'clock in the morning."

"Do you know who I am? Do you know who I am *to her*?"

Kate's father sighed heavily, his eyes steely. "I know you're trouble. I know you were in a fight with my nephew, Alex, and got expelled from school."

Étienne had flinched, reaching up to touch his bandaged nose that Alex had broken. "I drove all the way up here and I-I leave for military school tomorrow."

"Sounds like your parents know what they're doing."

He's saying no. He's saying no. He's not going to let you see her.

"Please." Étienne's heart beat faster and faster, panic increasing his frustration as he reached out to grasp the older man's arm. "I promise if I can just have five minutes with her—"

"Out of the question," said Mr. English, snatching his arm away and turning back toward the elevator.

"Please, sir!" begged Étienne, raising his voice, which ricocheted off the gilt walls and mirrors of the elegant lobby.

"Wait here for your father. If you get back in that car, Dante will call the police," he said, gesturing to the doorman.

Furious and frustrated, Étienne's eyes had filled with embarrassing tears. Kate was *here*. She was a few yards above his head, sweet and warm, asleep in her bed. Her chest was rising and falling with every breath, her lips slightly parted, the body he'd loved so tenderly was curled up and still with sleep.

This was his only chance. He *needed* to see her. He *had* to see her.

As Mr. English stepped back onto the elevator, Étienne rushed toward the older man, frantically trying to push past him and reaching wildly for the buttons, though he didn't even know the floor she lived on. Mr. English had fallen into the elevator wall from Étienne's push, but the concierge and doorman raced to the elevator, pulling Étienne out and forcibly restraining him in the lobby.

"Please!" he sobbed, pushing against the men holding him but unable to break free.

Mr. English straightened his bathrobe and ran a hand through his gray hair, fixing a lethal gaze on Étienne. "Stay away from my daughter. She knows what you did. She doesn't want to see you. If you *ever* come near her again, I'll have you arrested."

As the elevator doors closed, Étienne's eyes slowly shuttered, and his muscles went limp as the lobby attendants dragged him to a bench by the revolving front door to wait for his father.

She doesn't want to see you.

His Kate. His love. His heart. His first. His only.

She doesn't want to see you.

The ache in his chest had been so sharp and overwhelming, he hadn't moved from his seat on the bench until his father arrived. Following him like a sleepwalker back to the car, and deaf to his two-hour tirade as they drove back to Haverford, all Étienne could think was,

I lost her.

. . . and the fact that his lungs still breathed and his heart still beat in his chest seemed fantastical, because inside, he felt dead. The girl he loved more than anything didn't love him anymore. Just like that.

Even now, Étienne's hands fisted in his bed sheets as he remembered the feeling—the stark and utterly horrifying realization—that he'd somehow lost her. And in the weeks that followed, without a single letter from her forwarded to him at school, her father's words were proven as true. She'd turned her back on him, never even giving him a chance to explain exactly what had happened with Alex.

Swallowing down the lump in his throat, Étienne stood and hobbled without his cane, leaning on his bed, then dresser, then doorframe to make his slow way to the bathroom. As he turned on the hot water in the shower and stripped out of his boxers, he thought again that he shouldn't have kissed her last night. If losing Amy had prompted a night of furious drinking that led to a broken leg, losing Kate again would be . . . catastrophic.

Stepping into the steamy shower, he revisited the decision he'd made before going back to work last Monday

morning: blissfully free of Amy, he wasn't interested in a
serious relationship, not with anyone, and certainly not
with Kate English. Right?

And yet.

His brain filled with thoughts of last night: her lips
under his, her soft body pressed against him, the warmth
of her skin, the smell of her hair. Somewhere inside of
Étienne was the fifteen-year-old who'd loved her more
than he'd ever loved anyone else, before or since. Bending his neck and flattening his palms against the slippery,
copper-colored tiles, he thought of her face when he told
her Tony was gay and winced all over again remembering
her embarrassment and pain. Hurting Kate so long ago,
even inadvertently, had been an obscenity to Étienne, con-
trary to everything he felt for her, in opposition to his very
existence. His heart still longed for hers in a way that was
unceasing . . . and last night he'd discovered that his desire
to care for her and protect her was no less urgent than it
had been twelve years ago.

"No, Étienne. I didn't make any mistakes."

He drew a ragged breath as her words passed through
his head. Some part of him must have hoped there'd been
a misunderstanding—that she'd somehow never found out
about him and Alex or the comments that were inaccurately
ascribed to him. Some small part of him had naïvely hoped
she didn't have all of the information, that she was somehow kept from him, or hidden from him—that she hadn't
willfully deserted him.

But no. Her words last night had blown this final, pathet-
ically small hope to smithereens. She had believed her
cousin's version of events implicitly and without question,
turned her back on Étienne, moved on with her life and
forgotten him . . . and as she confirmed last night, it *hadn't*
been a mistake.

He could see she was still attracted to him, as he was to her, but she clearly didn't reciprocate the ridiculous fixation he had on her. She'd let her feelings die years ago, and even though he was unable to do the same, he needed to respect her feelings. Despite his longing for her, he needed to leave her alone.

He tightened his jaw.

Fine.

Before they met again at the airport tomorrow, he would apologize for kissing her and make a promise that it would never happen again. They would settle the outstanding legal issues that required their attention in New Orleans, and he would forbid J.C. to ever enter into a business agreement with English & Company again. And because he probably wouldn't get the opportunity to ever clear his name with Kate, he would have to make peace with the truth as he knew it— that he never could have hurt her as she believed he had—for three simple reasons . . .

He'd loved Kate then.

Just as he loved her now.

But maybe someday, if God was merciful, he'd find a way to get over her.

Kate couldn't very well pack a bridesmaid dress to wear in New Orleans, so she chose her least frumpy dress—a charcoal-gray sheath, slightly more fitted than the rest— and hung it in her garment bag with a simple black cardigan sweater and the heeled shoes she'd worn last night. It wasn't exactly sexy, but this trip was about business, wasn't it? Yes. Right. Business, not kisses.

She sighed, distracted by the memory of the kiss that had rocked her world last night.

Sitting down on the bed with butterflies humming in her tummy, she recalled Étienne's arms coming around her waist—the savage thrill that had shot through her body as he yanked her against his chest and covered her mouth with his. Everything Kate had been so desperately missing in her life, including hot, wet, sweet, messy, filthy kisses that made her toes curl, had suddenly been hers for a split second on that balcony last night. A protective hero, a compassionate savior, a stone-hard, hot, demanding, brooding sexpot of a man who wanted her, who claimed her, who took her.

She lay back on her bed as heat flooded her groin, making her muscles contract and relax with the memory of his passionate words, *"I've missed you so."*

Whispered so urgently near her ear, the words had sounded genuine. Could it possibly be true? How?

She didn't understand.

They fell in love. They had sex. She went back to New York, and then . . . nothing. After sending two weeks' worth of letters to him without a reply, Kate had gathered her courage to call his home before her overprotective parents got home from work. His mother had answered, and Kate had asked to speak to Étienne.

"I'm sorry, dear. He's not here," Mrs. Rousseau had answered.

"I see," Kate had murmured, "Will he be home later? Perhaps I can try ba—"

"He won't be here later," said his mother, an edge creeping into her voice.

"Oh. Well, um, can you tell him I called?"

"I suppose I can let him know. Your name?"

"Kate. Kate English."

"English?" she'd asked, sounding surprised. "Did you say Kate English?"

"Yes, we, um, we met over spring bre—"

"I know who you are, Miss English, and I'm quite sure my son doesn't want to speak to you."

"W-Wait. What?"

"He doesn't want to speak with you. Please don't call here again."

"But, Mrs. Rousseau, I don't—"

The line had already gone dead.

Kate had held the phone to her ear for several minutes, her lips parted in confusion and her heart thudding painfully against her ribs. When she called back again, she got a busy signal.

"I'm quite sure my son doesn't want to speak to you."

Kate had finally hung up the phone, walking slowly back to her room where she wept for hours. He didn't want to speak with her. He hadn't answered any of her letters, and he didn't want to speak with her.

At first, Kate had decided that her conversation with Mrs. Rousseau was a mistake of some kind: a misunderstanding, because Étienne *did* love her and *did* want to hear from her—she was sure of it. She continued to write two more weeks' worth of letters before Lib had insisted she stop. Only then, she'd started the long, painful process of letting go.

How could he "miss her so" *now*, but never do a thing to find her, to connect with her, to let her know that he still had feelings for her *then*? It didn't make any sense and the whole situation made her head hurt, because Kate was starting to wonder if there was more to the story than she knew. There had to be.

Or maybe she just *wanted* there to be.

Because the part of her heart that still belonged to Étienne, that still *loved* Étienne, had hoped for years he'd suddenly appear in her life with a completely understandable explanation for why she'd never heard from him again. But here he was, in her life, and no explanation had been forth-coming . . . yet.

The wrinkle now, however, was that Kate was starting to fall for him again. Another kiss like last night and—

Ring ring. Ring ring.

Her landline was ringing, which meant that either her parents or one of her cousins was calling, because no one else had her number.

"Hello?"

"Kate, it's Strat."

"Morning."

"Morning," he answered. "You busy?"

"Just packing for Naw'lins." *And thinking nonstop about Étienne.*

"Can we talk for a minute?"

She sat back down on the edge of the bed. "The dooms-day voice is back. Last time you called me with the doomsday voice Barrett had gotten into bed with J.C. Rousseau. Who's he in bed with now?"

"It's not his bed I'm worried about."

"Then whose?"

"Honestly? Yours."

She chortled. "Is that a joke?"

"You left with Tony Reddington at 8:57 last night. Étienne Rousseau promptly got into a tiff with Connie Atwell and left solo ten minutes later. I was wondering where he ended up."

"And you think I know?"

"I think you two were on the terrace together. I think he knocked back two double vodkas when he came out alone. You left soon after without saying good-bye, and he got into a fight with his date."

"Stratton—"

"You don't *know* everything," he blurted out.

Kate opened her mouth then closed it as a shiver trailed down her back. "About what?"

"Étienne . . . and you."

"What are you talking about?"

She heard Stratton gulp through the phone, which meant he was swallowing down a pretty thick lump. "Alex and I . . . we made a promise never to tell you. You'd been through enough. And you never asked. Once in a while, when we were in college? You'd get drunk and mention Étienne . . . you'd ask me why he never called you, never wrote to you . . ."

"And?" she murmured, her heart hammering.

"It was because . . . he . . . he didn't love you, Kate. He *never* loved you. In fact . . . he disrespected you."

Her eyes glistened with sudden tears. "What? Wh-what do you mean?"

"That Monday after spring break," said Stratton, chasing the words with a heavy sigh. "He said some terrible things about you at school, br-bragging about your time together . . . and Alex heard, and, well, he beat up Étienne. He took care of it."

"What things?" asked Kate in a soft, stunned voice. "What things did he say about me?"

"He called you 'Easy English' and he made some lewd comments about your . . . the size of your chest. And—"

"Stop," gasped Kate. "You *heard* him say these things?"

"No," said Stratton. "Alex did."

"So Alex beat him up."

"Yeah."

"Then what?" asked Kate, her heart racing as these unknown pieces of her history were revealed to her so many years later.

"Well," said Stratton, taking a deep breath, "when the Monsignor came outside, Étienne had managed to get on top of Alex, and he was in the process of landing a couple of good punches to Alex's face. A few of Alex's friends pulled him off and . . ."

"And what?"

"He was expelled."

"*Étienne?*" Kate winced. "He was expe—But Alex started it!"

"Kate!" exclaimed Stratton. "Alex was defending *you*."

"I know," she said quickly. "I didn't mean . . . I know that. I'm just trying to get my head around all of this. Then what?"

"Then nothing. Alex's friends vouched for him, saying Étienne started it. It wasn't Étienne's first fight. He was expelled and sent away to some military academy in the South, thank God. Plus, the Rousseaus started spending their summers in France." Stratton paused. "We really didn't see him much after that . . . until I ran into him again a couple of years ago."

Stratton used to be the next-door neighbor of Étienne's ex-girlfriend, Amy, before he and Valeria had moved to their own place.

He sighed heavily. "God, I hate like hell to be the one to tell you all of this, Kate. I'm sorry that—"

"Why didn't you tell me about this ten years ago?"

"We thought it would upset you to know he'd been talking about you like that. We didn't want him to hurt you any more than he already had."

A tear slipped down her cheek as she processed his words. "You were protecting me."

"Always, Kate." He paused. "Listen, now you know why we were so pissed at Barrett for taking the deal. We all talked last night after you left, and Fitz can go to New Orleans tomorrow. You shouldn't have to—"

"No," she said softly, but firmly. "This information doesn't change anything, Stratton. It's still part of the past. This deal is the future. I'm still going to New Orleans."

"Are you sure?"

"I am," she said, reaching up to wipe her cheek with the back of her hand.

"Was I right to tell you?"

"Yeah," she said, sniffling softly. "You actually answered a few long-standing questions for me."

"I wish *I* could beat him up for you this time."

Kate chuckled softly, reaching for a tissue to dab at her eyes. "No. It's okay, Strat. If memory serves, you warned me about Étienne a long time ago. I probably should have listened to you then."

"I never liked him."

Pausing for a moment, Kate let these words sink in, surprised by their unexpected impact. The child Kate once was had unquestioningly believed anything told to her by someone she loved. The woman, and lawyer, she had become, had learned to search a little harder for the truth.

"No. You never did." She paused again, her brain trying to put together an elusive thought just out of her grasp. "Why not? What was the real reason you didn't like Étienne?"

"He was a troublemaker, and—"

"Stop. The *real* reason, Strat. This was personal from the beginning."

"It's stupid."

"I'd still like to know."

Stratton sighed in that long-suffering way Kate had known all her life. "Freshman year at St. Michael's. He knew I liked Jillian O'Connor, who went to St. Bernadette's and was on our bus. He was sitting in front of me and overheard me say that I was going to ask her to the Christmas formal. Étienne stood up, grinned at me, then walked to the back of the bus and promptly asked her to go with *him* to the Christmas formal."

"He scooped your date."

Katy Regnery

"She said yes . . . and he winked at me when he sat back down."

"Is there where it all started? The rivalry between the Rousseaus and the Englishes?"

"Not really. In fairness, Barrett had stolen Bree Ambler from J.C. a few years before."

"Huh. Barrett stole Bree from J.C., so Étienne stole Jillian from you. And knowing how protective Alex is, I'm guessing he wasn't a fan of Étienne after that."

"Alex had been coaching me . . . you know, helping me practice how to ask Jillian. So, yeah, he wasn't too happy when I told him what happened. Like you said, there was always a rivalry." Stratton paused for a moment, and Kate could hear Valeria's voice in the background. "Sorry, Kate. I gotta go. It's Sunday morning, which means mass with Val."

"I understand," she said. "Thanks for calling, Strat."

"I hate dredging up the past like this, but I thought you should know, just in case . . ."

"In case?"

"In case you were getting any ideas . . . old feelings, that sort of thing."

"Ah," she breathed, glad he couldn't see her face.

"I hope I made the right decision to call. Safe travels tomorrow, Kate."

"Will do," she answered, and carefully hung up the mouthpiece on the receiver.

Her mind was spinning, but instead of forcing a train of thought or immediately jumping to more hurt feelings based on Étienne's conjectured comments about her on that fateful Monday, she waited to see where her thoughts landed. It only took a moment for one theme to eclipse the others, and surprisingly, it wasn't Étienne's purported comments about her.

The *rivalry* between her cousins and the Rousseau brothers added a new dimension to the dynamics of her week with Étienne. He'd never invited her to Chateau Nouvelle and she'd never invited him to Haverford Park. At the time, it hadn't occurred to her, because the Winslows' Westerly estate had been their sunny love nest, private from the prying eyes of protective cousins or little sisters. But perhaps Étienne had purposely kept their love affair a secret to avoid complications with her cousins or his brother, who wouldn't have approved of them dating.

She drew her bottom lip between her teeth and winced as she thought about Étienne's expulsion. Her eyes filled with tears and fluttered closed, as she realized she was the inadvertent cause of his banishment. He'd been sent to military school because of a fight *her cousin* started. She couldn't help but wonder . . . Did he ever get her letters? She had addressed them all to Chateau Nouvelle. She sighed deeply as she remembered Madame Rousseau's coldness. *"He won't be here later"* and *"I'm quite sure my son doesn't want to talk to you."* He wasn't there, because he was far away in Mississippi at military school. And he didn't want to talk to her because her cousin had beaten him up and gotten him expelled.

Suddenly his comment at their first meeting—*Why don't you go run and get Barrett to beat me up?*—which had seemed so incongruous at the time, made sense. It also told her something important: Étienne was under the impression that she knew about his beating and expulsion.

And what about last night when he'd said, *"We both made mistakes."* She now heard this comment through a different filter as well. What mistakes? What mistakes did he believe she had made?

"Oh God," she murmured, feeling light-headed as an awful question rose up in her head. "Did he ever get my letters at all?"

All these years, she'd assumed he'd used her, that he didn't love her, that their week together hadn't meant anything to him, and that could still be true, but for the first time in a long time, it was also possible that it wasn't.

As for the comments ascribed to Étienne that led to the beating? Stratton hadn't actually heard them from Étienne's mouth, though he insisted Alex did, and Alex had been furious enough to beat up Étienne and stand by as he was expelled. Would Étienne have said such things? Bragged about being with Kate? Called her a slut? Made disgusting jokes about her body?

Her heart clutched and her lips twitched, but she forced herself not to get emotional about that particular part of these revelations until she had a first-hand account of what had happened. Alex knew the truth . . . and Étienne knew the truth, and whatever it was, Kate wanted it. But as much as she loved Alex, her heart told her to seek her answers from Étienne, to trust Étienne instead of her cousin. Because Alex hadn't just been beating up Étienne to defend her honor, he'd also been punishing Étienne for his cruelty to Stratton, and it could have clouded Alex's judgment.

Buzz. Buzz buzz.

Buzz. Buzz buzz.

She hopped up from the bed and grabbed her phone off the dresser, gasping lightly to see Étienne's name pop up on her phone. She swiped at the screen quickly to read his text.

Kate, I'm sorry about last night. I had no right to kiss you like that, and I promise it won't happen again. The only thing I will be concentrating on from now on is the deal. You can count on me to be professional. —Ten

Kate frowned at the text, the words *I promise it won't happen again* making her feel both sad and annoyed. She didn't exactly know what she wanted from Étienne, but no more kisses sounded terrible. First and foremost, she wanted to understand exactly what had happened between them, but she also knew that would be self-indulgent. They needed to settle business first. Their personal history would have to wait.

I owe you an apology too. You were trying to protect me from getting hurt, and I said awful, presumptive things to you. I'm sorry. Thank you for warning me about Tony. He and I talked. I think we'll be able to remain friends. —Kate

Her phone buzzed again a moment later:

That's good, Kate. I'm glad to hear it. Despite what you may think of me, I never, ever intended to hurt you.

She blinked back tears as she read these words, because if his words were true—if Étienne had never gotten her letters or calls . . . if he had believed in her complicity with Alex's actions—then the injured party between them was not only her, as she'd believed for most of her life, but Étienne as well. She gulped, typing quickly before she lost her nerve.

I know that now isn't the time because we should both be focused on business, but when this deal is settled, do you think we could talk about what happened? Between us?

She pressed *Send* then took a deep, shuddering breath. What if he said no? What if he told her to go to hell?

Yes. I'd like that.

She exhaled raggedly, closing her eyes for a moment in relief. Her phone buzzed again in her palm.

As long as you don't wear that blue dress, or I won't be able to make coherent sentences.

A surprised giggle escaped from her lips and her tummy fluttered.

No promises :) See you tomorrow? she typed.

See you tomorrow, Kate, he answered.

She knew Stratton's intention in calling her this morning had been to warn her away from Étienne, but the opposite had happened. News of Étienne's expulsion and banishment hurt Kate's heart and made her question the truth of everything she'd believed for twelve years.

For so many years, she'd longed for an explanation for his behavior: why she'd never heard from him, why he'd let go. She finally felt like her questions might be answered, and her relief was palatable, even hopeful.

Aside from finally understanding the past, however, Kate didn't actually know what could come of their conversation. Settling the past was one thing, but a future together—after so much mistrust and misunderstanding—seemed unlikely. And yet, Kate felt her heart opening as she considered the possibility of belonging to Étienne again, the giddy burst of hope, the barely restrained longing.

"I have no expectations," she said aloud, but she took her simple white cotton underwear out of the suitcase and replaced it with black lace.

Kissing

By midweek, Kate and Étienne had developed a routine.

After breakfast, Kate would leave Haverford Park, and Étienne would be waiting for her on the other side of the hedge, in the backyard of Westerly. The Winslows' old groundskeeper, Friar, didn't seem to mind two teenagers canoodling in the rose garden or talking for hours on the swing. Étienne had known Friar since childhood, and he'd shared with Étienne that it was nice for *someone* to be enjoying the gardens that he kept carefully pruned for Mrs. Winslow, despite her absence. As long as Étienne and Kate were quiet and respectful of the gardens, he left them alone, which meant that as long as the sun was shining, Westerly belonged to them.

Kate woke up bright and early on Wednesday morning, but it seemed that her family had started to notice her long absences from Haverford Park.

Her Aunt Eleanora stopped by her room to speak with her, launching into a sermon about how Kate's parents had entrusted her care to her aunt and uncle, how little they were seeing of Kate (she had missed dinner on Monday and Tuesday nights while she was with Étienne) and asking how Kate was spending her days. Kate had hastily explained that she was spending time with the Story sisters and though her aunt had looked slightly dubious, when Kate mentioned that she was friends with Betsy from summer camp, Eleanora had finally relaxed. As she left Kate's bedroom to play in a tennis tournament, she turned back and told Kate she expected to see her at dinner for the rest of the week.

On the way downstairs Kate passed Weston who changed direction to chase after her, begging her to go riding with him again.

"Later, Wes?" she asked, looking at her watch and cringing to find it was already after eight. She was losing time with Étienne and couldn't help feeling impatient.

"*When* later?" he whined.

"Um . . . four?"

"Four o'clock? You promise, Kate? You'll be here?"

"I'll try," she said, tousling his hair with one hand and crossing the fingers of the other behind her back.

In the vestibule, Alex caught up with her.

"Barely seen you since Sunday," he said. "Let's catch up. How about lunch in town today?"

"I'm, um, I'm seeing Betsy for lunch," she lied, looking away from him.

"Tomorrow?"

"Um, sure, okay," said Kate, thinking she'd have to come up with an excuse to get out of riding with Weston today and lunch with Alex tomorrow. She hated that she was going to let down her cousins, but she couldn't imagine spending time with her family when she only had a few days left with Étienne. She wanted to spend every possible moment with him.

"Great. Tomorrow it is. Noon?"

"Terrific," she said, hurrying to the kitchen to grab a muffin on her way out.

"Hey Kate," said Stratton, sitting in the same place he'd been on Monday, except with a different book.

"Hey," she said, grabbing a travel coffee mug from the cabinet over the coffeemaker.

"Going somewhere?" he asked, flicking his blue eyes to her cup.

"Um, yeah. Thought I'd go hang out with Betsy."

"Huh. That'll be tough . . . since Betsy and her sisters are in New York until Saturday."

She whipped around to face him. "Wh . . . How . . . ?"

"How do I know?" Stratton shrugged, giving Kate a disapproving look. "Because I was getting the mail when they drove by yesterday. Betsy rolled down the window and told me to tell you she'd see you at summer camp, and that she was sorry you two didn't get to spend more time together this week . . . which was weird since everyone in this family thinks you've been with her every waking minute."

Kate poured coffee into her cup, swallowing slowly before turning to her cousin. "Oh."

"Yeah."

He looked worried and annoyed, and Kate suspected that Stratton knew exactly what she'd been doing and with whom. "Are you going to tell?"

"That you've been spending all day, every day, at Westerly with Étienne Rousseau?"

Rushing to the counter where Stratton sat, Kate placed her hands flat on the cold metal, seizing his eyes. "I'm begging you—"

"I *should* tell. The Rousseaus are trouble! My God, Kate, your parents would have a fit."

Her eyes watered and her words came out in a rush. "You have no idea what they're like, Strat! No idea. I can't go anywhere, I can't do anything . . . this is my only chance to be *normal!*"

He stared back at her, his expression torn.

"Please? I'm begging you, Stratton. Please."

His face was grave as he mumbled, "Yeah, fine. I won't tell."

"Thank you," she said softly, taking a deep breath and swiping at her eyes.

Turning around, she opened the refrigerator and took out some cream, adding a drop to her coffee before replacing it.

Last night, Étienne had thrown pebbles at her window a little while after she'd gone to bed. She'd leaned over the sill to find him standing below, knee-deep in her Aunt Eleanora's rose garden.

"Hey," he'd whispered, looking up at her, the white of his teeth bright in the moonlight as he smiled.

"What are you doing here?" she'd squeaked, her breath hitching with surprise.

"Shhh. If your cousins find me here, we'll both be in trouble."

"What are you doing here?" she asked again in a whisper, drinking in the sight of him, her chest fluttering with excitement and surprise.

"I don't know." He shrugged, then murmured, "I wanted to see you."

She leaned her cheek on her hand, smiling down at him, overwhelmed by the deep romance of the moment and the strong yearning of her heart.

"Meet me in the morning?" he asked.

"Mm-hmm."

"Friar told me about a hidden spot at Westerly . . . a hammock behind some shrubs in the back copse on the other side of the bridle trail. Want to look for it?"

"Yeah," she said, chuckling softly and nodding. "A secret place. I love that."

"*Our* secret place," he said, staring at her intently before snapping off a rosebud and throwing it up to her. "*Bon nuit,* Kate."

"Good night."

She'd pressed the soft, tight petals near her nose as she watched him pick his way through the thorny roses and walk the long way back to the border hedge.

"Strat," Kate whispered, stirring her coffee distractedly. "I think I love him."

"That's categorically impossible," Stratton answered perfunctorily, straightening his glasses. "You only met him sixty hours ago."

"It doesn't matter," she insisted.

"Well," observed Stratton, "you're going home in three days. It'll be the world's shortest love affair."

She winced and her eyes prickled with tears, even though she knew Stratton hadn't meant to hurt her. She was grateful that he had already looked back down at his book so she didn't embarrass them both by bursting into tears. Instead she took a deep breath and blinked her tears away. The sun was shining and Étienne was already waiting for her. Nothing could ruin today.

Picking up her coffee cup, she started toward the back door when Stratton spoke again. "For the record, I don't have a good feeling about this, Kate."

"For the record," she answered softly, "it's too late for warnings, Strat."

He glanced at her briefly and nodded, but not before she noted the concern that darkened his eyes.

Leaving her conversation with Stratton behind, she ran out the door into the sunshine, sprinting as fast she could across the damp, dewy grass, almost slipping twice in her grass-stained white Keds, but not slowing down until she had reached the hedge and pushed her way through it.

And there, like heaven had delivered him, was Étienne, facing the hedge in distressed jeans and a gray T-shirt. His stormy eyes softened and relaxed instantly with her arrival, and his arms, which had been tightly crossed over his chest, loosened and fell to his sides. His whole face lit up as she approached him, his beautiful lips tilting up as the sun reflected off his mop of glossy, jet black hair.

The sound of her coffee cup hitting the ground was soft in her ears as her hands reached for his face, her palms pressing urgently against the warmth of his skin. They hadn't kissed yet, but the interruptions that had stalled her race to him this morning, in addition to her confession to Stratton, had added a longing—a fierce need—to her heart. This boy, who'd seemed so cool and smooth when they met, was deep and delightful, riveting and hilarious. He made her heart sing and her body tingle and in only sixty hours, he had become like water to her, like air, like anything that Kate felt sure she would die without, and all she wanted—all she wanted *in the whole wide world*—was to be wrapped in his arms and feel his lips touching hers.

"Kate," he whispered, his eyes both lost and seeking as he stared at her. "I got worried. I didn't know if you were—"

"I will *always* come to you," she murmured, her fingers flexing on his cheeks as she tilted her head back and leaned up on tiptoes to press her lips to his. They were warm and soft, pliant with surprise.

But then . . . like the act of kissing him had flipped a switch and awoken something fierce and vital inside of him, his arms came around her swiftly, desperately, pulling her against his body as his head tilted to seal his mouth over hers with a deep, guttural groan. His tongue pushed between her lips, seeking hers, and she moaned into his mouth, meeting him stroke for stroke, clumsily at first, then establishing a rhythm that made heat spread from the epi-center of their lips, unfurling like tendrils all over her body. His fingers curled into the small of her back, the strength of his muscular arms gripping her like iron bands, the hard-ness of his desire pushing into the softness of her belly, and she welcomed it, answered it, and equaled it with a lust and longing of her own, arching her pelvis into his and shiv-ering from the delicious flood of heat she felt deep inside her body. Her skin flushed as her blood rushed through her throbbing heart, and in that moment, Kate knew that she would never be the same again. She had fallen in love for the first time in her life, and no matter what happened from now until the end of time, Étienne Rousseau would own a piece of her heart.

He touched her lips gently with his—tiny kisses like the brush of angel wings—and then he drew away, his chest heaving with pants as his eyes searched hers uncertainly.

"Étienne," she said breathlessly, staring at his mouth as she rubbed the pad of her thumb over his kiss-swollen lips. "Can we do that all day long?"

His head fell back suddenly and the sound of his laughter was so unexpected and welcome, Kate joined him with one of her own as he picked her up and swung her around. When her feet touched back down to earth, he released her waist, raising his hands to palm her cheeks as he smiled into her eyes with tenderness and wonder.

"Until our lips bleed," he promised.

"Until we can't feel them anymore," she suggested.

"Until it's dark."

"Until we starve."

"Until forever," Étienne whispered, tracing the outline of her lips with one fingertip, before pulling her back into his arms and claiming them with his once again.

Chapter 7

Kate hadn't seen Étienne in the boarding area, so she was surprised to find him already sitting in the first-class seat next to hers on the plane. Even with his head bent, she could still make out the angles of his face as he looked down at his lap. His thick, black hair was glossy and slicked back, giving her a good view of his face: dark eyebrows, pale skin, a hint of midnight stubble accenting his jawline. Through any lens, any eyes, he was male-model gorgeous, and it momentarily stunned Kate that once upon a time, he had belonged to her.

"Good morning," she said, unable to keep her face from brightening into a smile as his green eyes looked up at her. He looked freshly showered and completely delicious, which made her so nervous, she babbled, "You must have gotten super special boarding."

Holding a white coffee mug to his lips, he took a sip then lowered it, grinning at her. "Platinum elite status. I started racking up miles on American when I was a teenager going back and forth to . . ." His voice tapered off and he dropped her eyes. He placed his coffee cup on the tray in front of him, and when he looked back at Kate, his face was hard. "Doesn't matter."

"I'll just . . ." she said, lifting her small rolling suitcase into the overhead compartment and hating the shift from warm hellos to awkward curtness. What had he been about to say? Military school? Had he started earning miles going back and forth to military school after her cousin got him expelled?

Kate swallowed uncomfortably, then sat down beside him, putting her purse on the floor in front of her seat and holding her briefcase on her lap. Darting a glance at Étienne, she found him shifted slightly away from her, looking out the window.

"I thought I'd review the possible buyer profiles on the way down," she said.

Étienne didn't say anything.

"From what I can tell, Hubbard Oil looks to be our best bet," she said, feeling guilty about something she'd had no part in and wishing there was an easy way to talk to him about everything. "They have the capital to—"

"Can I ask you something?" he said, turning back toward her, his eyes direct and searing.

She shrugged, trying to look casual, but every muscle inside her body clenched with anticipation of unpleasantness. "I guess."

His face remained expressionless but for his eyes, which churned as he stared back at her before finally asking in an unexpectedly congenial voice, "How's your friend, Libitz?"

She blinked at him before shaking her head in surprise and laughing softly.

"Not what you were expecting?" he asked, his gorgeous lips slanting up in a tempting smile. She knew that look—he was teasing her, and it made her belly flip-flop.

"Not at all," she said. "How in the world do you remember her name?"

"I remember everything," he said softly, holding her eyes.

And something deep inside of Kate woke up, stretching and unfurling as though she were a flower and he, the sun. It felt warm and intimate. So tender. And so familiar.

"Me too," she whispered.

His face lightened again. "So? How's Libitz?"

"She's good," said Kate, closing her briefcase and relaxing into her seat. "She owns an art gallery in SoHo. She calls herself prickly, but I think Lib's just an acquired taste . . . and she still calls me on all of my crap."

"So, she's still your best friend?"

Kate nodded. "Oh, yeah. I can't imagine not knowing Lib."

"Based on what you told me, I always thought she might be a good match for J.C.," said Étienne, his eyes twinkling.

"Lib with a WASP? Fat chance."

"Hey, now . . . *we're* not WASPs. First of all, we're neither Anglo, nor Saxon. We're French. And second of all, we're Catholic."

Kate chuckled, conceding his point. "Still . . . debonair player J.C. with prickly little Lib? I don't see it."

"She'd call him out on all of his shit," said Étienne, cocking an eyebrow and daring Kate to disagree.

"That she would," agreed Kate, smiling and shaking her head because she couldn't imagine it ever happening. With nil threshold for bullshit, Lib would likely deck J.C. before he could even make a pass at her.

Étienne took a deep breath, changing gears. "Bet she wasn't thrilled to hear about this deal with me."

"She had some choice words."

Étienne chuckled lightly. "Yeah. It's weird."

"It *is* weird," agreed Kate, laughing with him, remembering another time when they laughed together, staring up at puffy clouds in a spring sky, and it surprised her a little that the unexpected memory of his head on her belly didn't make her sad. For the first time in a long time, it felt like a good memory, not a part of something bad.

"So what crap does Lib call you out on?"

"The cats. The cousins. Tony. The—"

"Wait, wait, wait. The cats?"

The flight attendant brought Kate a cup of steaming coffee which she accepted gratefully before turning to Étienne with a grimace. "I have three."

"*Three cats*? I didn't even know you *liked* cats."

"How would you?"

"We covered a lot of territory that week."

Another quick memory of blue skies and sunshine blasted through her head. She'd told him everything about herself that week. How much did he remember? And why had he held onto the information? And why did her heart leap with hopefulness at the thought that memories of her had lived, vibrant and alive, in his head for all of these years?

"I'd never had one back then. My parents disapproved of pets. In fact, my first cat wasn't even mine. Shelby was my roommate's cat in law school. One day, Thalia—my roommate—decided she didn't want to be a lawyer, packed her bags, and moved to Malibu to be a surfer, leaving most of her stuff, including Shelby, behind. She was . . . a special cat. Sweet and loving, like a little human on the inside."

"Hold on. We'll get back to the cats in a sec. Your roommate quit law school and moved to Malibu on a whim?"

Kate giggled. "Yeah. Thalia was interesting. Her plan was to study Human Rights Law, then move to the third world and *liberate*. She always said, 'We need to liberate the people, Kate! Get down with the plan!' She had blonde dreadlocks. I guess she was raised on a commune and was like this odd transplant from 1968 or something. I admit, her whole philosophy sort of went over my head."

Étienne chuckled before asking, "So . . . did Thalia get busted for narcotics more than once?"

"Now that you mention it . . ." joked Kate in a singsong voice before shaking her head. "No. Not that I know of. But she smoked a lot of weed."

"I'll bet." He grinned at her. "So, Thalia heads to Malibu and Kate is left with Shelby."

"Yes," said Kate, sipping her coffee. "And we loved each other."

He flinched.

It was slight, almost imperceptible, but as she said the words about loving Shelby, he visibly flinched, and a huge lump suddenly rose up in Kate's throat. She took another sip of coffee, looking up as the flight attendant came back to ask what they wanted for breakfast. Kate was grateful for the interruption, and by the time they'd placed their breakfast orders, Étienne was composed again.

"So, Shelby was the first . . . how many have there been since?"

Was it crazy that her mind immediately reinterpreted his question to: "So, I was the first . . . how many have there been since?" She stared at him, wondering if he was also somehow aware of the double entendre. She almost answered, *A few, but none who ever owned my heart like you.* Her cheeks grew hot as she stared at him, grappling to reset her brain and answer his question appropriately.

"Um, cats?"

He looked curiously at her, raising one eyebrow.

"A few," she said meekly.

His eyes flashed. "But you never forget your first, huh?"

Her stomach quivered and she lifted her hands, pressing her cool fingers to her cheeks. "She was a . . . special cat."

Étienne nodded, holding her eyes, his breathing suddenly ragged and audible. Kate's own chest heaved up and down with panted breaths, and without warning her mind flashed back to Stratton's words from yesterday: *He never loved you. He disrespected you.* And as she stared back at Étienne, a sudden anger rose up within her.

"*Her* love was true. Not fickle," she said sharply.

"We're not talking about your cat," said Étienne. "And here I thought we'd agreed to leave our personal history at the door until after the deal went through."

"I'm not the one who asked about Libitz!"

"Fuck," he muttered, clenching his jaw and shaking his head. "I'm going to be straight with you, Kate . . . within five seconds of you sitting down, the tension between us couldn't be cut with an ax. *Forgive me* for trying to alleviate some of it by asking you an innocent question about your best friend."

Innocent. Right. Kate narrowed her eyes. "If you're so eager to chat, why don't I ask you a question about someone in *your* personal life."

"Fine, Kate," he shot back. "Have at it."

"Amy Colson."

Étienne's nostrils flared as he took a deep breath, staring at Kate with a sudden and intense irritation. Finally, he shrugged. "You know what? Fine. Believe it or not, I have nothing to hide. You want to talk about Amy? Let's talk about Amy."

Étienne was trying to control his temper but was having difficulty, and he sensed Kate was in the same boat. Her eyes were wide and furious as her hands moved to her lap and reached under the briefcase to buckle her seatbelt.

He took a deep, frustrated breath, glancing out the window for a minute as the plane moved forward on the runway and he wondered if this—this, this, this . . . *knowing* Kate, and *being around* Kate, and trying to figure out what the hell *happened* with Kate, and giving a *fuck* about Kate, all of it—could possibly be any more goddamned difficult and if it was even fucking worth it to try to sort it all out?

There was a veritable sea of shit to wade through . . . their history with each other, why they lost touch with each other and let go, her cousins and the part they played, her father, her understanding of his relationship with Amy, his suspicions about Stratton. All of it stood between them like a moat of misunderstanding, hurt, and recrimination, and yet they didn't walk away from it. They kept circling it, walking up to the edge of it, just short of leaping in. It stunk and rolled his stomach, and yet all he could think about was grabbing her hand, jumping in, and holding on tight until they found their way to the other side.

Why?

Why would he ever consider jumping into a steaming, stinking, complicated, painful pool of shit?

WHY?

He took another deep breath as the answer came to him. Because all of it—Stratton, Amy, how and why they lost each other, the fight with Alex, his expulsion, her indifference—*all of it* paled in comparison to what they'd felt for each other for one unforgettable week. Because the years that had passed, and the lovers they'd enjoyed, and the lives they'd lived couldn't diminish or destroy what they'd experienced that week. Because wading through the messy, mucky shit of anger and recrimination was worth it if they could recapture a once-in-a-lifetime love. Because if wading through the shit was their second chance to claim it, then Étienne was just about ready to strap on some waders and jump.

He turned to her. "I'll give you the entire history of my relationship with Amy. Can you be open-minded? Because it may or may not mesh with fu . . . with *your cousin's* version of events."

Her pinched expression relaxed just a bit, though her lips were still pursed when she said softly, "I'll try."

"Tell me what you heard," he said, bracing himself for ugliness.

"That you cheated on her. Regularly. That you played mind games, letting her believe you were faithful and then denying it when she found out you weren't. Make-ups and break-ups. Pain. Suffering."

"Not all of that is incorrect."

Her face fell and she gasped softly. "Oh."

"But the same circumstances can look very different when seen through a different lens."

"You're saying I got the wrong spin on the same events?"

"Something like that."

"But I trust my source. He doesn't spin things. I doubt he even knows *how* to spin something."

"Your source. Stratton."

She nodded sadly. "Stratton."

Étienne reached for his coffee and took another sip before asking, "Have you ever met Amy?"

"No. Not in person."

"Never spoken to her?"

"No."

"So you only know what Stratton told you."

"Yes."

". . . and he only knows what Amy told him."

Kate cocked her head to the side, considering this. "That's probably true. He may have heard other gossip or conjecture, but his main source was Amy."

"Off the topic of Amy for a minute, because I'm still building my argument . . ." Étienne's eyes asked for lenience and she nodded for him to continue. "If I asked the Atwell sisters about Barrett, Alex, and Weston? What would they say?"

"Nothing good," she said in a soft, firm voice.

"I'm not trying to put you on the defensive, Kate . . . but there are two sides to every story. Now in regard to Amy . . . do you want to hear my side?"

"I do."

He could see it in her face: her pursed lips had relaxed, her eyes were open, her body had shifted a bit toward him in her seat. Like any lawyer worth his salt, Étienne knew that he won the first round of reasonable doubt, but one major roadblock still lay in the way of Kate really *hearing* him.

"I have to ask this because you're prejudiced . . . Can you keep my history with Amy separate from *our* history?"

She flinched, taking a deep breath and holding it as she searched his face. "*Our* history. I'm not even sure what our history is anymore."

"*Chaton*," he said tenderly, refusing to be drawn into a conversation about them when she had only asked him yesterday if they could save it until after the deal. "Can you keep it separate?"

"I can try."

He leaned toward her a little, speaking softly near her ear as she stared down at her lap, occasionally nodding to let him know she was listening. He told her how he met Amy at college and how he'd liked her initially until she'd become too clingy. He detailed Amy's terrible loss—the night her parent's had died and how it had been impossible to break up with her. He told her about Amy's grief and how she'd changed as the years moved on, finally showing Étienne her true nature: fiercely possessive and unreasonably jealous. Kate didn't ask him any questions as he related these details to her. Their breakfast came and they ate as he continued his story. He was almost finished as the flight attendant cleared their trays away.

"Amy and I were together for five years, Kate. Five *years* when we probably shouldn't have even been together for one. We were young and we were wildly incompatible. We had our ups and downs, make-ups and break-ups; we were like any other idiotic college couple, but Amy's jealousy made the relationship toxic. One day we'd be together, the next we'd be broken up. Did I sleep with other women during the times we were broken up for a few weeks? I did. So, *I assumed*, did she."

"Did she?" Kate asked, finally looking up at him.

"I don't know. She led me to believe that she did . . . with your cousin. But the more I think about it, the more I believe that wasn't actually what happened but instead what Amy wanted me to think, that her behavior was technically above reproach, making her a victim and me a villain." He paused for a moment. "I'm not going to lie: the lines were probably blurred here and there. There were times, after explosive or ridiculous fights, when I wasn't sure if we were together or not. And during those times she may have believed I had cheated on her.

"It was exhausting. It was confusing. But, look at me, Kate. Look in my eyes." She did and hers were so searching—so beautiful and blue and clear—that his breath caught, hope and desperation mingling in his heart as he gazed back at her. "I swear to you . . . When Amy and I were *together*, I was faithful to her."

Kate couldn't explain how she knew he was telling the truth, but she did. Perhaps it was because her job compelled her to be able to sort out the veracity of situations and testimony, to know when a witness was reliable and to know when she couldn't put someone on the stand because they simply weren't credible. It didn't matter how she knew, she just did. She believed him.

"I believe you," she said. "And you have to believe me. Stratton never slept with her. Never. Not once. I promise you that." She smiled, chuckling softly, ruefully. "He wanted to. But he didn't."

"I think you're probably right," conceded Étienne.

"I have to reframe all of this, and that's hard for me, because Stratton was sure that you were mistreating her. So positive. And he wouldn't lie to me. I don't think he's capable of it."

"You believe he's purehearted?"

"I do."

"Then he wouldn't know if he was being manipulated, Kate. Didn't it ever seem odd to you that she strung him along like she did? Sleeping over at his place, but never dating him? Running to him when she was sad, but leaving him in the dust the minute she and I were back together? Every time we broke up, Amy insinuated that she was sleeping with your cousin. You insist they never slept together, and I'm more inclined to believe you than her. And if I do, the pieces will fit together for both of us. Think it over. Think about what you know, not what you heard. She played him like a fiddle, Kate. She played me like a fiddle, too."

Based on everything she knew, especially the way Amy had used Stratton, which had always bothered Kate, Étienne was telling the truth. She leaned against her seat back, her cheek against the slick leather as she gazed at him, searching his face, and asked him one last time, "So, you *never* cheated on her?"

"Not willfully," he said. "Kate, I stood by her side when her parents died. I held her hand and dried her tears and carried her to bed when she couldn't stand up anymore. I cared for her, even though she was hell to get along with. I know what she said about me. I know she painted herself as a victim and me as a villain. I always told myself it didn't matter who knew the truth, because *I* knew it. But for the first time, it's important to me that someone else knows it too, so here it is: When I understood Amy and I to be together, I never cheated on her with another woman. Not once. Never."

Kate couldn't help the small smile that spread her lips and made her eyes feel soft. He leaned his cheek on the back of his seat too, mirroring her, staring at her with heartbreaking tenderness and something that looked a lot like relief.

"Closing arguments?" he asked her, cracking a smile.

Her grin grew bigger. "Go for it."

"We'd been broken up for twelve hours when she left on a business trip for Japan for two weeks. While she was there, she got engaged . . . to a stranger." Kate had heard about this, but now it made her see Amy in a whole new light. Not as someone who finally had found well-deserved happiness, but as someone who wasn't nearly as committed to her relationship with Étienne as she would have had the world believe. "Does that sound fickle or faithful to you, *chaton*?"

"Fickle," she said, her hand suddenly reaching for his as her mind processed what he'd endured at Amy's hands. "I'm sorry."

"I'm not," he answered softly, lacing his fingers through hers.

Étienne let her take his hand because he would never refuse Kate his touch or his body or his heart or his soul. It seemed they belonged to her now as they had then, so long ago. He raised her knuckles to his lips, smiling into her glistening eyes.

But he realized, as his heart swelled with a never-forgotten love, that he *had* cheated on Amy. In fact, he'd been cheating on Amy since the day he met her, from the very beginning. Staring into Kate English's bright blue eyes, the truth slammed into him like a freight train and he knew: all along, he'd been cheating on Amy with his heart, because his heart had always belonged to Kate.

Loving

After two straight days of making out in the sunny nooks and crannies of Westerly's gardens, during which he refused to think about Saturday, Friday had finally dawned, and it was impossible for Étienne to avoid its tragic reality: Kate was leaving tomorrow.

Before meeting Kate, he hadn't known that it was possible to fall for someone so quickly, so completely. But the deep feelings he had for Kate were more real than anything he had ever felt before. He was falling in love with her, of that he was certain.

Since Wednesday, their physical relationship had moved at breakneck speed, manifesting itself at a level commensurate with their growing feelings for each other. Last night, wrapped up in a thick blanket he'd brought from his house, they'd been almost naked together in the Winslow's secret hammock, his plaid boxers rubbing against her white cotton underwear as he rocked against her, cozy in their intimate cocoon.

By now, Étienne had touched all but the most sacred parts of her body—tenderly, reverently—with his lips and fingers, trailing both along the secret recesses of curves and folds, peaks, valleys and plains, dropping gentle nuzzles and passionate kisses, discovering her, exploring her, learning what made her sigh and what made her giggle. Unlike the other girls he'd been with, Étienne was completely aware of Kate all the time, almost as though they were plugged into each other—two halves of a greater whole that was only complete when they were touching, seeking, finding love.

Between kisses and touches, they lay next to each other under the stars, wrapped in each other's arms, talking about their hopes and dreams. Both wanted to be lawyers one day. Neither wanted a marriage like their parents had, which felt

more like business than love. They talked about the sort of
parents they'd like to be one day. Kate said she'd trust her own
children more, let them make mistakes and be a soft landing
for them when they were hurting. Her own parents, she said,
were both stifling with their affection and overly controlling
with their rules and expectations. His, on the other hand, were
more lenient, but had almost no tolerance for trouble or mistakes. So, Étienne could do what he liked, as long as he didn't
cause a ripple on the water. The minute he did? Their judgment was harsh and their sentencing grave.

Her arms had tightened around him. "But you take so
many risks! What if they found out you use their car?"

Étienne had shrugged. "I honestly don't think they'd
care . . . as long as I don't *make* trouble or *get into* trouble. If
I can drive it to town without having an accident or getting
pulled over? I don't think they could care less."

"And if you *did* get caught?"

"There would be consequences and I would accept them."

"Just like that?" Kate had asked.

"Just like that," he'd murmured, smiling at her reassur-
ingly before bending his neck to kiss her some more.

This morning, she'd pushed through the hedge a little
after seven as planned, early enough to avoid the English
Inquisition and for him to arrange for their breakfast.

"You left a note?" he asked, pulling her into his arms and
sighing into her hair as she leaned into him, clasping her
hands behind his back and laying her cheek on his chest.

"Mm-hmm," she murmured. "In the kitchen. I said that
I was jogging with Betsy, then getting breakfast in town."

"You're sure Stratton won't tell?" he asked, his eyebrows
furrowed. He trusted Stratton English about as far as he
could throw him.

"No," said Kate. "He promised he wouldn't. Besides, I'll
run back at lunch to check in."

They'd learned that if Kate checked in periodically for meals, her aunt and cousins weren't as suspicious about her activities. But today, their last day, he hated thinking about any moment not spent together. He tightened his arms around her, resting his cheek on top of her head and breathing in the clean, fresh scent of her shampoo.

I'm going to miss you, he thought, unable to detach himself from the finiteness of the moment. *I'm going to miss you so fucking much, it's aching like nothing I've ever felt before.*

"This is brutal," she finally murmured, the movement of her jaw soft on his chest. "Tell me you have something good planned for today."

"Not much," he admitted, feeling as miserable as she, and yet fighting that feeling because he didn't want to waste the day feeling sad when they still had time together. "Just you and me. Talking. Walking. Watching bunnies fuck in the sky."

She'd giggled softly then, and he relaxed a little.

"And making out?" she asked looking up at him.

"Lots of that," he confirmed, dropping his lips briefly to her nose. "Plus, Friar uncovered the pool and said we could use it if we wanted to swim . . . since it's our last day."

"I didn't bring a suit," she said.

"I grabbed one from the laundry room. It's Jax's . . . or Mad's."

"Who are both tiny compared to me," said Kate, giving him a look.

"Which just means I get to see more of you," he teased.

"Part of your evil plan?" she teased with a smile, darting a glance to the picnic basket at his feet. "Breakfast?"

He nodded. "In the rose garden or the copse?"

"The patio," Kate suggested. "A proper breakfast."

"Very good, Miss English," he said, stepping away from her and picking up the basket. He offered her his free hand and she took it.

All things considered, it had been a good day. They'd spent the morning sitting at the cast iron patio table on the Winslows' back terrace, eating croissants and sharing coffee from a thermos. Kate told Étienne all about the summer camp she attended in New Hampshire with Betsy and he told Kate about his grandparents' apartment in Paris that had views of the Eiffel Tower, promising that someday they'd go there together. He showed her the finished portrait which, he felt, still needed a lot of work, but her eyes misted as she touched the brush strokes reverently.

"Someday it'll be yours," he'd said, and she'd lurched across the table to kiss him.

As the sun rose higher, they put on swimsuits and got in the pool, playing games that always ended with Étienne grabbing Kate and kissing her as she wrapped her legs around his waist and buried her fingers in his dripping hair.

She never returned to Haverford Park for lunch, so she insisted on returning for dinner, despite his pleas that she stay with him. Promising to return as soon as possible and meet him at the hammock in the copse, she'd finally kissed him good-bye and slipped back through the hedge.

Étienne had run back to Chateau Nouvelle to shower and shave quickly, avoiding J.C. who'd returned last night, before heading back to Westerly. As he ambled across the lawn at twilight, he'd finally surrendered to the immense heaviness of his heart. Tonight when he told her "Good night" he'd essentially be saying, "Good-bye."

He reached the hammock and unfurled the thick blanket, laying one half across the netting carefully and letting the other half, which he would wrap around them later, droop to the ground. And then he lay down, staring up at the growing darkness of the sky and emerging stars, telling himself to live in the moment and enjoy the time he had left with Kate instead of grieving the time ahead when they'd be apart. But for Étienne, who had many acquaintances but no close friends with whom to share his deepest thoughts and dreams, losing Kate was hurting on several levels: he'd miss fooling around with her—the warmth and pliancy of her body—of course, but he'd also miss his friend.

"Room for me?" she asked from several yards away, picking her way through the shrubbery that concealed the quiet grove.

"Always," he answered, shifting over a little to make room for her and propping himself up on one elbow that sunk partway into the netting.

She was barefoot, wearing jeans and a T-shirt, with her hair back in a ponytail. Simple and innocent and breathtakingly lovely, just looking at her made his chest hurt.

Sitting down on the edge of the hammock, she reached up and pulled the elastic from her hair, shaking it a little, then swung her legs up and lay down beside him on her back, looking up at his face.

"This is it, I guess," she said, her voice thin. As she locked her eyes with his, the hammock swayed gently.

"For now," he answered, watching a tear slide from the corner of her eye into her hair. It glistened like a moving diamond, and strangely, it broke his heart and comforted him at the same time. He didn't want her to be sad, but he wanted her to love him as much as he loved her, and her tears somehow felt like tangible proof that she did.

She clenched her jaw, looking away from him, beyond him, at the sky.

"I'll go home. You'll move on," she said softly, pursing her lips together like she was trying to stop crying.

"Kate," he said gravely, "look at me."

She blinked, turning her head a little to focus on his face.

"I won't." He felt miserable and desperate, his throat thick and his eyes burning as he tenderly palmed her cheek. "I promise I won't move on. I won't because I can't. Because I . . . I love you. You're the only girl I've ever loved."

She flinched, her breath catching as she searched his eyes.

"I love you, too," she murmured, reaching for his face and pulling his head down to hers.

Her lips tasted salty from her tears, and they were a little slippery, so he licked them gently, nipping softly until her mouth opened to him. She whimpered as his tongue found hers, stroking the slick heat in a gentle rhythm as his hands moved to her T-shirt. He pulled at the hem and Kate shifted, struggling to pull it over her head. Their mouths were only apart for a moment, but when they collided again they were feverish and wild, his hands reaching behind for the clasp of her bra as he shifted to settle on top of her. Kate wiggled under him, and he pulled the straps from her shoulders, sliding his hands down her arms before covering the soft, sensitive skin of her breasts with his palms. Her nipples beaded immediately, and her hands found the bottom of his shirt, pushing it up, her nails grazing the skin of his chest as she frantically tried to bare his chest to hers. Étienne reached behind his neck and pulled off the shirt, throwing it to the ground and kissing her fiercely, his fingers gently pinching and massaging the taut peaks of her breasts as his hips thrust forward. He skimmed his lips to her ear, sucking the lobe between his lips and grazing it gently with his teeth.

"Kate, Kate, Kate," he murmured into her ear, and he felt her shudder beneath him. When he drew back, he saw that her face was glistening with tears and he reached up to cup her cheeks, gazing at her with all the tenderness in his heart. "Please don't cry."

"I love you," she said softly in a broken voice. "I'm so glad I met you, but I'm so sad I have to leave you tomorrow. It's so unfair. It's so . . . terrible."

"I love you, too," he said, bracing an elbow on the netting and rolling off of her a little so that his full weight didn't rest on her. He pulled the blanket around them and looked into her eyes, trying to be brave for her as the hammock swung gently from his movements. Despite the sadness he shared with her, he couldn't bear her tears. He had to try to reassure her. Pulling her into his arms, he whispered near her ear, against her hair, "*Chaton*, this isn't an ending, it's just a beginning. You'll go back to New York, but we'll still talk. I'll call you and when you can, you'll call me. We'll write. We'll see each other, too. I'll take the train up whenever I can, and when you come back to see your cousins, I'll be waiting." He drew back to look at her, and her eyes were wide and sad, and he felt his courage failing. His voice broke as he confessed, "If I think of tomorrow as an ending, I'll go crazy, Kate. I'll go crazy."

"Étienne . . ." She pulled her bottom lip into her mouth, her glistening eyes locking on his, "Remember last night? When I stopped you?"

During an especially passionate kiss, he'd wiggled out of his boxers, then reached for her panties, pulling them down a little so that his erection could rub over the soft curls that concealed her sex. It had been hell to stop, but Kate had slid her fingers between their bodies, pulling up her underwear first and then his, and Étienne had respected her gentle refusal.

He nodded, his heart thundering with hope. "Mm-hmm."

"Tonight . . . I don't want to stop tonight. I want to do it. I want my first time to be with you."

"Kate," he groaned, his already-hard erection thickening in his jeans and pushing against her thigh. "I don't want you to regret anything. Maybe we should . . . wait."

"Why?" she asked, another tear slipping out of the corner of her eye and running into her hair. "We love each other.

We won't see each other again for a while. I want the memory of us . . ." She paused, searching for the right words, ". . . doing it. I want to remember what it felt like to feel you . . . like that . . . inside of me. I'm going to live on it until I see you again." She swallowed, her eyes wide and luminous in the moonlight. "Have you ever done it?"

He briefly considered lying so that one of them would theoretically know what they were doing. But this was Kate. It was impossible to deceive her. He dropped his lips to the warm valley between her breasts and whispered against her skin, "No. Not yet."

She sighed softly, her whole body relaxing as her fingers threaded through his hair. "So, I'd be your first, too. Don't you want that?"

He looked up, his eyes locking with hers. "More than anything, Kate, but—"

Kate wiggled a little—which was a rare torture because it made her breasts rub against his bare chest—and reached around her back, arching her pelvis up against his for a moment before falling back. His breath hitched from the sensation, but he was quickly distracted: she held up her fingers which clasped a foil packet that glinted in the moonlight. "I stole it from Alex's bathroom during dinner."

He reached for the condom, looking at it before glancing back down at her. "You stole this from Alex?"

She sniffled, swiping at her eyes and grinning for the first time tonight. "Uh-huh."

"You don't think he'll miss it?" he teased.

"He had, like, thousands."

"Ew." Étienne wrinkled his nose. "I'm not surprised."

"Étienne," she asked, arching against him, her breasts soft and nipples tight against his chest. "Can we not talk about my cousin right this minute?"

Her face wasn't glistening anymore, and though her eyes were still sad, they were expectant now too. Soft with love and dilated with passion, she gazed up at him like an angel.

"Are you sure, Kate? Are you sure you want this?" he asked softly, and in that moment he could feel it: his heart still thundered in his chest, but it didn't belong to him anymore, it belonged to Kate. And deep in his soul he knew it would belong to Kate forever.

"I'm sure," she whispered. "I love you. I choose you."

Holding her eyes, he nodded, then stared at her lips for a moment before leaning down to kiss them.

Chapter 8

"You nailed it!" exclaimed Kate as she slid into the cab, scooting over next to the far window to give Étienne a chance to maneuver into the backseat beside her.

After their talk about Amy on the plane, a great deal of tension had collapsed between them and after sitting quietly, holding hands for a little while, Kate had insisted that they review the potential buyers for the oil rigging part of Rousseau Shipbuilding.

A car met their flight and took them to the first of two meetings at which Étienne had offered to take the lead, impressing Kate with his vast knowledge of the enclave of the company that they wanted to sell. After two meetings, one with McKenzie Fuel and one with Hubbard Oil, it looked like they were about to commence a bidding war, which meant more capital for the Rousseau Trust and a faster resolution toward English & Company buying the company.

Étienne grinned at her. "Did you see Alan Hubbard's face when I explained that McKenzie was willing to pay thirty million?"

"I thought he'd burst a blood vessel," laughed Kate.

"He was so sure it was in the bag for twenty-two."

In addition to the pleasure of watching Étienne negotiate, Kate had felt something else stirring inside her heart. After talking about Amy and understanding Étienne's version of events, Kate felt something a lot like hope. Possibility. And while it frightened her on one level, she felt herself hurtling headlong toward it, like she hadn't known it before now, but her whole life had been a series of paths and journeys leading here: here to New Orleans, here to a second chance with Étienne Rousseau.

And yet, their personal history was still unexplained. Their personal heartache was still unresolved. She had asked for him to wait until after the deal to discuss their history, but she felt an impatience, an urgency to understand and move forward. *Now.* But with weeks of negotiations ahead, now wasn't the right time. It would be prudent to save the conversation until everything had been signed, stamped, and delivered. Only then could they spend the time needed to resolve their issues and figure out if a second chance was in the cards.

"Kate," he said, and she looked over at him, grateful to be distracted from her thoughts, her belly fluttering from the stark appreciation that darkened his eyes. "You weren't too shabby yourself."

"I don't get to do negotiations that often," she said. "Not like this, you know, in the field. It's mostly phone calls and boardroom meetings. This was exciting. It was . . . fun."

"The thrill of the hunt," he said, leaning toward her.

Her heart sped up as she leaned closer to him. "The thrill of the hunt."

"Kiss me, Kate," he whispered.

And though she knew it was a bad idea to kiss him again until they settled the broken, untied ends between them, she couldn't deny his request. Her heart sped into a canter as she leaned forward, closer to him. As he angled his head to the side, his nose nuzzled hers—the lightest touch—and his breath, hot and quick, dusted over her sensitive lips. His skin smelled of soap and she knew he would taste like coffee, and Kate felt her blood surge, making her whole body tingly and charged, the strength of her longing edging out any second thoughts. His face was so close to hers, she could feel the heat from his skin on her cheeks, the feather touch of his eyelashes as he closed his eyes. Their breath mingled and magnified like soft music in her ears and she closed her eyes, tilting her head to the side and leaning forward to touch her lips to his.

He was tentative at first, slow and gentle as he caught her top lip between his, then releasing it and taking her bottom lip before letting it go. A hushed groan, a low sound of pain or relief was released from his throat and vibrated against her lips.

"*Chaton*," he murmured, forming her name against her lips. "I've dreamed of this."

"Étienne." She sighed, pulling her lower lip between her teeth as she panted softly, her eyes still closed, her body humming with need for him.

He licked his lips, his tongue brushing against hers for a brief second before he leaned forward again and took her top lip between his again, holding it, claiming it, and then letting it go.

"You've missed me, too." He swallowed and his words were soft but urgent. "Tell me. Say it."

"Yes." She sighed in surrender. "I've missed you, too."

The soft sucking sound of his lips against hers made shivers course down her back and her hands, balled into fists in her lap, unfurled. Reaching blindly between them, they touched down on the starched fabric of his shirt. She flattened them on his chest and his breath hitched as he lowered his mouth to hers again.

Leaning into her, his arm snaked around her waist, he slid her across the slick seat of the cab, eliminating any distance between them. Her fingers, which grew bolder by the moment, skated up his chest, the backs brushing over the hot skin of his throat, which made him shudder against her. His kiss deepened, and he slipped his tongue between her lips and groaned her name into her mouth. Plunging her fingers into his hair, her thumbs caressed the soft skin behind his ears as her tongue slid against his.

Étienne had kissed Kate on Saturday night, but there was something very different about this kiss. He had asked and she had given. She wanted to be in his arms. She wanted his lips moving insistently over hers. She welcomed the leaping of her heart and the coursing of her blood. She felt alive and desired and aroused beyond belief and she wanted it— everything that Étienne was offering, Kate wanted.

The problem was, Kate wanted—no, Kate *needed*— answers, too. In other words, the timing was terrible.

She pulled away from him, opening her eyes and trying to catch her breath as her chest heaved into his. Panting softly, Étienne leaned his head down, his forehead pressed against hers as his eyes slowly opened.

"We have to talk," she said. "I need to understand."

"You wanted to wait," he said, his voice lower and his accent thicker than usual.

"I can't," she murmured. "I can't wait."

He leaned back and nodded, his fingers kneading gently against her lower back. She rolled her forehead away from his, dropping her cheek to his shoulder as he tightened his arms around her.

"We're almost at the hotel," she said, his fingers making such delicious shivers run down her back that she arched into him, pushing her breasts against his chest.

"My room?" he asked in a husky voice.

She shook her head against his suit jacket, leaning away. "I don't think that's a good idea."

"I think it's a *very* good idea," he answered.

"Please," she begged him, her breath hitching.

The cab pulled up to the hotel and Étienne leaned back from her, placing his fingers under her chin to tilt her head up.

"I'll call down to the restaurant and reserve a table in their quietest corner. Meet me for lunch? In half an hour?"

"Yes," she murmured, drawing away from him.

"And Kate," he promised her, his eyes darkening as he released her and reached for his wallet, "after we talk, we're going to finish what we started here."

As they checked in, Étienne refused to make eye contact with Kate. And in the elevator, he purposely stood as far away from her as possible. His body was raging with lust for her, hot and unsatisfied, and he barely trusted himself not to push her up against the elevator wall and have his way with her. Their kisses in the cab, teasing and tender before suddenly turning hot, had made his hunger for her vault from manageable to undeniable, and as he limped behind her, headed for his room, he had no idea how he was going to practice enough patience to talk to her about their past when all he wanted was to bury every inch of his sex into every inch of hers.

He stopped at his room, holding the key card but watching her make her way two doors down, her ass swaying lightly in a tight gray dress that was keeping his dick hard and his blood hot.

"Kate," he growled, tightening his jaw as she turned to look at him. With one hand holding her key card, she raked the other through her blonde hair and his erection swelled. "Part of me doesn't care what happened. I want you. I just want you . . . *now*."

She flinched, pulling her bottom lip between her teeth as she stared at him in the quiet hotel hallway.

"*I* care," she said quietly, holding his eyes with longing and sorrow. "I need to understand."

He fought against taking a step closer to her. "This heat between us. This . . . chemistry—you can't deny it. Don't you *want* it?"

"Of course I want it," she said, her voice breaking a little. "But it's like quicksand. You can't build on it."

It was his turn to flinch as his lips parted in surprise.

"You want to build something with me?" he asked without thinking, a shot of unexpected hope making his heart race even faster than the sight of her curvy body so close to him in the deserted hotel hallway.

She shrugged, but it wasn't a casual gesture. It was slow and her shoulder remained bunched and tense by her ears before finally falling. "Maybe. I don't know."

Then she slipped her card into the door and pushed her way into the room, the latch quietly echoing her departure.

He stared down the empty hallway for a moment before fumbling in his pocket for the key card and letting himself into the room.

"*Merde,*" he muttered as he left his suitcase in the entryway and flopped down on the bed.

Build something? Did he *want* to build something? He'd just gotten out of the worst relationship of his life. It was madness—sheer lunacy—to even contemplate something serious with Kate English. He scrunched his eyes tightly closed and listened to his sharp, jerky draw of breath before opening his eyes and staring at the ceiling.

"Build something," he mumbled, rubbing his hand over his jaw and feeling his chest tighten with panic as he thought about her words, "*Maybe. I don't know.*"

Because deep inside, Étienne *did* know. He'd known all along. No one had ever compared to Kate. It's just that for so long he'd believed a future with Kate was impossible . . . and he'd given up on the possibility of ever being with her again. Thinking about her face in the hallway, the fierce passion of their kiss in the cab, the way she touched his heart like no one had ever been able to . . . the only thing that was completely impossible was to hold on to some ridiculous idea about staying single when he had a chance to be with the love of his life.

And something else . . . he'd let his desire overcome reason when he told her he didn't care what happened . . . he'd never truly be able to trust Kate unless he understood why she walked away. He needed answers just as badly as she did, and then he intended to strip her down and pick up exactly where they left off. But to survive their conversation . . . he needed a cold shower first.

Sitting up, he loosened his tie and reached for his shoes, pulling them off. He was down to his boxers when his phone started buzzing. Inclined to ignore it so he could keep his mind focused on the important talk he was about to have with Kate, he picked it up quickly to silence the ringer when he caught a glimpse of the name on the screen: Amy. Amy Colson.

His eyes widened, and he gasped softly before throwing the phone down on the bed like it was on fire. He stared at it like a snake as it continued to buzz, his heart rate speeding up as he wondered why the hell his crazy ex-girlfriend was suddenly calling him after almost two months. And damn it if curiosity didn't get the better of him.

He picked up the phone and pressed *Talk*.

"Amy?"

A loud, ragged sniffle. Then, "T-Ten?"

She was crying. He'd answered the phone a million times to Amy's tears, and out of habit he sat down on the bed, resting his elbows on his knees and bending his head forward. "Amy? You okay?"

"N-no."

Étienne took a deep breath, reminding himself that Kate was two doors down the hallway and he was having the most important lunch of his life with her in twenty-five minutes. Still, he was so conditioned to care for Amy, he couldn't just dismiss her and hang up.

"Amy, I'm in the middle of—"

"I'm so s-s-sorry!" she wailed. "Can you ever f-forgive me?"

"It's fine," he said, assuming she was talking about how she had gotten engaged in Japan. "I'm glad you found someone. I just want you to be happy."

"Well, I'm n-o-o-o-o-t! K-Ken broke things off. He w-went back to T-Tokyo. Ten, I n-need you," she sobbed, hiccupping intermittently as she explained. "You were always th-there for me. You always c-came b-back to me."

"Amy," he breathed. "I'm not coming back this time."

"Why?"

"Because I'm in love with someone else," he said softly, the blessed relief of the truth making him feel calm and certain.

"Who?" she demanded in a surprisingly un-hiccupy voice.

He stood, limped to the window, and looked through the sheer curtains at the afternoon sun. "You don't know her."

"Is she a . . . a nurse or something? Someone you met while—"

"I knew her a long time ago," he said. "Long before you."

"Before me . . ." Amy was silent for a long time before whispering, "It was her, wasn't it? It wasn't Connie Atwell or Becca Flincher or any of the other girls who you were with when we broke up. It was her. She was always between us."

Étienne took a deep breath and nodded. "It was always her."

"Then what was I? A plaything?"

A sarcastic chuckle escaped his throat. "Hardly."

"Did you ever *love* me? Ever?"

"Yes," he said softly.

"But not like her?" asked Amy, her voice breaking again, and this time for real.

"No. I'm sorry," said Étienne, swallowing the lump in his throat. "Amy, I have to go."

"Are you with her now?"

Her bitter, jealous tone made unpleasant goose bumps rise up on his skin and whatever sympathy he'd been feeling for her suddenly dissipated.

"That's none of your business." He paused, thinking about all of the years he wasted with Amy, when the person he'd always wanted was Kate. "We're done, Amy. I hope you find what you're looking for. I really do. But we're done."

Without waiting for a response, he pressed *End* and threw the phone back down on the bed. Sitting down on the edge, he raked his hands through his hair, and no doubt prompted by his conversation with Amy, his own anger exploded inside of him.

It *was* always Kate. *Always.* And yet Kate had let her cousins, her father, and her fear dictate the course of their future. She'd allowed duty and lies to keep her from him while he'd longed for her every day since the last day he'd seen her.

Damn it, he needed answers, too, and he needed them now just as much as she did.

Grabbing his pants off the floor, he pulled them on, zipping them up and buttoning them quickly. He threw on his undershirt and swiped his key card off the desk, limping as fast as he could to the door. Barefoot and furious, he made his way down the hall and knocked on her door a moment later.

"Étienne?" she exclaimed, her eyes widening as she took in his unkempt appearance.

He pushed past her into her room, listening for the door to close behind him before turning to face her. "I lied. I care about what happened."

Kate was trying to catch her breath. His sudden appearance, wild-eyed and demanding, made her nervous. Not to mention, she was in the middle of changing and hadn't had a chance to button her silk blouse or tuck it into her favorite pair of jeans.

"What changed between the hallway and now?" she asked, her fingers quickly finishing the last three buttons, blisteringly aware that they were alone in her hotel room.

"Amy called. She broke up with Ken. She wants me back."

Kate sucked in a sharp breath. "Oh, I—"

"And I told her I was never coming back. I told her I was in love with someone else, that I've been in love with that someone else for as long as I can remember. Always."

Kate's face crumpled as she sobbed quietly, pressing her palm over her mouth, her eyes suddenly glistening with tears.

"And I thought she loved me too," he choked out, flinching as he said the words. "Which is why I don't understand how she could forget about me, how she could walk away from what we shared without a second glance, how she could take my heart with her and never . . . Why didn't you ask for my side of the story? Why didn't you at least let me tell you what happened before you decided that you didn't love me anymore?"

Stunned by his words, Kate stared back at him, shaking her head back and forth, lightheaded and confused.

He blinked his eyes furiously, wetting his lips before speaking again.

"Why didn't you write?" he asked softly, lowering himself to the corner of the bed and straightening out his injured leg in front of him. He looked up at her, his eyes miserable, beseeching, distraught. "You promised. You promised you would write. I was holding you in my arms and you were crying and you promised you would write."

He didn't know.

Oh God.

He didn't know that she'd written.

"Étienne," she sobbed, taking a step toward him. "I *did* write. I wrote you every day for a month."

His eyes widened, and he winced as he stared back at her in disbelief. "No."

She nodded, taking another step toward him to sit on the edge of the bed, a few feet away from him. "Yes. Thirty letters. One a day. None answered."

He shook his head. "I never . . . I never got one. Not one."

"I promise you, I wrote them." She shifted her body to face his, watching as he leaned his elbows on his knees and let his head drop. She continued, "I sent them to Chateau Nouvelle. I didn't know . . . I didn't know, at the time, that you weren't there to receive them."

His face whipped up to look at her. "What do you mean, you didn't know?"

"I didn't know that you were expelled from St. Michael's. I didn't know that you were sent to military school. I called your house, but your mother told me never to call again."

"What do you mean?"

"I gave her my name, and she said to never call again."

"When?"

"Two weeks after I left."

"You didn't know?" he asked, looking up at her with crushed, almost disbelieving eyes.

"Not until Stratton told me. Yesterday. That's the first time I ever heard about it."

He winced again, running his fingers through his hair, where they remained buried as he dropped her gaze. "They kept us apart."

"You parents?" she asked.

He looked up again, his eyes narrow. "And yours."

"Mine?" asked Kate, tilting her head to the side and frowning. She shook her head. "Mine never even knew about you."

"I came to New York to see you . . . before I was sent away. I saw your father. He told me that you didn't want to see me."

"N-No," said Kate, shaking her head as a sick, swirling feeling turned over her stomach.

"Yes," said Étienne.

"Please tell me that's not true," she sobbed, knowing that it was. Knowing in her heart that her father had sent him away and made sure he believed she didn't love him anymore.

"I can't. I wish I could. I drove to your apartment at three in the morning. I wasn't allowed to see you, to say good-bye, to explain."

She felt stunned, like she'd been hit by lightning or sucker-punched.

"Oh," she managed, the sound a whimper, an expression of pain and regret and disbelief. He hadn't gotten her letters. He never knew she'd called. And she'd never known that he'd come to her home looking for her. They'd been kept apart by their families. They'd been deceived.

Étienne stretched out his arm and let his palm slide across the slick material of the comforter, and Kate dropped her hand to her side so that he could find it, so that he could entwine his fingers through hers and bind himself to her, so that they could experience this deep regret, this terrible betrayal, together. They sat in silence for several long minutes, dumbstruck and still, as they made way in each of their heads—finally, finally, finally—for the truth.

When she was ready, Kate turned to Étienne, and without any prompting, he looked up at her, his eyes sad but clear.

"Tell me everything," she murmured. "From the moment we said good-bye."

Parting

Étienne's hand was warm, clasping hers tightly as they walked slowly back across the Winslows' lawn, every step taking them closer to Haverford Park and closer to their final good-bye.

"My parents would say this is just a wild crush," she said in a hushed, bewildered voice. "They'd tell me that I'll get over it."

"Do *you* think you'll get over it?" he asked.

"No," she whispered. "I love you. I don't think I'll *ever* get over it."

"Do you wish it was less than it is?"

"It feels boundless," she said softly.

"*My bounty as boundless as the sea,*" he quoted. "*My love as deep.*"

"What's that from?" she asked.

"*Romeo and Juliet,*" he said. "I reread that line last night, and it reminded me of you."

"That's how it is for me," said Kate, her chest hurting as her fingers tightened around his. "That's exactly how it is."

"And that scares you?"

"A little," she admitted. "Doesn't it you?"

"It's *not* a crush," he said firmly, ignoring her question. "It's love."

"Yes," she said, sighing the word like she had no control over its urgency to leave her lips.

"What we just did," he said softly, the slightest touch of uncertainty in his voice, "that was love, wasn't it?"

She stopped walking, reaching for his other hand and staring up at him in the moonlight. The reality was that it had been a little awkward. She'd started putting the condom on backwards, and he'd had to flip it around to help her.

And when he'd entered her, it had hurt a little more than a little; he felt much bigger than she'd anticipated, and it burned as he pushed inside. As he rocked into her, tears had fallen from her eyes. She'd stared up at the sky with his forehead resting on her shoulder, his breath quick and panting as he tried to move slowly so he didn't hurt her. "Is this okay?" he'd asked over and over again, and she'd answered "Yes" because it *had* hurt, but the pain hadn't made Kate consider stopping. Being so intimately joined with him felt right, felt necessary, felt like the only thing that mattered.

Once he was fully lodged inside of her, he'd taken a deep breath and stayed still for a moment, staring down at her face.

"I don't know . . . where you stop . . . and I begin," he'd panted softly, a sheen of sweat on his face and his body trembling because he was trying to hold himself back, but ultimately couldn't.

The second time, made possible by the condom in his wallet, had been slower, more deliberate, and more satisfying for both of them. The second time was everything about which the songs were written and the stories told. The second time felt like heaven, and afterwards they'd held each other for over an hour, breathing, barely talking, just savoring their last moments together.

Looking at his face now, her heart exploded with love for him, and she rushed to reassure him.

"Yes," she whispered brokenly, unable to help another useless tear from escaping down her cheek. "That was love."

He released her hands and slid his palms up her arms, over her shoulders, gently caressing her throat and finally landing on her face. His thumb swiped away the tear. "*You* are love, Kate English. Nothing will ever, ever change that for me."

"How do you know?"

"Because I defy any other plan for my life. I refuse it. Because *this* is real—me loving you and you loving me.

Because I swear to God, Kate, I will still love you on the day I die."

Her shoulders shook with the sudden power of her sobs and he pulled her against his chest, stroking her back. His words were rough and ragged as he said, "This is *not* goodbye. It's *not*. This is just . . . until we meet again. And we will, Kate. I promise you that."

Her tears fell in cascades, wetting his T-shirt. She didn't want to go home. She didn't want to leave him. She didn't want the uncertainty of their separation when being with him felt like home. She raged at the universe for allowing them to meet only to pull them apart so soon after, and she thanked God for the time they'd had, and the chance to love him and be loved by him.

When Kate could finally speak, she drew back, wiping her cheeks with the backs of her hands and looking up at his face.

"How? How can this work?"

"I'll call you tomorrow."

She shook her head. "My parents won't allow it. I'm not allowed to date yet and they don't let me talk to boys on the phone."

He grimaced, then nodded. "Okay. Write to me."

"But I don't have e-mail. They monitor *everything*. They—"

"I assume you have paper and pens?"

She nodded.

"And enough change to buy a few stamps."

She sniffled, nodding again.

"So write me letters." He took her hand and they restarted their slow walk back to the hedges. "Write to me . . . whenever you want to."

"Every day," she promised. "I'll write you a letter every day."

"And I'll give you my phone number. Surely your parents go out sometimes? In the evening? Call me then."

"They'd find out. They'd see the charge on the phone bill."

"To Haverford? You could say you were calling your cousins. Would they really inspect the number?"

She gave him a look. They were too smart for that.

"Okay, fine. Then look at your mom's calendar. Write and tell me when they'll be out, and I'll call you."

A sudden laugh escaped her lips; it was a sound of hope, and it made her lips tilt up in a small smile because he kept coming up with answers and solutions. It made her feel like he wouldn't give up on them. "I can do that."

"See?" He grinned down at her, squeezing her hand once. "When will you be back?"

"Definitely for the summer party at Haverford Park," said Kate.

"July," he said, grimacing. "Not before?"

"It's possible, but my parents are very busy."

"Then I'll come to you. I'll figure out a way. I'll tell my parents I have a big exam coming up and I need to go to the library all day, but instead I'll take a cab to the train station in Philly and come up to New York."

"Libitz will cover for me," said Kate excitedly. "I'll tell my parents I'm going to her place for the day to work on a project or study."

"Okay!" he said, his voice more boyish as he got excited. "And you'll come and meet my train."

"Yes!" she said, stealing a glance at his face. "I'll meet your train."

"I assume I shouldn't send letters directly to you . . . can I send letters to Libitz? Will she get them to you?"

"Yes, I think so . . . let me check with her. I'll send you her address if she says yes, but I'm sure she will."

"And maybe you can call me from her place sometimes?"

"I'll try," she promised.

"I'll tell you when I'm coming and you can arrange to get away for a day."

"I will," promised Kate. "No matter what it takes! Lib will help, too. And I don't care if I get in trouble. I promise I'll be there."

"Me too," he said. "No matter what."

In their excitement, they hadn't noticed that they'd finally reached the hedge. It loomed over them—a six-foot barrier that would separate them for several long weeks until they could find a way to see each other again.

"Will you work on your parents, Kate?" he asked, turning away from the hedge, his eyes wild as they caught hers. "So we don't have to sneak around and hide? Maybe if you explained everything, they'd let us see each—"

"No." Kate shook her head. "If they knew . . . if they knew how I feel about you, I think they'd try to keep us apart. But Étienne, college is only two and a half more years away. We could choose to be in the same city."

"Your parents won't insist you stay in New York?"

"Even if they do, I'll have more freedom. I can live in the dorms or share an apartment with Lib. I can make my own choices. I'll be eighteen by then with some money of my own. I'll be free and . . . we can be together."

"Two and a half years," he said softly, letting go of her hand and wrapping his arms around her. "It's not too bad," he said softly in her ear. "I'd wait a thousand years for you."

"I'm going to miss you so much," she sobbed, her tears falling fast now.

"You'll write to me," he said in a low, barely-controlled voice. "You promised."

She rested her head on his shoulder, staring at the hedge behind him. She felt the warm, fragile hopefulness of their conversation slip away, replaced with the cold, harsh reality of their farewell. She leaned back and looked up at him. "Well, I guess—"

"Kiss me, Kate," he said, his eyes suddenly glistening in the moonlight as he searched her face with a stark misery that mirrored her own and wrenched her heart.

She pressed her lips to his, a sad kiss, a kiss good-bye.

"I love you," he said, his voice hitching as he reached up with one hand and swiped at his eyes.

"Me too," she said. "I love you, too."

She stretched out her hand, touching his beautiful face, holding his pale, chiseled cheeks between her palms for the last time. Leaning forward, she kissed him gently one last time as her tears mingled with his.

Then, without saying "good-bye," she turned away from the love of her life and forced her feet to move forward. Looking back one last time, eyes swimming and hand raised in farewell, she waved before slipping back through the hedge.

Chapter 9

That Kate hadn't known about him coming to New York managed to shock Étienne, although it probably shouldn't have. Her father had been so absolute in his refusal to let Étienne see Kate, it was no wonder he'd kept it a secret from her. It hurt terribly to know that she'd been oblivious to his last attempt to see her, but at the same time, relief coursed through his veins like a balm. She had written. She had called. She hadn't turned her back on him, after all. All these years he'd believed she had stopped loving him, but she hadn't.

In the end, it was their families who had kept them apart.

They'd been star-crossed from the very beginning.

He tightened his fingers around hers and shifted closer to her on the bed. Just close enough to hear her breathing, to feel the slight movements of her body, the light tremors and quiet gasps, as he told her the truth of their long separation.

"You walked back through the hedge, and I stood there for an hour. Pacing, looking through the branches at Haverford Park. I considered throwing pebbles at your window, or just throwing caution to the wind and knocking on the front door and risking your cousins' anger to see you again, to say good-bye again. I was wild with frustration. I couldn't believe that we'd just had sex and now I wouldn't see you again for weeks. I couldn't call you, I couldn't e-mail you . . . I couldn't stand it."

He swallowed, squeezing her hand, and heaviness threatened to overwhelm him as he told her what happened next.

"It was late, but I could hear music coming from Dash Ambler's house, and he was about the closest thing I had to a good friend, so I walked across the street to his place and found him and Kurt Martinson sitting by the pool, drinking beer and listening to CDs. I had a few beers with them. When Dash asked where I'd been all week, I said I'd been with you."

"You did? You told him?" she asked in a surprised voice.

They'd been so purposely clandestine that week, and by all intents, they'd intended to keep their love a secret from everyone except Kate's friend, Libitz. Sharing their affair with his friends had never entered the conversation or been okayed by Kate.

Étienne nodded solemnly, remorse making him wince as he stared at her, still outlining the steps that ultimately doomed them. "Yeah. I was . . . maybe it was the beer, but I wanted to talk about you. I wanted someone to know that I'd fallen in love with you. If no one knew but you, I'd be all alone, because you were leaving. I just wanted it to be real. I just . . ." He huffed softly, squeezing her hand. "I shouldn't have told Dash and Kurt. I should have realized that telling them could make trouble for us. I should have kept it a secret, kept it to myself."

"What happened?" asked Kate, shifting toward him on the bed so that her hip was aligned with his and the silk of her blouse brushed against his bare forearm. Her thumb made soothing, but distracting circles against the heat of his skin, making it difficult for him to concentrate, but he forced his thoughts back to the story she needed to hear.

"Do you remember the story I told you a long time ago? About Kurt Martinson's sister, Johanna? How she—"

"The one Alex dumped, who . . . who hurt herself. I remember."

"Yeah." Étienne swallowed, his deep regret assaulting him like it was yesterday. Kurt had asked so many questions about Kate—who she was, verifying that she was Alex's younger cousin, and that Étienne had slept with her. Étienne was so blinded by his feelings for Kate, so distraught by her leaving, he hadn't really noticed Kurt's tone or line of questioning. It hadn't occurred to him that Kurt would use information about Alex's cousin to get back at him. "Yeah. Are you angry? That I talked about you?"

"No." She squeezed his hand gently. "No. I understand. I do. I felt the same way. I told Lib about you first thing. Please . . . tell me the rest."

"It was only because I was so in love with you." He raised her hand to his mouth, pressing his lips against her skin. "I was . . . bursting to tell someone and my sisters were too young and my brother hated Barrett, so I didn't feel I could trust him. I just didn't . . . Oh God, Kate, in a million years I never, ever would have hurt you like that. I should have used better judgment. I should have kept my mouth shut. I should have—"

"Please don't. Please don't do that to yourself." She reached up, smoothing his hair from his forehead and cupping his cheek with her hand. "I believe that you loved me. I believe that you didn't mean to hurt me."

He took a deep breath and nodded, lowering their hands to his lap. "J.C. and I were never exactly favorites of your cousins. Nor were they favorites of ours."

"I know about Bree Ambler," said Kate. "And Jillian . . . O'Connor?"

"Yeah. That was a shitty thing to do to Stratton."

"Yes, it was," said Kate, remembering Étienne's too-cool-for-you swagger and knowing that Stratton, as much as she loved him, wouldn't have stood a chance against teenaged Étienne.

"I thought I was settling some debt for my brother."

"I know," she said gently, dropping her hand from his cheek, but holding his eyes.

"The next day at school, I was getting high fives and slaps on the backs after mass, which I had missed because I was hungover and went to the infirmary for aspirin. I mean, everyone's coming out of mass and I had no idea what was going on. They're saying, 'Way to go, Ten!' Or, uh, 'Ramming Rousseau.' Even 'Easy English.' I had no idea what people were talking about. All of these comments, and I didn't put them together immediately. There I am in the courtyard as everyone's pouring out of the chapel, and Kurt comes up to me and tells me that he's sorry. He says he didn't mean for the whole school to find out. He was only trying to get back at Alex for dumping Johanna. He wanted to embarrass Alex by spreading rumors about you. And sure enough, Alex comes up behind me and Kurt's eyes get all wide as fucking Alex sucker-punches me in the side."

Kate's whole body flinched, her fingers suddenly tightening around his as she gasped. "No!"

"He was . . . so *pissed*. Throwing punches and telling me I disrespected his family, saying I should've kept my hands off of you. Kate, your fucking cousins throw punches before finding out what's real and what's not. Anyway, I was down for the count and he's on top of me and he breaks my nose. I hear it snap. Honestly? I have no idea how I managed to get on top of him but something else snapped *inside* of me, too. I was so pissed at Kurt, and at Alex, and at the world for taking you away from me. It was this crazy amount of rage, and suddenly I'm on top of Alex, whaling on him. Like, crying and snotty, totally out of control, punching his face like a bag."

Kate's chin had dropped to her chest and she was crying; Étienne could tell from the way her shoulders shook, and he couldn't bear it. Shifting slightly on the bed, he dropped her hand and pulled her into his arms, rubbing her back gently as she rested her head on his shoulder.

"Don't cry, *chaton*. Please."

"We'd just shared the b-best night of our lives, and that's how you spent the f-first day back to school. I can't bear it. I'm so *pissed* at Kurt . . . and Alex!"

"Kate, listen," he said, leaning back to press kisses to the tears dotting her face and dripping onto her pretty cream blouse. "Let's stop here. You and I didn't give up on each other. That's all that matters. We can talk about the rest later. We don't have to—"

She reached up and clutched his face, her red-rimmed eyes searching his. "Yes, we do. I want to get this over with and put it behind us, Étienne. Tell me the rest."

Releasing his face, she dropped her cheek to his shoulder as he drew her back against his chest and resumed rubbing her silky back. "Okay. So . . . when the monsignor came outside, I was on top of Alex, and he was barely fighting back at this point. All of his friends knew the rumors, and fucking Kurt never took responsibility, for fear that he'd get in trouble. Alex's friends vouched for him, saying that I jumped him in the courtyard for no reason. I was expelled that day for fighting, and my father enrolled me at a military school in Mississippi about twenty-four hours later."

"But your nose was broken too. Why wasn't Alex—"

"Expelled? He only had two months of school left . . . plus, his friends all swore that he only threw one punch in self-defense and happened to catch me in the nose."

"So your father sent you away," she murmured in a broken voice.

"I embarrassed him. Big time."

"And the consequence was banishment."

"It was," whispered Étienne. "I never would have said those things about you, Kate. Never ever. I loved the way you looked. I loved *you*. That someone else disrespected the time we spent together was obscene to me. The fact that those words got back to you and hurt you? That's tortured me for years. I thought . . . I thought that was why you didn't want to see me. And yet, I was pissed at you for not giving *me* a chance to explain."

"Étienne," she said softly, her jaw moving lightly against his shoulder and her voice dreamy. "I never knew. I never knew that anything was said about me—by you or anyone else. I never knew you and Alex got into a fight. The first I ever heard of it was yesterday. That my cousins are protective of me goes both ways. Alex fought you to protect my honor. But he and Stratton—and my father, apparently—hid the details from me to protect my heart."

His eyes fluttered closed, a mixture of relief and sadness, and he stopped speaking for a moment, waiting for the old frustration to spit and sputter inside of him: the fury for Kurt's betrayal and Alex's rashness, and the terrible injustice of his expulsion and Kate's loss. Surprisingly, it didn't come. It didn't happen. Instead, as he held Kate against him, smelling the fresh sweetness of her neck and feeling the softness of her hair against his throat, he only felt sad to have missed so many moments with her and relieved that she hadn't suffered from his purported words or sanctioned Alex's retaliation.

"Speaking of your father . . . do you want to hear the rest, counselor?" he asked gently.

"I don't . . . but I do," she murmured, pressing her lips to his shoulder before resettling her cheek. "Tell me."

"I was set to fly down to Mississippi on Friday and start school on Monday, and I was basically under house arrest, but by Thursday I was going out of my head. You hadn't sent any letters yet—"

"I had," she said. "I'd already sent three."

"I didn't get any, *chaton*. I guess they were kept from me. My parents knew I'd fought with Alex. There's no way they'd give me letters sent from anyone with the last name English. It was the same reason my mother hung up on you."

Kate nodded. "I think you're right."

"I had to try to see you before I left. I borrowed the car after my parents were asleep and drove up to New York. I walked into your apartment building asking for you. Your father came down and told me I couldn't see you and I tried everything. I pushed past him and tried to get on the elevator. I begged him." Étienne swallowed painfully, remembering the desperation of the moment, knowing Kate was so close and that he was forbidden to see her. "He told me you knew what had happened with Alex. He told me you didn't want to see me."

"That was a lie," Kate whispered, her voice breaking. "My uncle must have told him what happened between you and Alex. But I never knew. I was in love with you. If I'd known that you were there—right there in my building—nothing could have kept me from you."

Her words knocked the wind from his lungs and made his chest hurt for a moment, and he closed his eyes, tightening his grip around her. "Kate. Fuck, it was terrible."

She nodded wordlessly, loosening her hands from where they were trapped against his chest and winding them around his neck. "I'm so sorry."

"It wasn't your fault."

"Nor yours," she said softly. "But it was hell for me, too."

His heart clenched from her words. "Tell me your side."

Kate took a deep, shaky breath, her chest pressing into his as she straightened up and leaned back a little.

"I think I need a drink," she said. "You?"

"I wouldn't say no."

Kate dropped her hands from his neck and scooted away, picking up the phone and dialing room service. "Yes. Room 314. Sauvignon Blanc. Mm-hmm. Chilled. And beignets. A basketful. Thank you."

After ordering, Kate stood and walked to the windows, opening the sheer curtains and looking at the intricate wrought iron balcony of the house across the street. It was painted mint green, but peeling badly in several places to show rust and darkness underneath. *Why don't they just strip the paint?* she wondered. *Why don't they strip the paint and clean off the rust and in the end they'd have a beautiful dark gray balcony instead of something that looked messy and forgotten?*

Because stripping away the paint was an arduous process. It was easier to throw another coat of paint on the rust and pretend it was beautiful.

Getting to the heart of any matter is always arduous, she thought. *And getting to the heart of the matter when it's a matter of the heart is even more painful.*

It was a lot to absorb: some of it a relief, and some of it utterly heartbreaking. Her family—whom she'd always idolized so much—had done everything possible to sabotage her relationship with Étienne, and it made her feel very stupid, very, very sad and very, very, very angry.

Alex's hotheadedness aside—though she would have some choice words for him *and* Stratton someday very soon—it was her father whose actions hurt her the most.

As an adult, Kate didn't see her parents very much. They had retired to West Palm Beach a few years ago, and only came back up to New York for the obligatory holiday visits. The reality was that the chokehold they'd had on her life for so long was impossible for her to forget, and she was protective of her independence and privacy. There would always be a wedge between them.

She wondered, looking across the street at that rusty balcony, if maybe deep down inside she'd always suspected that her parents had something to do with her crushing loss of Étienne. Nothing overt, but perhaps she'd picked up on something in those dark days when she was crying herself to sleep . . . in her father's manner, in her mother's worried eyes, something whispered and overheard, but long-forgotten. Because the hurt she felt now wasn't new or peculiar, it was old and familiar. That her parents were overprotective had been a grudging reality in Kate's childhood and teenage life. But her father was supposed to love her, and instead, he'd engineered the breaking of her heart.

Coming up behind her, Étienne put his arms around her waist, clasping his hands beneath her breasts, and Kate leaned back into the solid warmth of his chest, closing her burning eyes as she drew a deep breath.

"It's heartbreaking."

"It is," he agreed.

"If they'd all left us alone . . . do you think we would have done it? Gone to the same college? Found an apartment together?" Tears slipped from her eyes as she remembered the hopeful naïveté of her fifteen-year-old self.

"Absolutely," he said firmly. "Nothing could have kept me from you . . . except *you*. I hadn't received any letters. I believed your father. I truly *believed* you were finished with me."

"I wasn't," she sobbed.

"I know that now," he said, his voice somehow tender and furious at the same time. "What about you, *chaton*? What was it like for you? After we said good-bye?"

"I don't have much to add," she said, opening her eyes and reaching out to pull the sheers closed as he adjusted his grip around her, one thumb grazing gently over the nipple straining against her blouse.

His voice rumbled low in her ear. "I'll take whatever you're offering."

Her skin tingled as he said this, her heart pounding with desire, with a longing to reconnect with and to him, and to somehow recapture what they'd lost in every possible way.

"I went home. I missed you every second. I told Lib as much about us as I could bear to part with. I relived every detail. I wrote you flowery, ridiculous letters of love."

"I wish I'd seen them. I would have treasured them." He dropped his lips to her throat, kissing her gently. "And then?"

Kate arched her back, leaning her neck to the side to give him better access to the throbbing skin there. "After two weeks with no answer, I called your mother. She told me she was sure you didn't want to speak to me."

"I was already gone," he murmured.

"I wrote to you for two more weeks. Long letters, crying every night, wondering what had happened, asking why you stopped loving me."

"I never did, *chaton.*"

"And finally . . ." Kate sucked in a deep breath as tears sluiced down her cheeks and her shoulders sagged. "I gave up."

His lips, which had been nuzzling her neck, suddenly drew back, though his arms around her tightened, like he couldn't decide how he felt about this.

"It was Lib who made me stop. She told me to give up. She told me it was over."

Étienne took a shaky breath from behind her then rested his forehead on her shoulder.

Her voice sounded strained and broken in her ears as she continued. "I'm so sorry I never looked harder for you, never tried to find out what happened. I just assumed you'd decided that I wasn't what you wanted. I assumed you'd moved on—"

"I promised you I wouldn't."

"I know," she sobbed, speaking faster. "But you were so beautiful and sophisticated . . . and I was so inexperienced and fat and—"

He whirled her around in his arms, grasping for her chin and jerking up her face so he could look into her eyes.

"*Assez!*" he growled, his eyes fierce and his voice unyielding. "Stop."

Kate searched his eyes as his chest slammed into hers with every breath, his throbbing heart pounding against her breasts.

"You were *everything* to me, Kate. I don't care that we only knew each other for a week. I don't care that we were fifteen. And I don't care that we haven't seen each other since. You were warm and funny, interesting and kind. You listened to me. You understood me. You *belonged* to me. We crammed more into those days than I ever could have thought possible—enough to live on for half a lifetime. I *never* forgot about you, I *never* stopped missing you, I *never* stopped wanting you, and I *never* stopped—"

"Don't say it!"

"—loving you," he whispered.

Her eyes blurred with tears, and she shook her head looking down at the hem of his undershirt against the skin of his throat. "That's not possible."

"It is," he insisted. "It *is* possible." He took her hand and flattened it over his heart, then covered it with his own. His voice was so tender, her knees buckled when he said, "Kate. *Amié chaton.* It's beating only for you."

She looked into his eyes, at the fierce churning green of them, and the fringe of black lashes that framed them. His cheeks, cut from white marble, were tense, but his lips tilted up just slightly, and a small laugh of surrender made him shake his head with wonder.

"I never said good-bye," he said gently. "Neither did you."

"We barely . . . know each other," she said in a weak, halting voice, so close to surrender. Her body leaned into his, her heat seeking his, her lips parting softly in invitation as she searched his eyes, his heart still hammering under her palm.

"That's not true at all," he retorted, palming her cheeks tenderly, his eyes never leaving hers for a moment. "And besides . . . I'm free. You're free. There's nothing stopping us from *getting* to know each other all over again. No parents. No cousins. No ex-girlfriends. No one to get in the way. Just you and me. Just us."

"Is that what you want?" she asked, hope surging past fear. "*Us*?"

"That's all I've ever wanted," he answered, nuzzling her nose with his before dropping his lips to hers.

Chapter 10

Knock, knock, knock.

"Room service."

With Kate's lips only a millimeter from his, their wine and beignets had arrived. Étienne exhaled in annoyance, turning his head toward the door, then back to Kate. "Let's ignore it."

Knock, knock, knock.

"Hello? Room service."

Kate grinned at him and shook her head. "We can't."

"*I* certainly could," he muttered as she pulled away from him to answer the door.

Étienne turned from the windows in time to see a uniformed waiter stride into the room with an elegant, linen-covered tray containing a silver wine bucket, two crystal glasses, and a basket overflowing with beignets. The New Orleans-style doughnuts covered with powdered sugar were one of Étienne's favorite local delicacies. While attending nearby Loyola University for two semesters of law school, he'd certainly eaten his fair share. His mouth watered as the waiter set down the tray on the coffee table in front of a small love seat, and Étienne reached for his wallet. Handing the waiter a tip, he shook his head subtly when the waiter gestured to the bottle.

"Leave the opener," Étienne said softly, anxious to be alone again with Kate as soon as possible.

The waiter winked at him, setting the corkscrew on the tray and heading back out the door.

After Kate locked the door, she turned back to him, walking partway into the room before shoving her hands in her back pockets. This move had the benefit of thrusting her chest toward him, which made his mouth water further, but as she rocked back and forth on her bare feet staring at him, he wondered if she was nervous.

Reaching for the bottle, he sat down on the side of the love seat closest to the windows and used the corkscrew to cut off the metallic cover. When he looked up, Kate still stood in the same place, watching him.

"I don't bite," he said, letting his eyes rest on her chest for a moment before looking back up. "Unless you ask me to."

She pulled her bottom lip into her mouth as her eyes widened. "I, um . . ."

"Kate?"

"Yeah?" she asked breathlessly.

"I'm teasing you."

"I know."

Her shoulders relaxed a little, but she stayed where she was, close to the bed, several feet away from him, watching but making no move to join him.

Placing the bottle on the floor between his feet, he twisted the corkscrew into the cork, remembering Kate as a teenager. What had he done then to lighten things up when she was nervous? He searched his mind, grinning as he remembered how much she loved talking about her best friend.

"Hey Kate," he said, looking at her as the cork was removed from the bottle with a pleasant popping sound.

"Yeah?"

"Tell me what Libitz would say about this."

"This?"

He poured two glasses of wine, letting the opaque liquid splash into the wide bowl of each glass as her question hung in the air between them.

"You and me. Bottle of wine. Hotel room."

He held a glass out to her, and she moved forward, standing across the coffee table from him and taking the glass. She raised it to her lips, taking a long sip.

"She'd tell me to jump you," said Kate softly, her eyes brightening with amusement as Étienne choked on his wine.

Damn.

Maybe she was right . . . there *were* things he didn't know about Kate English, like the fact that she was more confident than he remembered. His dick swelled in his pants, so he took another sip of wine, telling himself to calm down.

"I always liked Libitz."

"I thought you had her earmarked for J.C.," said Kate, offering him a teasing grin as she sat down on the corner of the bed, diagonally across from him.

"I like her. I don't *want* her."

Kate dropped her eyes and took another sip of wine.

Damn again. She was hot, she was cool. She looked nervous, then she talked about jumping him. His Kate had some wiles. She wasn't totally innocent anymore, and it made a wave of jealousy break over him as he realized that there had been other men in her life . . . and probably in her bed.

"Is that what you usually do?" he purred, throwing his arm across the back of the love seat in an effort to look casual.

"Usually?"

"When you're about to make out with someone? Jump them?"

"Am I about to make out with someone?" she asked saucily, wetting her lips before taking another sip of wine and holding his eyes over the rim.

"Yeah," said Étienne, wondering how much more teasing he could take. And *damn one more time*, because when they were kids, *he* was the tease. Now? Kate was holding her own, and his body was getting hotter and hotter from the verbal foreplay. "You are."

"No."

His eyes narrowed. "No . . . you're *not* about to make out with someone?"

She shook her head, her eyes darkening as she answered him. "No, this isn't what I usually do."

"So I'm special?" he asked.

She laughed softly, the sound breathy and sexy, before taking another sip of wine. "You *were* the first."

"What if I want to be the only?" he asked, as startled as she by the words, yet unable to stop them from leaving his lips.

She tilted her head to the side, her sexy teasing exchanged for a more serious look. "You want us to be exclusive?"

"Yeah," he murmured. "I want you all to myself for a while."

Her lips parted in surprise as she touched the rim of the glass to her lips and tipped it back to finish her wine.

Fuck, she was way too far away, though it was convenient she was sitting on the bed. He threw back the rest of the wine and filled his glass, standing up and making his way haltingly around the coffee table, to sit down beside her. He filled her glass to the brim, placed the almost-empty bottle on the floor, then turned to face her.

Her eyes were unguarded and tender as she gazed back at him, her nipples pebbled against her silky blouse, torturing him with every breath she took.

"There haven't been many," she whispered earnestly.

"I hate all of them."

She grinned suddenly, about to laugh. "Are you jealous?"

"Completely."

"Should I be jealous too?"

It was true that he'd had many lovers after Kate and before Amy—lovers and girlfriends and one-night stands. But his answer was simple. He shook his head slowly, taking another long sip of wine before placing his glass on the floor next to the bottle. "No."

"Why not?" she breathed, letting him gently pry her wineglass out of her fingers to set it on the floor beside his.

"Because the only woman I ever *really* wanted," he said as his fingers buried themselves in her glorious hair, his thumbs lightly stroking her jaw, "was you."

Though Kate's mind issued one fruitless, final warning against walking down this path with Étienne Rousseau for the second time in her life, her heart and her body had already surrendered. And if she was honest, she'd clock her hopes to the night Stratton had called to say that they were going to be working with the Rousseaus on a deal. She had fought for the deal just to be with Étienne again— just to have a chance to find out if what they'd shared had been in her head, or real. Understanding their unlucky history, their heartbreaking "almost," the wistful "could have been" that was stolen from them by the people they loved? It made her desperate to be bound to him again, to recapture what was ripped away from her so brutally long, long ago. Knowing he'd tried to connect with her, that he'd wanted her, that he'd always loved her blew the roof off of any lingering hesitation, and as his lips touched down on hers, her mind gave up the struggle and yielded to him completely.

She'd waited a lifetime to figure out what had happened between them. Why he'd rejected her love and withdrawn his. And to know now that he hadn't . . . to know he'd cared for her as much as she'd cared for him somehow started mending something that had broken inside of Kate a long time ago. And suddenly, all she wanted was to slide back into love with him.

Flattening her hands on his T-shirt, she smoothed them down to the hem, pushing the material back up the ridges of his smooth, warm chest as his tongue slipped into her mouth and his fingers abandoned her face to unbutton her blouse. She shrugged out of it at the same time he reached behind his head and pulled off his T-shirt.

Both panting, they stared at each other for a split second before colliding, their lips smashing and teeth clashing as Kate fell to her back on the bed and Étienne shifted to lie on top of her, kissing her with a passion and abandon, a primal hunger that flooded her body with heat and anticipation. He cradled her face with his hands as his tongue slid silkily against hers, the heat of his chest flattening her swollen breasts under his hard muscles.

His lips skated down her throat, pressing soft kisses and licks, resting on the throbbing pulse of her neck before sliding lower to the valley of her collarbone, where he sighed her name, "Kate, Kate, Kate" mixed with breathy French endearments . . . *Chaton* . . . *Mon coeur* . . . *Mon chere* . . . *Mon chou* . . . and Kate suddenly remembered he'd done that when they were teenagers. She'd been wrapped in his arms, the hammock swinging them lightly, their bodies joined together under an old blanket as sweet French words tumbled from his mouth and filled her ears. A disbelieving giggle started in her chest, rising to her lips where it escaped with a joyful sound.

Étienne leaned his head up from her chest, a lock of jet black hair falling to his forehead as he looked at her curiously, his lips glistening. "Are you laughing?"

"Mm-hmm," she hummed, pillowing her hands behind her head and smiling at him with wonder. "I'm smiling. I'm laughing. It should be impossible, but it's not. It feels like a dream, but it's not. I'm finally with you again."

"Not impossible," he said dragging his lips back and forth against the bare skin of her chest. "Not a dream."

"But still . . . unbelievable."

His lips tilted up as his eyes twinkled with happiness, and for a split second Kate saw so clearly the boy she'd fallen in love with—the hopefulness in his eyes, the devotion, the longing. As he slid up her body to look into her eyes, his rigid erection pushed insistently against the softness of her sex. A familiar warning, a promise made a lifetime ago. He cupped her face again, rocking into her gently to share his intentions, his desire.

"It's fate," he whispered. "*Stony limits cannot hold love out . . . and what love can do, that dares love attempt.*"

"*Romeo and Juliet?*" she asked, loving the feeling of his weight on her, the darkness of his eyes looking into hers, the feeling of him pressed so urgently against her.

"We're a little like them," he said, caressing her face. "Don't you think?"

"You mean our families keeping us apart?"

"Mmm," he murmured. "But we're not fifteen anymore."

"No," said Kate, raising her eyebrows and arching her pelvis into his. "We're not."

As she lifted her back, his hands took advantage, unclasping her bra efficiently, then reaching up to touch the straps and looking into her eyes as he drew them down her arms.

"I've never made love in the afternoon," said Kate, throwing her free arm over her eyes as a bit of self-consciousness made her swallow nervously.

"I'll be your first," he said. "Again."

"I'm not . . ." *fit*, she thought, averting her eyes as he pulled her bra away from her body.

"Kate, look at me. You're beautiful," he reassured her, reading her mind.

His soft, sharp inhalation of breath made her lower her arm, and she found him staring down at her breasts with reverence and longing. When he flicked his eyes up to hers, they were almost black. His tongue darted out to lick his lips and his voice was low and gravelly.

"I'm going to love you all afternoon, Kate. And when it gets dark, I'm going to love you some more. These," he said, leaning down to capture one nipple between his lips and tug lightly before releasing it, "are perfection. And you," he said, circling the other nipple with his tongue until Kate whimpered, "are the co-star of my dirtiest dreams."

For a very good girl raised in a very restrictive household, his words shot through her like a bolt of fire, and she grabbed his head, guiding him back to her breasts roughly, pushing the wet heat of his mouth against her chest until he was sucking on her again. His tongue made dizzying, electrifying strokes that made Kate's head thrash on the pillow, while his fingers gently pinched and twisted, making her breathing shallow and fast, her hips driving up at him with every long draw.

"I can't . . ." she murmured. "I can't . . ."

"Then let go, *chaton*," he said, before sucking her nipple back into the heat of his mouth, his damp fingers slipping into the waistband of her jeans. Finding the hidden nub of aroused flesh he only stroked once or twice before Kate screamed his name, her fingers flexing in his black hair, her head thrown back, her body tense then trembling as he brought her to her first climax.

"Oh, Kate," he panted, leaning up to unfasten his pants with one hand, and grinning at her, "This is going to be fun."

She laughed softly, feeling languid and hot, her body still convulsing gently with aftershocks as she heard his pants hit the floor. A moment later she felt his fingers on the button of her jeans, and she arched up so he could pull them, and her panties, down her legs. Completely naked, he rolled back on top of her, and Kate sighed as she felt the hot throb of his sex pillowed in the soft curls of hers.

"Do you want to go slow?" he asked.

"Later."

"Are you on the pill?"

"Mm-hmm," she murmured, spreading her legs, and drawing her knees up to welcome him.

"I want you so badly," he said, his voice breaking as he leaning down to nuzzle her nose, repositioning himself just slightly.

"Me too," she panted, biting his lower lip before sucking it between hers. "Please."

She felt the tip of his sex rest at the entrance of hers, his hips rocking slowly and gently against her as if still giving her a chance to say no. Reaching down between them, Kate grasped the steel length of him in her fingers then looked him in the eyes.

"Now."

He slid into her with a low groan, his eyes shuttering and his arms trembling as her fingers peeled away one by one so that he could impale her fully. When he was lodged inside of her to the hilt, he gasped like he'd been holding his breath, and then opened his eyes.

"Oh God, Kate."

Leaning down, he kissed her frantically, urgently, as their bodies recalled the rhythm from so long ago, how they fit together, the slick heat of her body sucking him forward as his throbbing thickness massaged the sensitive walls of her sex.

"I've missed you. I've dreamed of you," he said with a sigh against her neck, the heat of his breath making her tremble as her body stretched to accommodate him.

"Me too," she panted. "For too long."

He found her hands on the mattress beside them, fingers twisted into the crisp white hotel sheets, and he pulled them away, entwining his fingers with hers and gently moving both over her head where they remained joined.

Kate felt the stirring deep inside, the blessed relief, the growing swirling that told her release was imminent.

"Étienne," she whispered. "Come with me."

His eyes dark and heavy, he gazed deeply into hers and groaned the words, *Toujours, chaton,* before driving into her one last time and bellowing her name in ecstasy.

"What's *toujours*?" Kate asked him, her blonde hair falling across his chest in waves as he stroked her back gently.

"Hmm," he murmured. "It means forever."

He felt the slight tremble of her laughter against his pecs and flexed one in warning. "Quit laughing at me, woman."

She leaned up on his chest, blue eyes shining, bruised lips tilted up in a sweet smile. "You'll come with me forever?"

"Absolutely," he said without flinching. "I'd be crazy to turn down that invitation."

She grinned at him again before laying her cheek back down on his chest. "I don't remember it being like that."

"In the hammock?" It was his turn to chuckle. "I still don't know how we managed it."

"I loved that hammock," said Kate. "Even when my elbow or knee would slip through the mesh."

"Friar died two years ago," said Étienne quietly.

"No!" said Kate. "Our guardian angel."

"I went to the funeral. I think the Winslows were shocked to see me there. Which is good, I guess. It means they never found out we used their backyard as our little haven."

"He was good to us," said Kate, pressing her lips to his skin. "Without him . . ."

"We still would have found a way," Étienne said firmly, running his fingers through her hair. "It wouldn't have been easy, but after I met you on the trampoline that first night, a pack of wolves couldn't have kept me away."

"Why?"

"I don't know. I'd never met anyone like you. So innocent and confident and lovely."

She leaned up again, raising an eyebrow. "Innocent, yes. Confident, not really. Lovely?"

"Kate, we need to have a serious talk about how you see yourself."

"I have a mirror."

"Then you should know how mind-blowingly beautiful you are. Blonde hair and blue eyes." He reached for her probably still-sensitive breasts, placing his palms over the nipples, which puckered for him eagerly. "These." He pressed lightly until she fell onto her back and he leaned over her, trailing the index finger of one hand over the softness of her belly as the other kneaded her breast. "Your curves are all woman. So sexy." His finger continued its journey, his palm occasionally flattening as it dipped lower, probing the damp curls that smelled like him, and her, like recent sex. "Here. Where you're so sensitive."

She gasped softly, and when he looked up, her head was thrown back into the pillow, her lower lip caught between her teeth.

"I've never tasted you, Kate," he said softly, parting her lips with his fingers. "Another first for us."

She whimpered as he dropped his head, the tip of his tongue touching down on her rigid pink clit as her pelvis bucked lightly into his face. He chuckled softly, and she murmured, "More" as his tongue made a lazy rotation around her swollen flesh.

"More, *chaton*?" he teased her, knowing that the breath from his mouth would caress her skin and make her tremble.

"Yes," she moaned, fingers fisting into the sheets again.

Covering her mound with his mouth, he sucked strongly, his tongue laving over her slick, hot flesh, then flicking playfully as Kate's cries of pleasure grew stronger and louder until her whole body tensed, then exploded in tremors.

Étienne sat back on his knees, wrapped his arms around her waist, and jerked her onto his lap, fitting them together as her forehead landed on his shoulder and limp arms hugged him. He pushed up into her hot, trembling sex, panting into her neck as her still-quivering muscles sucked him into her body. He thrust upward and Kate moaned, her teeth biting lightly into the skin of his shoulder.

"Is this okay, love?" he asked her through panted breaths.

"This *is* love," she answered in a broken sigh, repeating the words she'd said to him the night they'd lost their virginity to each other.

"*You* are love," he responded, thrusting up into the heaven of her body one last time before stars burst behind his eyes, and his body emptied itself into hers.

Eating beignets in bed is messy, thought Kate, licking some powdered sugar from Étienne's abs, which were serving as a makeshift table.

"I love these," he said, grinning at her as he took another bite, which covered his lips in white.

Kate couldn't resist. She leaned forward, running her tongue over his lips as he stopped chewing.

"Me too," she answered with a flirty wink before grabbing another and popping it into her mouth. "Did you like going to school here?"

He shrugged, swallowing his mouthful of doughnut. "I guess. Amy was still up in Philly, so it was a long break for us . . . which was probably good. I sort of got used to the South while I was in Mississippi."

Kate flinched and he reached forward to place a gentle hand on her bare thigh. "Don't do that. Don't feel bad when I talk about it. You had nothing to do with why I ended up there."

"I'm angry that it happened. I'm so angry with Alex," she said sadly.

"It was a long time ago, and honestly, Kate? He really believed he was defending your honor. He did. I could tell. My nose could tell."

Kate thought about her cousins whose lives were so intricately entwined with hers. "How can this work? How can you date Alex English's cousin?"

"Are you nuts? How could I not? I'm in love with her."

Kate's eyes filled with tears at the sweetness of his simple admission, but the words—while delivered with a firm certainty—still didn't feel real.

"How is that possible?" she asked him.

He shrugged, reaching for another beignet. "Because I never stopped. I keep telling you that, counselor. At some point, you're just going to have to believe my testimony."

"Will you give me a little time?"

"Will you be my girlfriend while you're thinking it over?"

"Thinking what over?"

"Letting me come with you forever."

She was so surprised, she chortled, and a puff of powdered sugar showered them with white. Étienne dusted himself off, grinning at her. "Was that a yes?"

"You *really* want to be exclusive."

He nodded, all trace of teasing gone. "Don't you think we deserve that? More of this? More time? I don't want any distractions . . . on either side. I just want to be together and see what happens."

Kate took a deep breath then nodded at him. "Okay. But I get to tell my cousins."

Étienne's eyes narrowed and his mouth thinned to an annoyed line. "We'll discuss that later."

Sensing the discussion was going to be less playful than beignets and boyfriends, she relented. "Fine. Later."

"Hey, I've been wondering . . . why do you have so many cats?"

Kate grinned, popping another beignet in her mouth. "After Shelby died, I felt really lonely for another one, but when I went to the local shelter, there were about a hundred that needed foster homes. HIV kittens. Babies with injured eyes or legs. I couldn't go home with just one."

"So you went home with two."

She cringed. "Three. Annie, Oliver, and Cinderella."

"Literary orphans," he chuckled.

"Mm-hmm," she said. "They're all special needs, but I love them."

"Who's with them now?"

"Oh, I have someone come and tend to them. You know?" She bit her bottom lip wondering if he'd laugh at her dream of sponsoring a special needs feline shelter in Philadelphia.

"There isn't a shelter just for special needs animals in Philly. I was thinking . . ."

"About starting one? I bet my sister, Mad, would give you a hand. She's a softie too."

"I always liked Mad," said Kate, loving it that he'd jumped on board without ridiculing her or second-guessing her plans. "Are you close to them? J.C., Mad, and Jax?"

"Oh, yeah," said Étienne. "We have dinner together every other Friday night."

"That's right," said Kate.

"Uh . . . that's right? How do you know about my family dinners?"

Kate's cheeks flushed red and hot. She knew because Jax often mentioned them on Facebook. "Jax, um, Jax is my Facebook friend."

"Stalking me through my sister, huh?" he joked.

He has no idea how right he is.

She pinched his bare thigh. "As if! I can be friends with your sister without trolling for info about you!"

He grabbed her hand, shifting it from his thigh to his penis, which sprang to life, growing and thickening the moment Kate's fingers touched the hot flesh. She wrapped her fingers around him, caressing lightly as his eyes seared into hers.

"What do you want, Kate?" he asked her in a low voice.

"I want . . ."

"You want me."

"Yes. I want you."

"Good," he said, gasping as her fingers increased their pressure and speed. "Because I belong to you."

Kate leaned forward and dipped her head to take him in her mouth, laying claim to what was hers.

Chapter 11

"The sun's setting," said Kate, walking back into the room after a hot shower. Étienne had started with her, then left while she washed her hair, taking her key card and heading to his room to get dressed quickly before returning a few minutes later.

"How about dinner in the French Quarter?" he asked, looking casual and delicious in jeans and a black T-shirt.

"I'd love it," she said, pulling a brush through her wet hair before twisting it up into a chignon.

"Wear it down," he said softly, staring at her from where he sat on the love seat.

She smiled at him, pulling out two pins and letting the damp waves cover her shoulders. "I'm not used to wearing it down."

"The first time I ever saw you, all I wanted to do was run my hands through your hair."

"I know," she said, opening her suitcase to find some fresh panties and pulling them on under her bathrobe. "You were always reaching out to touch my hair. Even before we kissed."

"I still have that painting, you know."

This surprised her and she stopped what she was doing, turning to face him. "You do?"

"Every so often, when I wanted to torture myself, I'd pull it out and look at it."

"I'm surprised you didn't burn it," she said, overcome by the steadfastness of his heart during all of their years apart.

"How could I do that? I'd promised it to you. On the back of it, it says 'Property of Kate English.' Just in case anything ever happened to me, I wanted it to find its way back to you."

"Why?" she asked.

"To remind you of that week. So you'd know that you were loved, no matter what came after."

Kate crossed the room, straddling his lap and putting her arms around his neck. Her bathrobe loosened a little and he dropped his forehead to her bare chest, resting there. He didn't reach for her breasts, or try to pull off her panties. Wrapping his arms around her, he breathed deeply, the soft cotton of his shirt pushing against her chest as they held each other tightly.

"Can you fall in love with someone when you're fifteen and pick up where you left off twelve years later?" she whispered.

"I hope so," he said softly, his lips moving against her skin. "Let's find out."

Taking his cheeks between her palms, Kate lifted his head and pressed her lips to his—a sweet kiss, undemanding and loving. And he responded gently, his tongue making a leisurely sweep of her mouth before sliding tenderly against hers. His arms tightened around her, his fingers kneading her back through the thick terrycloth of her robe.

"Yeah. Let's find out," she agreed, kissing his lips one last time before climbing off his lap.

Picking up the bra she'd left on the bed, she let the bathrobe drop from her shoulders, appreciating the way his mouth followed suit as she shrugged into the black lace, covering her breasts and clasping it quickly in the back with a teasing grin.

"How about dinner in?" he asked, frowning as she pulled on her jeans.

"Nope. You're showing me Naw'lins."

"You're a tease," he said. "And your accent is terrible."

"I'm not the one who went to school here," she countered. She glanced at him sheepishly. "Speaking of school, I'm sorry I didn't say hello to you . . . at Harvard."

He pulled his bottom lip into his mouth. "Yeah, that stung. It was like further proof that you'd never been as into me as I was into you."

"All I could think was that you'd try to say hello and maybe offer some polite small talk after all we'd shared. I couldn't bear it."

"Honestly, I was so surprised to see you I have no idea what I would have said if you'd turned around."

"We're all about missed opportunities." She sighed.

"We *were*," he corrected. "You're not slipping through my fingers this time."

Kate grinned at him as she pulled on her blouse then grimaced when she realized he'd pulled off two of the buttons in his haste to get her naked earlier. She faced him, frowning. "Really?"

"Sorry. I wanted you bad, Kate English."

She shook her head, rifling through her suitcase, but coming up dry, except for her work-out clothes, which included a clingy, hot pink and black lycra shirt. "Then this'll have to do."

Étienne raised his eyebrows, giving her a leering grin as it stretched over her full breasts. "No complaints here."

An hour later, they sat at an outdoor table drinking hurricanes, serenaded by the jazz band in the adjoining bistro. It hadn't taken long for Kate to observe that every woman they passed, and every woman in the café where they sat, noticed Étienne. Their eyes flagrantly undressed him as their cheeks flushed with pleasure, but Étienne only seemed to notice

Kate, which somehow felt like a miracle to her, since she'd never been the type of woman to attract a lot of attention.

"Tell me something," said Kate, tilting her head to the side as she grinned at him. "Do you ever get sick of your adoring fans?"

He cringed, shaking his head at her. "It's nonsense. They have no idea who I am."

Kate nodded, remembering that he'd always felt just slightly out of step with his peers after being transplanted so abruptly to America. "So, who are you now? Who is Étienne Xavier Rousseau now?"

"Xavier," he repeated in a thick French accent. "Was I drunk when I told you that, Kathryn Grey English?"

"We never got drunk together," she said, taking a hefty sip of hurricane. "And quit evading my line of questioning, counselor."

He sighed. "Who am I? I'm a lawyer at my family's firm. I paint when I'm stressed. I like fast cars. I don't mind cats. Recently single." He glanced at her and winked. "Even more recently . . . taken. And you?"

"Same, except for the fast cars and painting."

"What do you do when you're stressed?"

"Adopt cats, see friends, read . . . troll Facebook for news about ex-boyfriends."

He pounded the table lightly with his fist. "I *knew* it!"

She chuckled. "Guilty as charged. When I heard about your accident, I . . . well, I couldn't stop thinking about you. It's not like I could call you or visit . . . but I couldn't stand not knowing if you were okay. I friended Jax and thank God she posts on Facebook about twenty times a day. I followed your whole recovery."

He reached for her hand across the table. "I tried to force myself not to think of you whenever you popped into my mind."

She squeezed his hand before releasing it and relaxing back in her chair. "It's so nice here. Let's stay forever. Let's not go home."

"We can't run away."

"Why not? We're grown-ups. We're lawyers. Let's move here and open our own firm."

"Kate," he said gently, "as tempting as that sounds, we have to go home."

"I'm furious at them," she said softly, her chin dropping to her chest as her cheeks blazed with heat. "I still can't believe the part they all played . . . my father, Alex, Stratton . . . even Weston, Fitz, and Barrett must have known about everything. My uncle would have called my father to tell him about the fight, so he knew too. They *all* knew. They all manipulated me, ruined our chance to be together, conspired to drive us apart. I-I don't know how to look at them, let alone what to say. They took away what I loved more than anything else in the world."

"They thought they were protecting you," he said, reaching for her hand again and not letting her pull away.

"How can you say that? How can you defend them when they did this to you, too?"

"I'm no fan of the English brothers, Kate. But I love you. As much as I hate what they did, I respect that they did it out of love for you."

"So you're just going to forgive them? All of them? Even your mother?"

His eyes hardened. "I don't know what I'm going to do about my mother yet, but yes, eventually I'll forgive her, too."

Kate's eyes swam with tears as she looked back at him across the table. "That's too easy. What happened between us broke my heart. It shattered my confidence. It made me believe that I wasn't worthy of love, that I wasn't desirable. Did I go to a good school and become a lawyer? Sure. But a part of my life was crippled by their interference, and I can't just blithely forgive them because they had good intentions. Not for me. And not for you." She bit her lip as a tear made its way down her cheek. "I love them so much, but this will change things between me and them, and I hate that so much, too."

"It will change things, yes, but maybe for the better," Étienne suggested. "Maybe they still see you as their little cousin Kate, and it's time for that to change. Maybe some good could come from this, *chaton*. Not just a second chance for us, but a better relationship with them, too."

She thought about this . . . about the way they'd tried to protect her from this deal, from Étienne, from anything that might disturb delicate Princess Kate in her ivory tower. If she was going to remain in Philly, she didn't want to live her life under that sort of protection. She needed for them to see her as an equal and as a strong adult woman who didn't need to be shielded or protected or coddled, and if they couldn't make that change, she'd need to find a new job.

"You're right," she said, taking back her hand as their waitress arrived with two steaming bowls of crawfish. "Things are *definitely* going to change."

Morning light streamed into Kate's room and Étienne's eyes opened slowly. He was holding Kate against him—her back to his chest—but she was still sleeping deeply, her breathing even.

It's a strange thing to suddenly have what you always wanted, what you always dreamed of. While Étienne's life had been privileged in some ways—wealthy parents, beautiful mansion, creature comforts—it had been hard too. Military school for over two years had taught him a harsh lesson in control and deprivation, but in a strange way, it had also been welcome punishment after hurting and losing Kate. In a way, he'd embraced it as the consequence of his stupidity in trusting the wrong people with important information. It made him grow up faster to be away from his parents and siblings. It taught him respect, discipline, and teamwork, and made him more independent and self-assured than he'd been as a young boy and teenager in Haverford. Ultimately, military school had made him a man.

As an extension of the Rousseaus' parenting philosophy, being a cadet had also reinforced the concept of punishment and reward, and somewhere in Étienne's mind his betrayal of Kate—by talking about her with Dash and Kurt—constituted a punishable offence. And though heartbreaking, it made sense that he would lose her, because he hadn't treated their love with the honor it deserved. He hadn't flaunted it or disrespected it, but what he'd learned in the long years apart from Kate, was that he'd had no business to talk about her at all. Ever. What he'd shared with her was too sacred for beer-bathed confessions around a swimming pool with neighbors. He'd lost Kate because it was his punishment. And he deserved it.

So why, he wondered, was she his reward now?

His life hadn't been so exemplary that he deserved another chance with her.

All he could think was that there must still be a debt to pay in order to be worthy of Kate, and he'd gladly pay it, for the rest of his life, just to wake up holding her every morning. She stirred in her sleep, pushing back against him, and he tightened his arms around her softness, burying his nose in her hair and breathing deeply.

They'd made love twice more last night after returning to her hotel room, but there was sadness behind Kate's eyes after their conversation about her cousins. She was angry with them, hurt and betrayed, and suddenly it occurred to Étienne that there *was* something he could do for her— something important he could do to deserve her: he could make his peace with her cousins so that his quarrel with them was neutralized.

He'd meant it when he said that he respected Alex for defending Kate's honor. At the time, as a raging, furious fifteen-year-old, he hadn't understood, of course, but during his tenure at military school, he had come to value that respect and honor were of paramount importance. Alex acted hastily, yes, but Étienne truly believed he was acting in Kate's interest, defending and honoring her in a way that Étienne had not.

Surely it would be easier for him and Kate to have a solid beginning if there wasn't infighting and old grudges between him and her family, right? He wasn't some fifteen-year-old who needed to sneak around with her anymore either. He would confront the English brothers head on, without his usual sardonic smirks, and once *his* fight was over, he could support her in her own.

But before meeting with Kate's cousins, he had one other very important piece of business to take care of in Philadelphia that didn't include the English family, and for that he would need to go back early so it could be settled today.

Carefully moving his arm out from under her, he pulled away from the warmth of her body, kissing her shoulder as he slipped out of bed. Writing a quick note which he left on the bedside table, he dressed quickly and left her room without a sound.

He had won Kate, yes.

Now it was time to deserve her.

Kate had to admit . . . Étienne's note bothered her. Waking up without him, she'd assumed he was in the bathroom or had run back to his room to shower. The note, which she finally found on the bedside table read:

Dear Kate,

Jax texted me to say she changed my flight and I didn't want to wake you, love. I will see you back in Philly this afternoon. You are my dream come true, chaton.

Your,
Étienne

It was sweet and loving, and yet Kate didn't like being left behind. She wished she'd had a chance to kiss him good-bye, to touch his face and look into his eyes and reassure herself that this time wasn't like last time.

It was almost absurd to contemplate after the past twenty-four hours, but what if she arrived in Philadelphia and he was cool or awkward? What if he regretted the rashness of his passionate words and decided that his freedom—especially after his painful relationship with Amy—was more important that any revived connection between them? She read the note over and over again, trying to calm herself, but she was anxious as she packed her bag, the room littered with evidence of their affair—beignet sugar, the wine bottle and glasses, the musky smell of their bodies colliding—only made her more worried somehow. They'd loved one another last night, just as before, but when real life greeted them back at home, would they be able to finally segue into a normal relationship?

Kate wanted so badly to believe she and Étienne were finally receiving the second chance they so desperately deserved, yet the fact of their first separation, and the emotional landmines it left behind, made her suspicious. He claimed to still love her, which she wanted to believe with every fiber of her being, but didn't entirely.

That fact that she still loved him—and always would—had been such a carefully guarded secret, protected in the deepest recesses of her heart. It was difficult for her to give words to the feeling, even now when he was, theoretically at least, standing before her and asking to give them a second chance.

How to break down the final walls of fear? *By loving him quietly*, her heart reasoned, *until you trust completely that he's yours and that he'll never hurt you again.*

And by calling Lib, she thought, *to talk some common sense into you.*

Knowing she had fifteen minutes before calling a cab to take her to the airport, she sat down on the bed where she and Étienne had renewed their love affair and dialed her best friend.

"KK?"

"Lib." She sighed.

"Oh, wow," said Libitz. "Let me get Duane to take over here and go into my office for a few minutes."

Kate smiled. It was creepy and a half how Lib could tell Kate's moods from a sigh.

A moment later she came back on the line. "So! You opted for restarting the conversation with Étienne Rousseau."

"You could say that," Kate said weakly.

"Or I could also say you've been boning him all night in New Orleans."

"Lib!"

"I'm not wrong, am I?"

Kate rubbed her forehead. "You're not wrong."

"Yay!" yelled Lib. "Kate got laid!"

"Seriously?"

"Well, kitten," she said slyly, in a reference to Étienne's nickname for Kate. "How long had it been?"

Kate cringed. "Over a year."

"I rest my case." Lib paused, and her voice was gentle and wistful when she asked, "How was it?"

"Fantastic."

"Good, good. And reassurances?"

"Oh, I don't know. He said he wanted to be exclusive and date for a while, see what happens."

"Well, that sounds promising. Not like a one-night stand, and believe me, I have a wide breadth of knowledge when it comes to one-night stands."

Kate chuckled and shook her head. "You ever want more than that, Lib?"

"Yeah," she said softly. "Someday. When I meet a guy who isn't a total jackass and still wants me to stick around. How about you? You want Étienne to stick around?"

"He says he still loves me."

"Whoa," said Lib. "Well, that's . . . that's serious."

"Yeah."

"Forgive me, but I would think you'd be screaming it from the hilltops, Kate. You've been stuck on this guy since forever."

"I want to believe it, but two weeks ago? He was a memory. A *bad* memory, Lib. Now he's back in my life, and I slept with him, and he wants us to date . . ."

"And the problem is?"

"I don't know if I trust him."

"From the moment I picked up the phone, I knew you'd hashed things out with him. I don't need to know what exactly happened between you two, but I am assuming that he wasn't the blackhearted asshole we always thought he was."

"Not at all. We were both . . . betrayed."

"Sounds heavy."

"It's a mess. Alex and Stratton. My father. His mother. Neither of us realized it at the time, but everyone who loved us was trying to keep us apart."

"That sucks. But you know what's interesting?" asked Lib. "You found each other anyway."

"We did, didn't we?"

"Not everyone gets a second chance. Don't blow it, huh?"

Kate sighed. "I won't. I'll try to . . . trust in it, have faith, not be scared . . . all that good stuff. My cousins are going to have conniptions when they find out."

"So? Let them have conniptions. They're not the ones boning the hot Frenchman. And as far as I can tell, it's really none of their business whose tongue is welcome in your mouth. You want Étienne in your life?"

"I do."

"Well then, Sheriff Kate, it sounds like you're going to need to kick a little English ass."

Touching down in Philadelphia a little before eleven o'clock in the morning, Étienne turned on his phone and noticing that the battery was almost dead, he didn't waste a moment in sending a quick message to Barrett English:

Back in Philly. Need to speak with you and your brothers, including Alex, ASAP. Please arrange. Will come to you at 3pm.

Satisfied with the message and not giving a rat's ass if Barrett was annoyed by the commanding nature of the request, he sent it then dialed the number of Chateau Nouvelle. For most of the trip, Étienne had had a chance to review his mother's decision to keep Kate's letters from him, and his anger had gone from a boil to a simmer. If he wanted answers, the best way to deal with his mother was directly and in person.

"*Bonjour?*"

"*Mére? C'est Étienne.*"

"*Mon fils! Quelle belle surprise!*"

"*Bon Jour. Je ai besoin de parler avec vous.*" I need to speak with you.

"*Aujourd'hui?*" Today?

"*Oui. Maintenant.* Right now. I'll come to you."

"Is everything all right? What is this about, Étienne?"

"I'll see you in an hour, mother."

Chapter 12

The cab stopped in front of Chateau Nouvelle and Étienne got out of the car haltingly, leaning on his cane more than usual. Between nonstop sex with Kate, a short walk in the French Quarter last night, and navigating two airports this morning, his leg was throbbing in protest.

"Étienne!" exclaimed his mother, opening the double doors of the large Mediterranean-style mansion and welcoming him home with a kiss on each cheek before dropping her eyes to his leg. "My poor darling."

Lilliane Rousseau had been a celebrated ballerina before marrying Étienne's father almost thirty-five years ago, and her body still maintained the spare, elegant lines of a dancer. Dressed in a smart Chanel suit and smelling of Number Nine, it was also a good bet that she was headed out for lunch.

"*Bon Jour, mére*," he said softly, allowing her to hold his cheeks without protest. Whatever she had lacked in parenting she'd made up for with a cheerful theatrical twinkle that all of her children adored, and when she turned on the charisma, it was almost impossible to be angry with her.

Finally dropping her hands, she stepped back from her son, closing the door then turning to face him.

"I am so sorry, darling, but I have a luncheon at the club in . . ." She twisted her wrist and glanced at her diamond-and-platinum Tiffany watch, ". . . twenty minutes. Can we visit quickly?"

Par for the course. His parents had never really wanted to be "troubled" by their children. They loved Étienne and his siblings in their own way . . . as long as their children didn't disrupt their lives too much.

"Of course," said Étienne, following her into a small parlor to the right of a massive staircase. He sat down in his father's favorite leather chair that smelled of cigar smoke and Dior *Eau Sauvage*.

Lilliane sat across from him, balanced on the edge of a needlepoint wingback chair like a bird, her perfectly made-up face inquisitive, with a polite, polished smile tilting up her pink lips.

"Mother," he started, clearing his throat, "when I was fifteen, right around the time you sent me away to school, I may have received some letters."

His mother blinked at him, her smile fading just a touch as she smoothed her skirt with expertly manicured fingers. "I don't know what—"

"I know that you received them. I know why you kept them from me. Because they were from Kate English."

When his mother lifted her eyes, they were stony and narrow. "That family had already taken enough from ours."

"Kate wasn't trying to take anything. I'd already given her my heart."

His mother's lips parted in surprise as she stared at him, clearly moved by his quiet declaration. "But her last name—"

"Was English," said Étienne. "Like her cousin, with whom I fought."

Lilliane nodded, like she was seeing pieces of a long-forgotten puzzle come together. "You fought over *her*."

"In a manner of speaking."

His mother sighed, sitting back in the chair and shrugging, but her face looked conflicted with guilt. "I thought I was doing what was best for you. We'd given you a fresh start. Hearing from that English girl could have interfered."

"Like I said," he told her, her voice tight with control, "I understand why you did it."

"Then why are you here?" she demanded, waving a hand in the air with irritation. "To tell me what a bad mother I was?"

Étienne shook his head. "No. To ask if you still have them."

"All these years . . . and you think I kept them?"

"I don't know. But if you still have them, they're mine, and I want them back."

Lilliane took a deep breath and stood up, walking across the room to a small desk in the corner where she sometimes handled her correspondence. Turning a key in the lower drawer of the desk, Étienne listened to squeaking sound of it opening. When his mother turned around, she had a crisp, new-looking manila envelope in her hand.

"I don't know why I kept them," she said, crossing the room and offering the gold envelope to her son. Étienne's breath, which he'd been holding, released in a rush as he reached for the envelope, unfastening the clip on the outside to find thirty unopened letters neatly filed inside.

When he looked up at her, his mother's eyes were glistening.

"She meant a lot to you?"

"*Means* a lot to me," said Étienne, refastening the envelope and standing up. "I love her."

With his cane in one hand and the envelope in the other, he turned toward the entrance of the room, walking back to the front door. His mother took his elbow, walking slowly beside him.

"I know I wasn't the best mother," said Lilliane. "But when your father collected you and drove you back from New York that night, I recognized the wild look in your eyes. The misery. I knew that whomever you had gone to see meant a great deal to your heart. I hoped that you would forget her, since she was part of *that* family, but I couldn't bring myself to throw away her letters."

Étienne swallowed past the lump in his throat and turned to face her as they reached the front door. "Thank you for keeping them. *Merci, mére.*"

In an instant, Lilliane brightened, fixing on her face the same polished, polite smile that she'd perfected over the course of her life. "Of course, darling. Anything for you." Pressing her cheeks to his, she chuckled lightly in the doting way of a good mother. "*Au revoir*, darling."

"Good-bye, mother," said Étienne, stepping out into the sunshine as the door closed behind him.

As Kate waited in the boarding area at the New Orleans airport, she still felt troubled about Étienne's abrupt departure, and it didn't help that the two texts she'd sent to him had gone unanswered. They were only a sentence each—one about missing him when she woke up and the other asking if he wanted to have dinner when she got back to Philly that evening—and as each moment ticked by without a response, she felt more anxious and more like a fool.

He seemed so sincere, but his words from so long ago rang clear in her head. "*I don't have girlfriends. I have flings.*" And even though they'd been said by a cocky fifteen-year-old trying to impress her, she couldn't keep herself from wondering if she had been a fling too. Her stomach flipped over and her heart clenched at the notion, but once the idea had taken root, she couldn't help the way it spiraled, the way it taunted her and made her second-guess her decision to allow Étienne back into her life.

By the time the business class cabin was welcomed to board, she was a wreck, and that was precisely the moment her phone rang.

"Hello?"

"*Chaton.*"

"Étienne." She sighed with relief. "Why'd you leave?"

"There were some things I needed to do on my own."

"Like what?"

"Do you trust me?"

"I-I want to," she said, trying to shove aside her misgivings.

"Meet me at English & Company at three o'clock."

"At English & Com—"

"I've asked for your cousins to meet us. We're going to talk to them together."

The gate agent made another announcement about Kate's flight and she took her place on line for boarding.

"It's *my* fight," she insisted. "Not yours. They're not going to take me seriously if we show up together."

"You're wrong. It's not your fight. It's *our* fight. And they will take you seriously. I'll make sure of it."

Kate bristled.

He didn't understand. She was sick of everyone protecting her. First her parents, then her cousins, now Étienne? As much as she loved them all, she wanted to stand on her own two feet, and Étienne was undermining that goal.

"I'm an adult and they're *my* cousins."

"And they had me expelled from school and cut out of your life."

"You don't get it . . ." she said, handing the gate agent her ticket and lowering her voice as she walked down the jet way. "I need to do this alone."

"No, Kate," he said gently. "You need to be *heard*. You don't need to do it alone. Because you're *not* alone."

"Yes, I am—"

"No," he said firmly. "You've been alone for a long time, and gotten used to it. The odd cousin out. The only girl, who needed to be protected. Well, I'm not trying to protect you, *chaton*. I *want* you to say your piece. But I'm going to be standing right beside you when you do because there are a few things I need to make clear, too."

Taking her seat, she nodded at the flight attendant who indicated that Kate needed to put her phone away. "I have to go."

"Think about what I said, Kate. If we want this to work—you and me together—we need to *be* together in their eyes, from the very beginning."

"I'll see you later," she said softly, feeling deeply conflicted.

"Trust me," he answered, before hanging up.

Kate turned off her phone and tucked it into her bag, accepting a bottle of water from the flight attendant and looking out the window with a pounding head.

Trust Étienne Rousseau. Therein lay the problem. Despite her love for him, for many long years Kate had convinced herself that Étienne was the last person on earth whom she could ever trust. Étienne stood for pain and longing, for rejection and heartbreak. And now, in the course of a few days, she had discovered his constancy, his blamelessness, and his love for her. It was hard for Kate to rewire twelve years of instincts where Étienne was concerned, but as the plane left the runway, she heard his words in her head again.

You need to be heard. *You don't need to do it alone. Because you're* not *alone.*

Then she leaned her head against the window and closed her eyes, willing her mind and heart to accept the truth of his love and find the courage to return it without fear.

As soon as Kate walked into the lobby of the building where English & Company was headquartered, Étienne read the apprehension on her face. Selfishly, part of him didn't care because he was just so damn glad to see her, which must have registered on *his* face, because hers answered the feeling almost immediately, breaking into a lovely, relieved smile, and walking straight into his arms.

"It's ridiculous that I missed you so much." She sighed, her breath warm on the skin of his neck.

"I know exactly how you feel," he murmured into her ear, aware that their passionate embrace was attracting attention and not caring. "Where are we staying tonight? Your place or mine?"

She chuckled lightly. "Mine, I guess. I have to get home to the trio."

"After this I'll run home for a few things then come straight to you. Deal?"

"Deal."

"You ready for this?" He leaned back from her, searching her eyes and finding them worried, but determined.

Kate's mouth narrowed into a grim line. "Yes. I didn't like it at first . . . you coming with me. Something about it felt weak, but I thought about what you said. I'm not alone. I want you in my life, as you should have been all along. I want them to have to acknowledge that we're a package deal, whether they like it or not."

He smiled, lacing his fingers through hers and using his cane to help guide them to the elevator.

"My guess is not," he said as she pressed the *Up* button.

"Too bad," she said curtly.

He looked to the side, at the stony profile of her beautiful face. Kate was going into this meeting with guns loaded.

"*Chaton*," he said gently as they stepped onto the elevator. "Remember that they love you."

Her shoulders relaxed a little and she squeezed his hand, nodding, but she didn't turn to look at him, the muscles of her face still tense.

Well, he thought, looking straight ahead as the elevator conveyed them higher and higher, she had a right to her anger. They'd been cheated from years they could have spent knowing and loving each other as he detoured through the shitshow that was Amy and Kate endured sharp moments of loneliness and self-deprecation. They deserved some answers. But mostly, they deserved peace.

Without dropping Étienne's hand, but accommodating his awkward stride by slowing her own, Kate opened the doors to English & Company, nodding at the receptionist before turning down the hallway toward the conference room.

As they walked by the floor-to-ceiling windows, Kate caught sight of her uncle, Barrett, Fitz, Stratton, and Weston all seated at the conference table, and as she entered the room, her eyes lifted to find Alex's face on the TV screen. She stood just inside the door of the room, clasping Étienne's hand, and looked each one of them in the eye, starting with her uncle and ending with Alex.

Their reactions were varying degrees of displeasure and disapproval as their eyes flicked to her fingers entwined with Étienne's, but her anger—her fury—made it easy to stare them down. She would not be cowered. She would not be rebuked.

"Thanks for assembling everyone," said Étienne in a clear, firm voice from beside her, and it occurred to Kate that he addressed Barrett, who nodded once, tersely.

"Didn't leave me much choice. I assume the business was—"

"This isn't about business," said Étienne, shooting a quick look at Alex, whose eyes, Kate noticed, were narrow and angry. "This is about me . . . and Kate."

Stratton huffed angrily, looking at Kate with an expression of such disappointment, it hurt her heart to see it.

"I told you who he was . . . what he said about you . . . and you got together with him? That's great, Kate. Great choice."

"Strat," she said, pulling out a chair with her free hand and sitting down as Étienne maneuvered to sit in the chair beside her. "You have an old grudge against Étienne. But that ends today."

"I have *many* grudges against Étienne," said Stratton in a cold voice, "and I highly doubt anything that happens here today is going to change that."

Kate looked at the TV screen where Alex looked as pissed off as Stratton.

"And you?"

"What *about* me?" he challenged. "What about *you* carrying on with this asshole?"

Étienne tensed beside her, but Kate squeezed his hand, asking him to let her handle it. "You want to jump into it? Fine with us. You beat Étienne to a pulp and got him expelled."

Alex lurched forward. "Because of what he said about you, Kate! Jesus! I was just defending you!"

"You *heard* him say these things?" asked Kate in a level voice.

"Yeah. I mean, I-I know he said them."

"Because you *heard* him," Kate said again.

"Yeah."

"Where?" she asked.

"Um, at mass . . . that morning."

Kate shook her head. "He wasn't at mass that morning. He was hungover. He was in the infirmary getting aspirin."

Alex's eyebrows furrowed together as he stared back at Kate and dug in his heels, "I heard it."

"Where? Not from Étienne," she said.

"You heard Ten say those things about Kate, right Alex?" asked Stratton, straightening his glasses.

"*Everyone* was saying it," bellowed Alex. "And he'd just pulled that shit with Stratton and Jillian O'Connor a few weeks before. He was fucking with our family, Kate."

Stratton's eyes shot to Kate and Étienne and then back to his older brother. "Alex, wait a second, you never heard Étienne say those things about Kate?"

"He didn't hear anything," said Étienne in a low, level voice, "because they were never said by me. They were things I never would have dreamed of saying about Kate."

Stratton stared at Étienne, sizing him up from across the table. "But everyone said—"

Étienne turned away from Stratton dismissively and looked at Alex. "It was Kurt Martinson."

Alex's face registered instant recognition and surprise as he stared back at Étienne, crossing his arms over his chest.

Étienne continued, a sour look on his face as he stared back at Alex. "I told Kurt and Dash Ambler that Kate and I had been together, and Kurt wanted to embarrass you, Alex, so he told the whole school, in lewd terms, what had happened between me and Kate. And you took the bait."

Alex stared back at Étienne, seething. "That's not how I remember it."

"Interesting, Alex," mused Kate. "Because you actually don't seem to be remembering it at all."

"I was protecting you, Kate."

"I believe that you love me, Alex. But, you acted rashly because you had an old score to settle with Étienne. An old score that actually started with Barrett," she added, turning her eyes to her eldest cousin.

"Me? What the hell? I wasn't even living at Haverford when all of this went down!"

"No," said Étienne, "but you were living there when my brother was dating Bree Ambler, weren't you?"

Barrett shifted uncomfortably in his seat. "Bree said they'd broken up."

"Yeah," said Étienne acidly. "She just hadn't told J.C. yet."

"So, Barrett stole Bree from J.C., and Étienne stole Jillian from Stratton. Are we all up to speed?" asked Kate, looking around the table. She shifted her glance back to the TV screen where a belligerent Alex looked like he'd rather be anywhere than at this particular family meeting. "Then *your* ex-girlfriend's brother spread a nasty rumor about me to get back at you, but instead of checking your sources, you went after Étienne. And you got him expelled."

Alex clenched his jaw and swallowed, then looked down.

Kate turned to Stratton, who looked about as uncomfortable as Alex. "And all those times I cried to you during college . . . you never told me that Alex had beaten him up and gotten him sent away. You let me believe he didn't love me."

"Because I didn't think he did," said Stratton softly.

Kate nodded.

"I do," said Étienne in a cool, clear voice. "I love Kate. I've loved Kate since the day I met her."

"Well," said Stratton in a terse voice, his eyes narrowing, "that explains why Amy always felt like you were cheating on her."

"Oh you know what, Stratton?" exploded Étienne, banging his free hand on the table. "Fuck you! Did you sleep with her? With Amy?"

"Unlike you," said Stratton, "I have morals."

"Some moral high ground," sneered Étienne. "Amy was pretty clear that every time she wasn't in my bed, she was in yours."

"She was." Stratton cleared his throat. "Or on my couch. But I didn't *sleep* with her. She was always talking about *you*."

"And you don't think we were played?" asked Étienne, his eyes shooting daggers across the table.

"Étienne," whispered Kate, her eyes begging him to calm down. His nostrils flared and he flexed his jaw, looking down at the table.

"Strat," said Kate gently. "I know you cared for her. But Amy wasn't exactly who you thought she was."

"I know she was jerked around by *him*!"

Étienne huffed quietly beside her, and Kate turned to look at his bent head before rounding on Stratton. She'd had just about enough of the accusations hurled at Étienne.

"No, she wasn't. No more than she jerked him around! And you! Did you know she's not engaged anymore?" Stratton's surprised expression confirmed he didn't. "Did you know she called Étienne last night and asked for him to come back to her? Strat, you have one of the purest hearts I know, but she manipulated you just like she did Étienne. You're smart. If you look back on everything, you'll start putting it together, but I swear to you, Étienne wasn't the monster that she claimed him to be."

Stratton looked away disgustedly, crossing his arms over his chest.

Kate looked around at her uncle and cousins before glancing back at Étienne, who'd raised his head. Sensing that she was about to deliver her closing arguments, he gave her a small smile and nodded slightly, loosening his fingers from hers as if to say, *I'm right here if you need me, but you should do this part on your own.*

Kate flattened her hands on the table, taking a deep breath before she looked up.

"I love all of you," she said, capturing the eyes of each of her family members in turn. "But I love Étienne too."

She heard his soft, sharp gasp from beside her, and it made her lips tilt up in a smile as she glanced over at him and nodded. He reached for her hand again, weaving his fingers through hers, before urging her to continue with his eyes.

"I love him, and your actions"—she glanced meaningfully at Barrett, Stratton, and Alex before leveling her gaze at her Uncle Tom—"and those of my father, kept us apart for many years. Let me be very clear: I don't require your protection. I don't require your approval. I don't require your permission. And all of you are going to need to get used to seeing Étienne's face, because he's welcome wherever I am. I love him and I choose him."

Her uncle and cousins each nodded at her solemnly after this short speech, until she got to Alex, who looked at Étienne.

"If I was wrong," he offered belligerently, "I'm sorry."

"I understand," said Étienne. "You thought I disrespected Kate."

"I would have bet my life on it."

"You would have lost." Étienne squeezed Kate's hand. "To be clear, I'm completely in love with your niece and cousin. She's the only woman I ever really wanted, and Stratton? You're right that I cheated on Amy in my heart, but you're wrong about Amy as a person. Maybe you'll figure that out one day or maybe you won't, but you don't know her like I do. I guarantee you that.

"The bottom line is that Kate and I didn't have much of a chance the first time around, and as long as all of you are willing to bury the hatchet, I was hoping we'd have a better chance this time."

Barrett cleared his throat, looking across the table at Étienne with a shrewd glance before shifting his eyes to Kate. "Does this mean that Étienne Rousseau is going to need an invitation to my wedding?"

Kate felt her lips tilt up—grateful when Barrett's did the same—until she was laughing softly, nodding at her oldest cousin. "I think it does."

"You free to come to my wedding?" asked Barrett, sizing up Étienne with a cautious smile.

"If you're lucky, you'll get out of being a groomsman," said Weston. "These guys are pretty demanding at weddings."

Kate watched, her heart bursting with pleasure, as Étienne grinned back at her cousins and answered, "If Kate's going to be there, I'll be there too." He reached across the table and offered his hand to Barrett. "I'd be honored."

Tension broken, they all stood as Alex hung up to take a call and Étienne crossed the room to shake hands with Fitz and Weston. As he joked with Barrett, Fitz, and Weston about weddings, Stratton made his way around the table to Kate, finally standing in front of her with a troubled look.

"I don't know. It's a lot to take in."

"Tell me about it," said Kate.

"I've always felt guilty that I knew about you two and didn't blow the whistle. I could have protected you better."

"You made the right decision to keep my secret. I'm grateful for that."

"If I was wrong about him, I'm sorry. But only time will tell."

"It certainly will."

Stratton nodded once, then passed Kate on his way out of the room, pressing his lips to her cheek before leaving.

"Kate," said her uncle from behind her, and she turned to face him. "In my brother's defense, he was only trying to protect you. When that boy arrived at his apartment that night, well, he knew about the fight with Alex, and I think his only goal was to protect you."

"I'll have to take it up with him, Uncle Tom," said Kate, thinking that she only saw her father once or twice a year, and by then she might want to concentrate her energy on introducing him to Étienne instead of rehashing the past. "Or not."

"You were the only girl in the family. We just wanted—"

"I know. But no more."

He nodded at her, his blue eyes looking tired and sorry. "No more, Katie. I promise." He kissed her forehead and started out of the room, then turned around at the door. "If you decide to get married, though, good luck finding a date. These guys have the calendar pretty booked," he said hooking a thumb at his sons before slipping out of the room with a wink.

"Cart before horse, Uncle Tom!" Kate exclaimed then gasped as she felt two strong arms encircle her waist.

"Oh, I don't know," said a lightly-accented French voice close to her ear. "It doesn't sound like such a bad idea to me."

"Étienne!" she said, spinning in his arms as the rest of her cousins filed discreetly out of the boardroom. "We have to date a while. We need to get to know each other again and I don't even know what you want for dinner tonight, and besides, you haven't met the trio yet, and—"

Grinning at her with that old twinkle in his eyes that Kate had first fallen in love with, Étienne lowered his head, and whispered, "Kiss me, Kate."

And she did.

Epilogue

Two months later, there wasn't a dry eye in the gardens of Haverford Park when Barrett English looked into the face of Emily Edwards, whom he'd loved since he was a child, and promised to love her for the rest of his life. Kate, who stood beside bridesmaid, Molly McKenna, had entered the church first, since she had the added responsibility of reading a verse from First Corinthians. Now she looked across the minister and happy couple to the groomsmen, almost all of whom were looking at their mates: Fitz at Daisy, Alex at Jessica, Stratton at Valeria, Weston at Molly, and Étienne . . . at her.

Asked to join the wedding party at the last minute when Barrett's college roommate came down with the flu three days ago, Étienne had graciously accepted and it had thrilled Kate to be able to walk down the aisle with her boyfriend instead of a stranger.

Even more thrilling was the fact that over the past couple of months, Barrett, Fitz, and Weston had accepted Étienne as a friend, inviting him to all of the bachelor prewedding events. Étienne and Fitz, who were both lawyers, had a lot in common, and Kate was always delighted to spend more time with Daisy, who was due to have baby Caroline any day.

A tense peace existed between Étienne, Stratton, and Alex, but Kate trusted their relationship would get better over time. After all, Kate had no intention of letting Étienne go, so her cousins would simply need to accept him eventually.

"So," said Jessica, leaning over Alex to chat with Kate later at the reception. "Alex won't tell me any of the good stuff about how you two got together. It sounds so jolly secretive! How'd you get to know each other? Where'd you meet?"

Kate had stared at Jessica with her mouth open as it dawned on her that Jessica's family home, Westerly, had, in fact, been where she'd fallen in love with Étienne. She glanced at his face, split with the same smile she wore, then turned back to Jess.

"We met over spring break a long time ago."

"Here? At Haverford Park?"

"Mm-hmm." Kate nodded, feeling Étienne's fingers slip through hers under the table. "Here and there," she said, glancing over at the hedges where they'd said their final farewell so long ago.

"Did I see Jax here?" Jess asked Étienne, unaware of the subtext in her questions and Kate's answers.

Étienne nodded. "Yep. Jax, Mad, and J.C. are all here."

"I'll have to catch up with them," said Jess. "It's been ages."

"And it's been ages since you've danced with me," said Alex. Grinning at his fiancée, he turned to Kate. "We've been practicing with Val . . . for the wedding."

"Like he needs practice," said Val, rolling her eyes. "Smoothest dancer I ever saw, and the wedding's still three months away."

"Any excuse to get his woman on the dance floor," said Stratton, "which seems like a very fine idea to me."

Kate watched as Stratton and Val joined Alex and Jess on the dance floor.

"What do you say, Molly? Want to . . . dance?" Weston grinned wickedly at his girlfriend, offering his hand to her.

"Weddings are sort of our thing," said Molly to Étienne, winking at Kate before slipping out a side door nowhere near the dance floor.

"Ooooph," Daisy sighed, massaging her tummy through her bridesmaid dress. "She's kicking like crazy tonight."

"You want to head home, mama?"

"I think I'll just go upstairs and lie down."

"Room for one more with you two?" asked Fitz, his eyes soft with love.

"Always room for you," said Daisy, letting him help her up and waving good-night to Kate and Étienne.

"I never thought I'd say this," said Étienne, watching them go, "but I like your family."

"They're growing on you, right?"

"If you had told me six months ago that I'd be in one of the English brothers' weddings? I'd have told you that polar bears would sooner take over hell."

"Would you have believed that you'd be sitting here next to me?"

"I think I always hoped," he said, taking her hand in his and kissing her knuckles tenderly.

She still hadn't gotten used to how beautiful he was . . . not after countless nights in his arms and innumerable mornings watching him sleep. Even now, as he watched the couples dancing, his profile was so stunning it made Kate's breath catch. And he belonged to her.

He belongs to me, she thought with wonder.

Two months together had proven that Lib was—of course—right when she said that it wasn't impossible to meet the love of your life when you're fifteen. It's not necessarily that Kate had fallen more in love with Étienne since New Orleans, but she trusted the love they had. In living their lives together—half at his place and half at hers—she was learning that he was everything she'd ever dreamed of in a man . . . possibly because the man of her dreams was the adult version of the boy she'd so loved. Whatever the reason, for the first time in Kate English's life, she was completely, blissfully happy.

"I have something for you," said Étienne, still staring out at the dance floor. "Two things, actually."

"What? Like a gift?"

He shrugged, still not looking at her, but his lips were smiling slightly like he had a wonderful secret. "Something like that."

"I'd planned to give this to you on our first anniversary, since paper is traditional, but it turns out I can't wait that long."

"Not to mention we're not married," said Kate, laughing. "I don't think those rules apply to dating couples."

Étienne reached into his vest pocket and pulled out an envelope. Kate could tell it was old as he handed it to her, but her mouth dropped open as she saw the flowery script that had addressed the letter. It was hers. It was one of her letters to him. Her fingers trembled as she took the envelope in her hands, her eyes watering so that she could barely make out the words. Turning it over she found it was unopened, still sealed like the day she'd sent it.

She raised her eyes to his, "But how?"

"Turns out my mother kept them. She gave them back to me."

"All thirty?" asked Kate.

Étienne nodded. "Every single one."

"Have you read them?" she asked, clutching the letter to her chest as a tear rolled down her face.

"No," he answered, reaching into his other vest pocket and slipping to his knees on the floor in front of her. When he opened the little white box holding a dazzling diamond engagement ring, his eyes met hers. "I thought . . . we could read one every anniversary for the next thirty years."

"Oh," gasped Kate, covering her mouth with her free hand as her tears fell double-time. "Are you . . . Are you doing this? Right now? Here?"

His smile was tender and loving as he peeled her hand from her mouth and held it in his. "I'm doing this right now. I told you a long time ago that I defied any plan for my life that didn't include you. I swore to God that I would still love you on the day that I died."

"I-I remember," said Kate, through shallow breaths and soft sobs.

"I said that we were real, that me loving you and you loving me was real."

Kate nodded, her shoulders shaking as tears coursed down her face.

"We lost each other in the worst way and somehow found our way back. That's a miracle. You're a miracle to me."

She couldn't speak, so she just stared at him, all the love in her heart pouring from her eyes.

"Kate English, who I lost and found, who *is* love and my own personal miracle, and whom I will still be loving on the day that I die . . . will you marry me?"

And Kate, whose heart had been broken into a million pieces and put back together, who wanted the first boy she ever loved to also be the last, who wanted a lifetime of hot, wet, sweet, messy, filthy kisses that would make her toes curl forever . . .

. . . said yes.

THE END

The English Brothers continues with . . .

MARRYING MR. ENGLISH

THE ENGLISH BROTHERS, BOOK #7

THE ENGLISH BROTHERS
(Part 1 of the Blueberry Lane Series)

Breaking Up with Barrett
Falling for Fitz
Anyone but Alex
Seduced by Stratton
Wild about Weston
Kiss Me Kate
Marrying Mr. English

Turn the page to read a sneak peek of *Marrying Mr. English*!

Chapter 1

Vail, Colorado
December 1981

"C'mon, Ellie," pleaded Eve Marie. "They're, like, rich."

"They're *all* rich," said Eleanora Watters, hustling into the kitchen of Auntie Rose's Breakfast-All-Day Chalet with an armload of dirty plates.

Eve Marie followed her through the swinging door.

"But they seem *ni-i-i-ice*," she whined.

"They *all* seem nice," said Eleanora over her shoulder, nodding at Manny as he took the dirty dishes and winked at her.

"But these two really *are*."

Eleanora turned to face her younger cousin, pushing a stray lock of blonde hair behind her ear and planting her fists on her hips. "Like the last ones? And the ones before them?"

Eve Marie had the decency to look embarrassed.

"When are you going to learn, Evie? They're all rats. Rich, old, entitled, grabby rats. They come to Vail looking for a young waitress or hotel maid to warm up their bed for a week, and once they've had their fun, they leave. Do you know *who* they leave?"

"Us," said Eve Marie dolefully.

"Us," confirmed Eleanora. "And are we harlots to be thusly used?"

Eve Marie screwed up her face in confusion.

Eleanora rolled her eyes, rephrasing, "Are we hos, cuz?"

"No," said Eve Marie, though there wasn't much conviction in her voice.

"No, we are not," said Eleanora crisply. "We deserve better than that, Evie."

Images of home flashed through her mind at lightning speed before she could stop them: her father's grubby double-wide, choked by a rusty chain link fence . . . the hellhole of a bar where her tips hadn't been worth the slow death of her dreams . . . and—she touched Evie's cheek gently with her knuckles as a fierce burst of protectiveness flared within her—her stepuncle's leering eyes and filthy, grabby hands.

Eleanora dropped her hand and lifted her chin with determination. "If we keep our legs closed and our options open, we just might find it."

She turned to the warming lights and picked up two plates of pancakes and bacon for table two before bustling through the swinging door, back into Auntie Rose's main dining room. Designed to resemble a rustic ski lodge, the restaurant was a favorite of skiers and snowboarders who wanted to fill up on a hearty breakfast before hitting the slopes.

"Will you at least, like, say hello?" persisted Eve Marie at her cousin's shoulder, her voice almost drowned out by John Lennon's "(Just Like) Starting Over" blasting through the ceiling speakers.

Eleanora ignored her cousin and plastered a smile on her face as she carefully delivered the plates to the table. "Stack of hot cakes, side of oink. Bon appétit."

"Looks great," said the man on the left side of the booth, reaching for her wrist. He handled her gently but firmly, looking up into her eyes. "Now how about making it delectable by giving me your number?"

Without fighting for her imprisoned hand, Eleanora flicked her eyes over him. He was wearing a cream-colored Irish wool sweater—the type that sold in the local boutiques for hundreds of dollars—and had sunglasses in his heavily gelled hair. Vuarnet? No. Versace, she noted, glancing at the stem close to his ear. His hair was salt-and-pepper, and his eyes were lazy but hopeful as he grinned at her with what he probably believed was charm.

"My number . . . hmm." Eleanora sucked her bottom lip between her teeth, then released it with a provocative pop. "Sure. Okay."

He looked surprised but delighted, tightening his grip on her wrist to pull her closer. "Oh, yeah?"

"But which number?" said Eleanora, tapping her chin in thought. "So many to choose from . . ."

"Oh, I meant your—"

"—my age? It's twenty-two. To your what? Forty-five? Or the number of years between us? Roughly twenty-three. Or my birth date maybe? Nine, three, fifty-nine. And yours? Well, I'm guessing it ends in . . . hmm . . . *thirty-six*? How about *those* numbers? Probably not what you were looking for, though. Ooo! I know! Maybe you're one of the good ones and you've fallen madly in love with me and you want my ring size? It's a six. No. Come to think of it, you don't look like the type to buy me a ring, so how about the serial number on my father's shotgun? It's four, three, six, oh, oh, seven—"

"Forget it," said the man, his face bright red as he dropped her wrist.

"Sure thing."

"You're a bitch," he muttered, looking up at her with narrowed, angry eyes.

"Maybe. But I'm not a chump," she answered, ripping the bill from her pad and placing it on the table before turning on her white Keds and heading back toward the kitchen with Eve Marie at her heels.

Tom English watched the sassy little waitress make her way back across the bustling dining room, chuckling softly as he admired everything from the sharp way she'd taken down that dickweed to the way her tight ass swayed back and forth under the big white bow of her pink gingham dress.

"Wow!"

Pulling his eyes away from the waitress with a stab of regret, Tom looked across the table at his companion, Van, raising his eyebrows.

"Talk about sharp nails!" said Van.

Tom chuckled again, picking up his coffee cup and taking a sip of the strong brew.

Van sneered as his eyes tracked the blonde. "You couldn't pay me enough to go out with a girl like that. I don't care how hot she is. That guy had it right. Bitch on wheels!"

Tom's grin faded as he placed his mug back on the table and looked up at his friend. "I don't agree."

Van scoffed, rolling his eyes. "Are you effing kidding me?"

Tom shifted his gaze back to the kitchen, hoping for another glimpse of her. "Nope. I thought she was fairly spectacular."

"Fairly spectacular," mumbled Van, grimacing as he shook his head. "Well, you're not known for your taste in women. I hope to God she's not the friend the cute brunette was referring to."

Tom, on the other hand, desperately hoped she *was* because he had zero interest in the vacuous brunette, but that spitfire blonde? Oh, man. She was something different.

And he could sure use the distraction.

In just four days, Tom English was going to lose every cent of his fifteen million dollar inheritance, because his fiancée, Diantha Montgomery, of the Philadelphia Montgomerys, had run off with her ski instructor, leaving Tom high and dry the night before their wedding.

It's not like he was heartbroken—he hadn't been marrying Di for love. No, theirs had been an agreement, a marriage of convenience. Tom's thirty-second birthday was in four days—on Christmas Eve—and unless he was married by the final day of his thirty-first year, his eccentric old codger of a grandfather would disown him. Tom had heard the lecture a thousand times:

A good woman makes a man honest, makes him work harder, makes him true. If you don't have a good woman in your life by age thirty-two, you don't deserve a cent and you won't get a cent. I'm not letting some devil-may-care wastrel playboy squander my millions!

Diantha, more than happy to pocket a cool million in exchange for saying "I do," had planned a lavish wedding in Vail, and they'd invited dozens of friends and family to witness the temporary nuptials. The plan was to stay married for a few months, secure Tom's inheritance, and then get a quiet divorce and go their separate ways.

But when Di didn't show up to her own rehearsal dinner last Friday, things didn't look good. A tearstained note shoved under Tom's hotel room door confirmed the rest: *Paolo and I have fallen in love and decided to elope. We're leaving for Italy tonight. I'm so sorry, T! Love, Di*

While all the guests had returned home, Tom remained in Vail with his erstwhile best man and sometime investing partner, Edison Van Nostrand, for the week that should have been Tom's honeymoon. Time had certainly flown by with Van as their entertainment coordinator—today was Friday and Tom's birthday was Tuesday.

He shrugged and swallowed the rest of his coffee. If he was being cut off in four days, he may as well enjoy his last few days as a "devil-may-care wastrel playboy."

Van had asked their waitress—cute, airheaded brunette Eve Marie—to meet them at the bar of the Hotel Jerome tonight for some fun. The young waitress, checking out Van's brand-new Rolex, snapped her gum and offered Van a sparkling smile as she promised to "do her best" to find a friend for Tom.

Van brightened suddenly, looking over Tom's head with a lascivious grin. "Hey, angel, don't break my friend's heart and tell him *your* friend said no."

Tom shifted in his chair to find Eve Marie standing behind him, wringing her hands nervously. She blew a small bubble with her gum and sucked it back quickly, snapping it between her teeth.

"Um . . . she's not my friend; she's my cousin." She shifted her eyes from Van to Tom. "And she needs *you* to, like, answer a question first."

"Me?"

The waitress nodded at Tom, her cheeks flushing. "Yeah. She's, like, um, well . . . she needs to know your favorite book."

Without skipping a beat, Tom asked, "Fiction or nonfiction?"

This question proved a bumpy road for Eve Marie, who froze, staring blankly at Tom.

"Which one," he asked slowly, "do you think she wants to know?"

Eve Marie chewed once, then held up a single finger and hurried away. Tom watched her beeline to the feisty blonde (yes!), who was taking an order across the dining room. Tapping her cousin on the shoulder, Eve Marie cupped her hands around the blonde's ear for a moment, then leaned back expectantly. A second later, she returned to Tom.

"Fiction. Ellie said fiction."

"Now we're getting somewhere."

Tom chuckled softly, nodding at Eve Marie, who sighed happily, like she'd finally done something right.

"My favorite book of fiction. Hmm . . ."

Glancing around Eve Marie, who was twirling a long strand of teased hair around her index finger as she chewed her gum and eye-fucked Van, Tom looked across the dining room at—what had Eve Marie called her? Ellie?—Ellie, who still had her back to him, writing on her pad. Pocketing the pad, she held out her hand and collected the menus.

When she turned around, her eyes slammed into his, almost like she'd known he was staring at her all along. With the menus pressed against her chest, she stared back at him for a long moment, her posture straight, her blue eyes keen and bright. When her lips wobbled just a little, he realized she was trying not to smile, and he suddenly felt his own lips lift into a grin. But that broke the spell they were under, and she dropped his eyes quickly, heading for the kitchen and disappearing behind the swinging door without a second glance.

He didn't realize he was holding his breath until his lungs started to burn and he exhaled with a soft puff.

"Uh, Tom?" asked Van in a low voice, utterly captivated by gum-snapping, eye-fucking Eve Marie. "A book. Name a book. For the love of God, *please* name a book."

Ellie seemed brighter than average—she was quick with numbers and interested in books—but she looked young too, which meant she'd be impressionable. He considered lying. He thought about saying *A Clockwork Orange* (to seem edgy), or *The Catcher in the Rye* (to seem deep). But in the end, something about those clear, blue, unsmiling eyes made him feel ashamed of even considering deception, and he heard "*The Swiss Family Robinson*" fall from his lips instead.

Eve Marie winked at Van before looking down at Tom with glistening lips and a sexy smile. "Hmm?"

"Tell her my favorite novel is *The Swiss Family Robinson*, and ask her the name of her favorite poet."

"Uh . . ." Eve Marie stared at him for a moment, then shrugged. "Okay. Be right back."

She sauntered away toward the kitchen, and Van adjusted his pants, grimacing. "Fuck, she's hot. How many hours is it until tonight?"

Tom looked at his watch. "About ten. But I assume you're buying her dinner first, so more like ten and a half."

"Fuck," Van muttered again. "Dinner better buy some tail."

On cue, Kenny Rogers started crooning "Lady" overhead, the lyrics *Lady, I'm your knight in shining armor and I love you* an ironic follow-up to Van's comment.

"That's real nice."

Though, judging from Eve Marie's come-hither glances, he doubted Van would have much trouble securing that tail. Him, on the other hand? He wasn't so sure. Ellie didn't look like a girl who put out as easily. Her appearance wasn't contrived to seek attention—it didn't appear that she wore makeup, and she kept her hair in a plain, tidy ponytail—and yet she was so naturally beautiful, every pair of male eyes in the room naturally gravitated toward her.

It felt like forever waiting for Eve Marie to return.

"So?" asked Tom, his anxious heart stuttering, hoping the little spitfire liked adventure fiction as much as he did.

"Elizabeth Burnett Browning," said Eve Marie.

"Barrett," he said reflexively.

"Huh?"

"Elizabeth *Barrett* Browning," said Tom.

"That's what I said."

"No, you said—"

"So, we good?" interrupted Van, leaning across the table to give Tom a look that begged him to shut the fuck up and stop arguing with the waitress he was aching to bang.

"Um, no," said Eve Marie, wrinkling her nose. "Now she needs to know your favorite *non*fiction book too."

"What the actual fuck?" exclaimed Van. "Is she a waitress or an English professor?"

Eve Marie turned away from Tom to look at Van with wide, innocent eyes. "A waitress. But she goes to college. At Colorado Mountain College over in Edwards."

"Wow," said Van sarcastically. "Colorado Mountain College! You don't say!"

"I *do* say," said Eve Marie earnestly. "She saves up her tips every month to pay for it. She's, like, supersmart."

"What does she study?" asked Tom, kicking Van under the table so he'd stop being an asshole.

"Bookkeeping," said Eve Marie. "Because math is a . . . a . . . oh, I remember! A universal language." Tom smiled at her, forcing himself not to give her a round of applause since she'd worked so hard for the answer. "But she also reads a lot of books. Ellie's, like, *always* reading books. Since as long as I've known her, and that's forever because I'm three years younger. It's, like, her favorite thing to do."

"Too bad partying isn't her favorite," said Van under his breath.

"Nope. That's *my* favorite," said Eve Marie, arching her back provocatively as she slid her gaze to Van.

Van chuckled, nodding at her with appreciation before glancing at his friend. "So, Tom, what's your all-time favorite nonfiction tome, huh?"

Tom glanced at the kitchen door, wishing Ellie would come out for a second. He'd like to look into her eyes again. He'd like to see her reaction as he answered *The Joy of Sex* or *A Moveable Feast* or . . .

He looked up at Eve Marie and grinned.

"Tell her if she wants to know my favorite nonfiction book, she has to be my date tonight."

Look for *Marrying Mr. English* at your local bookstore or buy online!

Other Books by Katy Regnery

A MODERN FAIRYTALE
(Stand-alone, full-length, unconnected romances inspired by classic fairy tales.)

The Vixen and the Vet
(inspired by "Beauty and the Beast")
2014

Never Let You Go
(inspired by "Hansel and Gretel")
2015

Ginger's Heart
(inspired by "Little Red Riding Hood")
2016

Don't Speak
(inspired by "The Little Mermaid")
2017

Swan Song
(inspired by "The Ugly Duckling")
2018

ENCHANTED PLACES
(Stand-alone, full-length stories that are set in beautiful places.)

Playing for Love at Deep Haven
2015

Restoring Love at Bolton Castle
2016

Risking Love at Moonstone Manor
2017

A Season of Love at Summerhaven
2018

ABOUT THE AUTHOR

USA Today **bestselling author Katy Regnery** started her writing career by enrolling in a short story class in January 2012. One year later, she signed her first contract for a winter romance entitled *By Proxy*.

Katy claims authorship of the multi-titled Blueberry Lane Series which follows the English, Winslow, Rousseau, Story and Ambler families of Philadelphia, the five-book, best-selling A Modern Fairytale series, the Enchanted Places series, and a standalone novella, *Frosted*.

Katy's first Modern Fairytale romance, *The Vixen and the Vet*, was nominated for a RITA® in 2015 and won the 2015 Kindle Book Award for romance. Four of her books: *The Vixen and the Vet* (A Modern Fairytale), *Never Let You Go* (A Modern Fairytale), *Falling for Fitz* (The English Brothers #2) and *By Proxy* (Heart of Montana #1) have been #1 genre bestsellers on Amazon. Katy's boxed set, The English Brothers Boxed Set, Books #1-4, hit the *USA Today* bestseller list in 2015 and her Christmas story, *Marrying Mr. English*, appeared on the same list a week later.

Katy lives in the relative wilds of northern Fairfield County, Connecticut, where her writing room looks out at the woods, and her husband, two young children, and two dogs create just enough cheerful chaos to remind her that the very best love stories begin at home.

Sign up for Katy's newsletter today: http://www.katyregnery.com!

Connect with Katy

Katy LOVES connecting with her readers and answers every e-mail, message, tweet, and post personally! Connect with Katy!

Katy's Website: http://katyregnery.com
Katy's E-mail: katy@katyregnery.com
Katy's Facebook Page: https://www.facebook.com/KatyRegnery
Katy's Pinterest Page: https://www.pinterest.com/
    katharineregner
Katy's Amazon Profile: http://www.amazon.com/
    Katy-Regnery/e/B00FDZKXYU
Katy's Goodreads Profile: https://www.goodreads.com/author/
    show/7211470.Katy_Regnery